Copyright © 2019 by Ron Tucker

All rights reserved.

This book is a work of fiction. Names, characters, and incidents are the product of the author's imagination or are used fictitiously. Any resemblance to actual events, locales, persons, living or dead, is entirely coincidental.

No part of this book may be reproduced in any form or by any electronic or mechanical means, including information storage and retrieval systems, without written permission from the author, except for the use of brief quotations in a book review.

Edited by Melissa Ringsted of There For You Editing.

Cover design by Robin Ludwig Design Inc. www.gobookcoverdesign.com

❦ Created with Vellum

TRIAL BY FIRE

HIGH SCHOOL SIDEKICK, BOOK 2

RON TUCKER

1

"Dónde está la biblioteca?"

A month into sophomore year, my Spanish class is still trying to grasp the proper sentence structure when speaking Spanish. I'm supposed to take two years of language classes in high school, even though I severely protested it to my parents. I mean, what's the point of learning a language when I can just pop a linguistics pill from the Justice Alliance and start speaking any language I want?

Since taking down Vacuus last year, everything has been pretty smooth in King City. Mr. Mimic, my superhero mentor, and I have had some really great training sessions, and he's even let me man the control station in Alliance headquarters from time to time. Not long, mind you, but it feels great being trusted by everyone again.

Supron's still strict, but every now and then he'll offer a pointer on how I can handle a situation better, or a more logical and concise way of dealing with something. Yeah, it feels great knowing I'm back in good graces with everyone.

This year I have three classes with Pete, my best friend. Spanish being one of them. All throughout summer, Pete was begging me to visit Alliance headquarters. Since he knows my secret identity, he thinks he has free rein over any and everywhere I go.

"Come on, it'll be so cool!" he pleaded for what must've been the fiftieth time one day at the mall.

"Pete, you know I can't just bring you along. The only way to get you back behind regular touring areas is if you're hurt or it's some kind of emergency."

"I know, I know."

He stopped pleading that day but has continued asking since.

I might be a little annoyed by it, but I'm glad he knows the truth. I was keeping my powers and the fact that I'm a sidekick from him for months, and when he finally found out, he didn't freak out on me. Or get mad at me, which he had every right to, since he came out to me and I basically blew him off because of an emergency. But we've grown closer since all of that went down. When I have to leave for Justice Alliance business, he knows the deal, and doesn't hold it against me.

"¿Señor Garcia?" I hear my teacher say, but my mind is elsewhere. I have my Spanish book open, but inside my phone is on, and I have it connected to the Justice Alliance app, scanning for any possible crimes.

I know Melissa, also known as Mighty Miss, is on duty right now. I asked her to send me an alert if anything is happening, even if it's just a simple jaywalking case.

She's a year older than me, which Pete teases me about dating an older girl. I still can't believe we're dating. After everything that happened, she was there for me when my world was falling apart, and I thought I might lose everything.

Technically, she is an alien from a different planet, but

she's amazing. And spending more time in the bunker I've kept at Alliance headquarters, we've had a couple of hot make-out sessions. Did you know girls from other planets are amazing kissers?

Yeah, things are good.

"¿Señor Garcia?" I hear my teacher, but an alert pops up on my phone.

[Alliance encoded message] MM: Sorry, Worm. Hydro and I have to take out some B-Level criminals. I was going to send you an alert, but Majestic told us to get to it.

Reading the message, I let out a small groan. Since she's from another planet, she doesn't need high school. Daniel, also known as the sidekick Hydro, took his GED and doesn't need it either. High school sucks when I could be out fighting crime, teleporting all over the city.

"Mr. Garcia!" my teacher shouts.

"Dude," Pete whispers, kicking my chair.

"Huh?" I look up, catching Pete's snickering first, then my teacher's furious gaze. A scattered round of eye rolls and laughs from the students roll in.

"Do you know the answer to the question?" my teacher asks, a line across his brow. "¿Hacer saber la respuesta a la cuestión?"

"Uh ..." My mouth drops open, unable to think of anything. Needless to say, I have not been taking my Spanish class very seriously.

"¿Hay un problema? Estás bien?" he says, the entire class still looking on. When I don't answer, he furrows his brow. "Are you okay?" he asks, enunciating each word slowly.

"Oh, um, y-yeah," I stammer out. He starts to turn

around when I stop him. "Actually, sir? No. No, I think I need to go to the nurse's office."

"What?" Pete whispers behind me.

The teacher shakes his head, and then casually waves at me to leave the room.

"Sorry, I gotta go." I turn around, whispering to Pete, "B-List. Gotta meet."

Over the course of the last couple of months, Pete and I have come up with a shorthand verbiage to talk about my sidekick life. "B-List" is used when it's a supervillain attacking, but not a high-threat one. "Hit the tracks" is that I have to go in for training, and "varsity" refers to Mr. Mimic, Supron, and Ms. Majestic. There are a few others, and we've gotten really good at speaking the shorthand, making sure my secret identity stays safe.

Leaving the classroom, and with no one in the hallway, I teleport to the top of the closest building where the fight is happening. I've become much more comfortable dropping my pants out in the open, and switching into my uniform, so I suit up.

I've tried wearing my uniform under my clothes, but it feels weird. Not to mention, it bunches up and it's uncomfortable. It's not spandex, which my favorite comic book superhero, Crimson Cowl, has his suit made of. No, in the real world, superheroes have their suits made of mevlar, a super-enhanced material. Sidekicks use the same stuff. It's comfortable by itself, and I carry it everywhere in my backpack.

Leaving my bag on the roof, I run and jump off the side of the building. Teleporting in the air, I land next to Melissa, who's fully decked out in her Mighty Miss uniform. Her uniform has dark brown leather pants and a leather armor top, and her forehead tiara comes down into a mask over her eyes. Over the summer, she was bequeathed a sword from her people. Even though she always tells me her people are not Amazonians, she looks freaking hot wielding that sword.

She snaps her head to the side as I catch her off guard. "I thought you had class?"

"Yeah, but Spanish is lame," I say, giving her a smirk under my visor.

"Aren't you Hispanic?"

I nod. My mom has tried to teach me Spanish over the years, but I've never been interested in it. I know I should be, but every time she starts talking to me, I kind of just zone out. There are moments when I wish I'd take it more seriously because it would be kind of nice being able to communicate with my abuela better. But, like I said, I can just take a linguistics pill and *boom*, all set.

"Heading east, three blocks up!" Daniel yells at us, flying through the air on a bed of water.

Daniel draws his power from the moisture in the atmosphere. We got off to a rocky start, especially since I always call him by his regular name instead of his codename. But he's been helpful over the summer. I wouldn't say we're friends now, but definitely allies. Even though he did walk in on me and Melissa making out one time, and still teases me about it.

I teleport three blocks up and see the B-Listers; it's Bonnie and Clyde. I know, not the best name, but the Alliance doesn't come up with the villain names, that's usually the media. And they bestowed on them the high-profile bank robber names because they knock over banks. And they do it with guns. Such creativity, I know.

The reason they're B-Listers is because their guns aren't regular six shooters; they use a pair of ion-blasters from the black market. This attempt is their third heist in two weeks. The reason the Alliance hasn't caught them before is because their ion-blasters look like normal guns. The first time they robbed a bank, the police thought they were just normal bank robbers, so they didn't call for any backup from the Alliance. But during their last robbery, they shot a civilian, and now everyone knows.

"Worm, Fourth Avenue!" Daniel calls out to me.

I can see their car, but there's a traffic jam straight ahead. They're going to have to turn east or west, onto Fourth Avenue. Daniel flies ahead of their car and goes west, so I teleport onto a building on the east side. Onlookers are all around, and I can see people standing on the sidewalk, pulling out their cellphones to capture what's happening.

At the end of the street, Daniel's pulling a ton of water out of the atmosphere, and forms a huge wall of liquid, blocking off the road. With the traffic ahead of them, they're going to have to turn toward me.

Screeching tires ring out, and Bonnie swerves the car side to side. Clyde leans out of the window, aiming his gun at me. I can't let him get a shot off because, even though I can teleport, there's still a ton of civilians lining the street.

I run at the car and teleport, landing on the roof of it. Clyde looks up, surprised, and points the gun at me. Grabbing his hand, we quickly teleport away, and I pop us up on the top of a streetlight, letting him hang. He drops his gun and I quickly grab it, teleporting back to the Alliance evidence room to drop it off before jumping back.

Reappearing back on the scene, I watch as Bonnie swerves, losing control of the car. It begins to fishtail, spinning, finally coming to a crashing halt when it hits a small, blue pickup truck. The bed of the truck strikes a lamp post, and my eyes widen, watching it fall. Standing right in the path of where the lamppost is falling is a little girl with her phone out, recording the chaos.

My body tenses. Just before I can teleport to her, Melissa jumps from out of nowhere, and catches the falling light post with her hands. Yeah, she has super strength in addition to flight, and being an amazing kisser.

Tossing the post to the side, she kneels down to the little girl. "Are you okay?"

"Are you kidding? That was awesome!" the little girl exclaims. I guess having King City inhabited with superheroes for over fifty years has made normal civilians numb to near-death experiences. "Can I get a selfie with you?" she asks.

Melissa seems shocked for a moment, then smiles. "Sure." She leans in close to the girl as she snaps the picture.

Daniel flies over to us, skidding along on a sheet of water. Before he can say anything, clapping starts to ring out all around us.

"Yeah!" someone yells.

Another person fist-pumps the air and screams, "Woo!"

Sirens begin to echo in the distance, and we look at each other, knowing the police will be here soon.

"So, who's gonna do it?" Melissa asks, her gaze bouncing between both of us.

"Well, that was a pretty cool save you just had," Daniel replies.

"But Worm teleported the guy out of the car," she counters. We all turn our attention to Clyde, still hanging from the streetlight, and chuckle.

"True," I say. "But seriously, this time it's all you, Hydro."

After sidekicks or superheroes take out the bad guys, someone has to stay behind and deliver a press conference. We let reporters ask questions, and help the police file any paperwork. It's something we all do, and as tedious as it is, it's actually a little bit of an honor. We're representing the Alliance when we do it.

"Are you guys serious?" he asks.

"Absolutely," I reply. "You organized us, blocked off the west side of Fourth Avenue with the water wall. We were able to take them down easily thanks to you."

Daniel raises his shimmering eyebrows, the sheen of blue water covering his skin, masking his identity. "Wow. Worm, I don't think you've ever said that many nice things about me."

"Take it while it lasts," Melisa says, chuckling.

I offer my hand to him. "Nice work, man."

He returns the gesture, and gives me a handshake.

The sirens stop as the police arrive, the flashing lights from the cruisers radiating off of the windows from neighboring buildings. Reporters start to show up, and they all rush over to us.

"You ready?" I ask Melissa, offering her my hand.

Instead of taking my hand so I can teleport us back to Alliance headquarters, she steps closer, wrapping an arm around my waist.

"Ready." She smiles. It's the first time we've been this affectionate out in public, and I can't help but feel my face get red.

It doesn't help that I hear someone across the street yelling, "Yeah! Go, Worm!"

The comment makes Melissa start to blush. "He's just jealous," she says, trying to counter it.

"Of course he is," I reply with a smile. "I would be, too."

I teleport us back to headquarters just as the reporters start firing questions at Daniel.

2

As soon as we teleport into the Alliance control room, Melissa taps the side of my helmet, retracting it back into my earpiece, and starts kissing me. To say we've gotten closer ever since last year would be an understatement. I'm not ashamed to admit that I told my parents I had extra training sessions with Mimic over the summer, when, in actuality, Melissa and I would just spend the time making out in my room. My bunker inside of headquarters has almost become like a home away from home for me now.

We aren't able to enjoy the kiss long, though. Someone releases a very obvious cough, letting us know we aren't alone in the control room. Both of our faces instantly turn red.

Turning around, we see Supron peering down at us. Not with an annoyed or angry expression, but definitely a face that says to knock it off. Mr. Mimic and Ms. Majestic are both part of what people like to call the Trio. The top three superheroes not just in King City, but the world. Of the three, Supron's looked at as the leader of the Justice Alliance by the general public, as he's been Supron for as long as there's been superheroes. No one knows how old he is. I'd say he'd have to be at least sixty, but he looks like he's in his early thirties.

He has a natural leadership air about him. His light brown hair stays in place, and has a hard, square jawline, and crystal blue eyes. In addition to super strength and flight, he has the power of lightning manipulation, and tiny lightning bolts dance over his skin when he's powering up. With his red and gold uniform, and his matching colored cape, he comes off as more than regal. It's almost godlike.

"You're both still on the clock," he sternly announces.

Ms. Majestic walks in after him, smirking. "Nice work out there, you two."

The compliment helps ease the tension, but we both separate. As much as we have made out, we do try to keep it professional when in front of others at headquarters.

"Did the news conference start yet?" I ask, walking over to the control desk.

Inside of the control room, the main desk houses five large monitors that anyone on duty can use to scan the city, be kept abreast of any criminal activity, and access the Alliance databank servers.

Majestic sits down in the main chair at the desk. "Just starting now."

She hits a button, popping up the news conference on a screen in front of us.

"Hydro, how come no real heroes came out today?" a reporter asks, off camera.

All sidekicks are used to being marginalized like that. We aren't the real heroes, like Mimic or Supron. We're sidekicks. Unfortunately, a lot of the media look at us as lackeys. The only two times a sidekick usually gets recognition is when they're officially promoted from sidekick to superhero, or when they're initially revealed as a sidekick, after their first mission. It still stings that my first mission last year was a total fart-show, with me teleporting away from a fight, and people thinking I ate worms to access my powers.

For the record, once again, my codename is Worm because when you teleport you travel through wormholes. Luckily, it's grown on me since then.

Much to Daniel's credit, he doesn't cringe at all when the reporter hits him with the question. On the contrary, he stays composed and confident.

"First of all, Worm, Mighty Miss, and I *are* real heroes. We're sidekicks, and Supron has complete faith in us, letting us take down Bonnie and Clyde by ourselves. And I think we did a great job."

"Was anyone hurt?" a reporter shouts.

"Only Clyde's ego, when Worm left him hanging from that light pole."

Reporters off screen can be heard laughing.

"Hydro, what's the deal with Worm and Mighty Miss? They seemed awfully chummy when he teleported them out of here."

I instantly feel my face go flush. I keep my eyes locked on the monitor, not wanting to look around and see Supron or Majestic giving me a side eye.

Daniel smiles at the reporter. "They're just friends."

Last year, Daniel and I got off to a rocky start. Frenemies might be too harsh of a word, but we definitely had our differences. So, as he stands there in front of the cameras, and basically the world, and keeps our private lives private, and doesn't even deliver a cheap shot with some kind of sarcastic remark, it impresses me. Not only have we grown up more in the last year, we've also developed a real camaraderie.

"Thanks, everyone," he says, before releasing a wave of water underneath him, flying off into the air.

Majestic switches the screen over from the press conference to other watch screens, and the room falls quiet. I finally look over at Melissa, who stares back at me, both of us unsure if we should address the elephant in the room of the media pointing out our relationship. Before either of us can say anything, Supron interrupts our silence.

"Both of you, follow me."

After my incident last year, I was put on probation for six months. Even though I was trying to help Mimic, I'd broken protocol, and acted on my own. I served my penance and have been on a few missions with Mr. Mimic since, but this was really the first one I'd been on without one of the Trio there. Unsure what's happening, I mouth to Melissa, *"What's going on?"*

She raises her brow, shrugging.

We walk down a hallway, the white tiles matching the bright walls, into a conference room where Mr. Mimic and Doctor Grandside are waiting. Doc has helped me a lot since becoming a sidekick, so I'm not sure what's happening.

"Nice work out there, you two," Mimic says, instantly cutting the suspense. Doc nods in agreement. "Hydro is almost here, so we felt it was time for something."

Majestic and Supron walk around the table, sitting next to Doc and Mimic.

"Take a seat." Doc gestures to both of us.

We stare at one another, nervously. From behind, Daniel depowers from being Hydro and jogs into the room. Walking around the table, he sits down and his eyes dart between Melissa and me. Mouthing the same thing I did, I lift my shoulders.

"Nice work on the press conference, Hydro." Supron stands in front of us, a proud smile across his lips. "We've been keeping track of everything, and we wanted to say that you have all really impressed us."

"Hydro, you handled yourself with poise out there," Majestic says. "Not only leading the group today, but in that press conference."

"Mighty, every time you're out in the public, you act with confidence, and always keep an eye out for any civilians in harm's way," Mimic says.

"Worm, you've rebounded nicely from your probation period last year," Supron adds. I look at Mimic nervously, who smiles and nods in agreement. "You're still a little erratic, but you're efficient and you've learned to rely on others and not just jump into the frying pan, but instead plot out a plan of action."

Melissa, Daniel, and I all exchange looks, caught off guard by the commendations.

"So, we want to offer you all your first opportunity of guarding over King City without us," Mimic says.

"What do you mean?" Melissa asks.

"We've received a distress call from the Camdrion Galaxy," Majestic explains, her tone turning from friendly to one more serious. "The Star-Guards have been fighting a war with a blood-thirsty alien race, and they need help. Mimic, Supron, and I are going to travel and offer our assistance."

"What?" Concern overtakes me.

"It'll be okay," Mimic reassures. "We plan to only be off-world for a few weeks, but if this fight proves difficult, it could last longer. We've talked it over and we think you are all ready."

Doc finally speaks up. "I'll be taking on a more hands-on

role, not just residing in the medic-bay and laboratories, but I'll be on the command post. I'll issue out the alerts, and you three will take to the streets, watching over King City while they're off-world."

The three of us exchange glances—our faces a mix of concern over our mentors venturing to another galaxy to fight an alien race, and excitement at the prospect of guarding the city on our own. Not to mention, the feeling of being trusted by them.

All four of them stand up from the table.

"Wait, you guys are leaving right now?" I ask.

"Yes," Majestic answers. "Granite and Lazerbeam will both be on call in case things get too serious. Their cities are very quiet, so they don't have a lot going on."

"This is ... incredible." I smile. "Thank you, guys."

Daniel stands up from his chair. "We promise, we won't let you down."

"We know," Supron responds, sounding nothing but confident. He walks around the table and offers his hand to Daniel, who shakes it, before giving his mentor, and surrogate father, a hug.

Melissa does the same with Majestic, as Mimic stands next to me, giving my shoulder a reassuring squeeze. I really want to hug him. Ever since he's become my mentor, I've learned so much from him, both about being a superhero and about life. However, I control my emotions, and give him a firm handshake, a smile still plastered across my face.

All three then turn and exit the room, leaving us standing around the table with Doc.

Daniel breaks the silence first, shouting into the air, and pumping his fist, "Yes!"

I look over and smile at Melissa, who returns the expression. "Pretty awesome, right?"

Trial By Fire

"Totally," she answers, grabbing my hand.

Doc knocks on the table, bringing us all to attention. "Now the real fun begins." He smiles, but it's more mischievous than commendation. "Hydro, you're on command watch starting now."

"Yes, sir," Daniel answers and leaves for the control room.

"You two." Doc points between Melissa and me. "Mighty, you'll be on command tomorrow. Robbie, since you have school, you'll take every other weeknight and weekend duty."

"You got it." The smile never wavers from my face.

"Until then, I guess you two are dismissed. If something comes up, I'll alert you."

Melissa and I are hand in hand, about to leave the room, when Doc stops me. "Robbie, can you meet me down in Lab Three?"

"What for?" I ask, looking at Melissa as she slows by the doorway. She gives me a smirk and nods. A silent code between us about meeting back in my room.

"Well, I've been running the tests on your blood and things appear as normal as they have the last few months, but I'd like to run a couple more."

Last year, when I embarrassingly teleported away from my first mission, Doc found some kind of anomaly DNA strain in my blood. When I teleported, I somehow time-jumped back two seconds, but he's never been able to figure out what's trigged the anomaly. Since then, he's been running tests every couple of months. However, he hasn't found anything that looks like what my blood looked like during that first outing.

"Uh ..." I glance back at the doorway and find Melissa gone. "Doc, can it wait until later?"

"It should only take an hour or two. I'd really like to inspect—"

I hear his words, but my mind is completely somewhere else right now. "Can we do it tomorrow? I'll swing by right after my class."

"Well, we can, but—"

"Great!" I cut him off and practically run out of the room. "Thanks, Doc."

There's no way I'm going to miss a great make-out session with my super-hot, alien girlfriend.

3

I'm so excited about us getting the opportunity to watch over King City, the next day at school it's all I can think about. The first thing I do when I see Pete is spill the beans and continue to talk about it through the classes we have together, in between classes, and at lunch.

"This is a major step!" I whisper excitedly to him, as I grab my soda and take a drink. "I mean, I've told you before, sidekicks can go years before getting an opportunity like this."

"How come you're still in class?" Pete asks. "This should be able to grant you, like, time off or something."

I roll my eyes, my excitement finally dipping a bit. "I know. Mimic had already left, so I asked my parents about it when I got home, but they said no. Mostly because Mighty and Hydro don't have school and can stay at headquarters while I'm here."

"Bummer."

I shrug off the comment, still feeling the excitement of everything. As much of a responsibility that's been entrusted to us, the anxiousness to show not only Mimic, but King City itself, that I can be looked at as a *real* member of the Alliance is immense. I would've never thought that just over a year ago, when my sidekick training started, I'd be getting this chance, but here we are. I can't wipe the smile off of my face for the entire lunch.

"Hey, you think since you guys are kind of in charge now, I can get that behind-the-scenes access?" Pete asks as we leave the cafeteria.

I roll my eyes, laughing. "Dude, I can't get you back there. Why are you so antsy to tour anyway? You already met Doc last year."

"I know, but it was just so cool. I mean, there's a lot of stuff I haven't seen, too."

"Uh, yeah. That's because it's off-limits to civilians."

He grumbles something, shoving his hands into his pockets, as we keep walking.

I can't help the side eye I give him, but he doesn't notice. He's been bringing up visiting headquarters more and more, and I'm not sure why. Ever since I accidentally revealed my secret identity, I've tried to be as open with him as I can, while still attempting to keep things I need to keep secret, a secret. I don't want Pete to feel like a third wheel or anything, and as far as I know, he doesn't. So, I'm not sure why he's been persistent on visiting headquarters.

I try to change the subject. "I know it's early, but I was thinking ... Homecoming is a little over a month away, and things are going really good with Mighty right now."

"Oh, yeah?" He eyes me suspiciously.

"It's not like I've asked her or anything, but I'm pretty sure I'll be bringing her to the dance."

His eyes nearly double in size. "Dude, how is that gonna work?"

Trial By Fire

"Well, she'd have to use her regular name. Which means, if we double, that you know ..." I trail off.

"What?"

I look around, making sure no one is close enough to hear. "We'll have to tell you her secret identity."

"Are you serious?" Pete asks, shocked and excited.

"Yeah, but play it cool. I still need to ask her. What's more important than that is you."

"What do you mean?"

"Come on." I look at him expectantly. "I mean, we'll need to find you a date."

He instantly rolls his eyes. "Robbie, no way. We've talked about this before. I'm not ready to go out in public, let alone a dance with a date."

"Come on, dude. You're my best friend, and I'm not letting you sit out homecoming. We'll find you a date. Hey, what about that guy in English?"

"What guy?" Pete stares at me, confused.

"You know, that dude with the spiky hair."

"Brad Kessler? He's not gay."

"What? How do you know?"

"Because I sit next to his girlfriend in geometry."

"Oh."

"And besides," he says, taking a drink of his soda, "you're the only person who knows. I want to go, but I don't want to freak out over it."

"But, Pete, think about it—"

My counter-argument comes to an abrupt halt when we turn a corner, and I accidentally bump into Jasmin, knocking the books she's carrying down to the ground.

We stand there, almost frozen in time. Ever since I broke up with Jasmin last year, I've tried to keep my distance. Not only for her, but for me, too. It hurt too much to see her. I've had a crush on her for years, and I finally got enough nerve to ask her out last year. We even went to homecoming.

For a little while it was going great. Even though I was keeping my secret identity from her, I thought it would work out. But when Vacuus' minion stole her phone at the dance, acting like he kidnapped her, I knew it would've been all too easy for her to get caught in the crossfire. I couldn't risk that. So I lied, told her I never really liked her, and we broke up.

After the breakup, we both tried to avoid each other as much as possible. This year we don't have any classes together, so that's made it a little easier, but it still sucks. This is actually the first time I've come face-to-face with her since last school year.

"Shoot!" My eyes widen and I look over at Pete, before landing them back on her. "I-I'm ... sorry."

The words are difficult to get out because she looks as beautiful as she always has. Last year she put silver streaks in her hair, but this year it's her normal chestnut brown, with what appears to be highlights. Her hazel eyes widen, before they soften a bit as she lets out an uncomfortable smile.

I kneel down to pick her books up at the same time she does, and our eyes lock again. "Here you go." I hand her a book, as she picks up her other one. "Sorry, I didn't see you there."

"It's okay," she responds, her voice only a little louder than a whisper.

"Sorry," I repeat, unable to think of anything else.

She lets out a small laugh. "Robbie, it's fine. It was bound to happen, right?"

I nod, unable to keep my eyes off of hers. "Yeah, I guess so."

Pete and Maria, Jasmin's best friend, stand off to the side, quietly watching the interaction.

Finally gaining some semblance of coherency, I stand a little straighter, my nerves calming down. "Hey, so ... we're sophomores now."

"Yeah?" She quirks an eyebrow.

I let out an embarrassed chuckle. "Right. What I'm saying is, we still have three years of this. Jas, I don't ... I don't want this to be awkward all of the time."

She flashes an accepting smile. "Me either."

I let out a sigh of relief. "Okay, cool."

"Cool," she replies.

The awkwardness I'm trying to fight lingers. "Well, uh, I guess I'll see you later."

"Okay." Smiling, she starts to walk in the opposite direction with Maria.

Pete and I continue on our way, but I turn around and see them walk off, with Maria whispering something to her.

"Yeah, that wasn't uncomfortable at all." Pete rolls his eyes.

"Yeah," I reply, letting out another sigh.

Before I have time to dwell on it, my cellphone vibrates. An emergency alert from Doc displays across my screen.

"Yes!" I fist-pump, my attention immediately returning to my excitement of watching over the city.

"Are you serious?" Pete asks, excitement also in his voice.

"Wish me luck." I look around, making sure the coast is clear, and teleport away.

Teleporting to the top of King City Tower, the tallest building in the city, I can see Daniel flying through the air a block away, and it looks like he's chasing a guy who's engulfed in flames.

"Worm, you with us yet?" Mighty says into my comm piece.

"Just got here. Top of King Tower."

"Good. It's two fire-powered guys, but they haven't been hurting anyone. They've just been causing damage all around."

"Where's the second?" I ask, and teleport to a neighboring rooftop.

"We aren't sure," she responds. She sounds like she's running on the street level. "I'm on the chase with Hydro, and keeping watch over civilians. The other one was last sighted by the harbor, but we haven't gotten any more intel on it."

"I'm on it." I teleport over to Third Avenue, which is near King City Harbor. "Doc?"

"Still nothing," he answers in my earpiece. "Nine-one-one calls were made ten minutes ago, but we don't know where he's gone."

It's the middle of the day, so lots of people are still at work on the dock. I walk along cautiously, noticing more and more heads turning, noticing me. A few workers and bystanders pull out their phones and start taking pictures.

"Lots of people out here, Doc."

"I know," he replies, and I can hear him tapping away on a keyboard. "King City PD and Fire are on their way to help with crowd control. If he does pop up, try to move it away from the civilians."

"Copy that."

A large ship is docked, and I can see a number of shipping containers lined up on it, so I teleport over to the top of them, to get a better view of the area. Looking around, the civilians still stand by, watching me move, but nothing seems out of the ordinary. Someone is driving a forklift off in the distance, and a few workers are loading some crates onto a ship. Everything is perfectly normal.

"Mighty? Hydro? Still no movement over here. You guys good?" I ask.

"All—" Daniel starts, then lets loose a grunt. "Good."

"This flame guy still hasn't attacked anyone, but he's causing all kinds of trouble, knocking over streetlights, billboards, and he's even blown up a couple of cars."

"Need backup?"

"We're good, Worm. Keep an eye out over there," Daniel answers back.

"Doc?" I ask, tapping the side of my helmet. I feel like I'm not helping at all.

"Stay where you are, Worm."

"Copy that."

I teleport around a few more times, from one container to another, then to the top of a nearby building, but it's all calm. After about fifteen minutes, all of the onlookers from before have gone back to their business when my communication piece chirps in my ear.

"Worm?" Melissa says.

"What's up?"

"We lost the fire guy. How's lookout on your side?"

I scan the area for the umpteenth time, finding nothing. "Whoever this guy is, or wherever he went, he's not here now."

"All right, let's meet back up at HQ."

"One second," Doc chimes in over the comms. "We just got word from KCPD. The Turbo Trio escaped lockup. Who's free?"

"I got nothing," I answer, getting ready to teleport away.

"I'm still helping a few people over here, waiting for the fire department," Melissa says.

"I'm free," Daniel adds.

"All right, Worm and Hydro. It's down near King City High."

"On it!" I call out, a little more excitement than probably necessary lacing my voice.

I'll be honest, I've wanted superpowers ever since I was little. I thought superheroes were the coolest thing ever. But when I actually got them, as cool as it is to teleport, when I became a sidekick, I finally realized that having these powers means taking things seriously. Life-and-death situations can be faced at a moment's notice now that I'm part of the Justice Alliance.

But I'd be lying if I said I never thought about making a save in front of everyone I went to school with.

Teleporting to the top of King City High, I scan the sky for the Turbo Trio. Basically, they're glorified bank robbers, who are C-List supervillains. They use turbo-fueled jetpacks as their main getaway transportation, and there are three of them. Thus, Turbo Trio.

Off in the distance I see Daniel sliding through the air on a sheet of water, and then one of the trio flies around the building. I look around, searching for the other two, when I hear my name called out from down below.

"Dude, check it out! It's Worm!" a student calls out. Glancing down, I see a crowd of students have gathered to watch.

"Worm, behind you!" Daniel yells into my comm piece.

Returning my attention to the situation at hand, I look back right in time to take a solid punch from another member of the trio. Losing my balance, I fall off the side of the building, but regain my composure mid fall, and teleport down to the ground safely. Out of nowhere, Pete is standing in front of me.

"Ro—" He cuts himself off. "Worm!"

"What's up, man?" I ask, giving him a smile.

Teleporting across the street, I try to keep the fight away from the rest of the students, who are now becoming a bigger crowd, pulling out their phones to take pictures and record the fight. The first trio member buzzes by me, and I teleport as fast as I can, landing on top of him, crashing him down to the ground. I grab his jetpack off of him and pull out a pair of cuffs, wrapping them around him wrists.

"One down, Hydro," I call out.

"On your six!" he yells back, and I teleport out of the way just as one of them zooms past me.

Jumping across the street, I watch as Daniel skids to a stop in front of the second thug, forming a water ball the size of a basketball over his fist, and knocks the trio member out cold. The crowd of students erupts into cheers.

"Where's the third, Worm?" he asks.

Trying to block out the cheering from the crowd, I scan the area. Across the street from the high school sits a large group of buildings, but I know he couldn't have gotten far, and he won't be able to get away without the other two.

See, the trio's jetpacks not only run on turbo-fuel, but the high-tech equipment built into them means they work best when all three are in the air. So, if one of the jetpacks is out of commission, the other two aren't going to last very long.

"There!" I point, as the third member comes flying around a building, heading directly toward me.

"He's coming in hot!" Daniel calls out.

The rest of the students begin to understand what's going on, and start to back up, giving us room. Daniel walks over to the left, on the roof of a building, while I hold my position on the rooftop across the street, keeping my eyes locked on the trio member.

"Worm, how about we try out that new move?" Daniel asks, and I can hear the smirk in his voice.

"Are you serious?"

"Totally."

Over the summer we worked on a few things that might be able to take enemies off guard. An attack that they aren't expecting. With a grin, I nod over at him, knowing this is the perfect opportunity.

"Let's do it."

He starts to swirl a bunch of water around himself. The flying criminal notices and changes directions. A huge tornado of water begins to form about him, and the students down below start hollering in anticipation of whatever's to come. I teleport from my location to the other end of the building Daniel's on, and start running at him.

At the speed the trio member is flying, it looks like we're both going to collide into Daniel at the same time, who's now formed a giant orb of water. The crowd below quiets down, no one understanding what's happening.

"Now!" I call out, and Daniel jumps off of the building, landing down below, sending the huge waterball into the sky.

The flyer zooms past him and I slide to my knees, then teleport high into the air, right where the waterball is. The trio member hits the reverse thrusters on his jetpack and turns around, just as I touch the sphere of water, and teleport the entirety of the liquid directly at him.

A huge splash sounds as the criminal crashes into it, and Daniel keeps liquid surrounding the final member of the trio, as if he was locked into a huge hamster ball made of water. Running out of air in the waterball, the flyer reaches for his throat, and Daniel floats the orb down to the ground, finally bursting the bubble. The criminal drops to his knees, gasping for air, and I jump to him, locking him in cuffs.

A massive eruption of cheers comes from the onlooking students. Sirens blare, and the police arrive on scene and rush over to the trio members, taking them away. For a C-List villain group like Turbo Trio, not many media outlets show up, so that means there isn't much needed in the way of a press conference.

Daniel turns to me, giving me a thumbs-up. "I can't believe it actually worked. Nice job."

"Yeah, you too." If I didn't know any better, I'd say our very civil alliance was turning into an actual friendship.

Daniel glides back in the direction of Alliance headquarters, as the student body looks on. I can see Pete watching everything, and he appears to be absolutely giddy. It reminds me of his constant requests of going back to headquarters, and now I know I'll have to take him sooner rather than later.

Behind him I catch sight of Jasmin and Maria. The visor on my helmet blocks my eyes, but if I didn't have it on, I could swear she'd be locking eyes with me. I cast a grin, and I'm surprised when she smiles back. It almost looks like she blushes a little.

With not much else to handle, I'm about to teleport away, when an odd urge takes over. I can't help it. I just took down a group of supervillains in front of everyone I go to school with. Sure, they're C-listers and Daniel helped, but still.

I teleport in front of Jasmin, causing a sudden yelp to escape her.

"Hey, cutie."

Her face turns a dark shade of red, and Maria's eyes pop open, staring at her. I have my uniform on, my helmet with visor so you can't see my eyes, and the collar of my uniform has a voice modulator so she can't recognize my voice even if she wanted to. But I still don't stay long. Students whip around, all with their phones out. Scanning the area, I see Pete in the distance.

His eyes bulge out, and he mouths "*What are you doing?*"

I flash a cocky grin and then teleport away.

4

The rest of the week goes by without any other incidents that require us to get involved, so I'm unfortunately left to be a normal high school student. Pete is quick to question my playful flirting with Jasmin as Worm throughout the entire week.

"It's not a big deal, Pete," I repeat to him. Today is the fourth time he's brought it up.

"It's totally a big deal!" His voice gets slightly angrier and higher, as we sit at our lunch table in the cafeteria. He scans the area, making sure no one is paying attention, before bringing his eyes back to me. "First of all, you're going out with Mighty, remember?"

"Of course I remember, but I didn't do anything. I just said hi." I chuckle before opening my bag of potato chips, rolling my eyes again.

"Oh, don't you—" He cuts himself off, lowering his voice. "Don't you pretend you just said hi. I may have been ten feet away, but I heard you. I'm not saying you're a flirt, Robbie, but you do know how to be charming."

"Careful, Pete, I might start thinking you're a little jealous." I laugh.

"This isn't funny. I'm your best friend, so I hate to say this, but I think I'm more of a gentleman than you."

My mouth drops open, genuinely surprised. Scanning the cafeteria, the low buzz of chatter continues with the other students, but I lower my voice, keeping my gaze locked on him. "Excuse me?"

"Yeah, that's right. I'm not saying you're gonna cheat on Mighty, but if I know you like I think I do, you won't be able to help yourself. Especially with a girl you've liked since forever."

"That's messed up, Pete."

He must notice I'm genuinely hurt because he suddenly slumps down from his overbearing posture. "Robbie, come on. I don't mean to be mean, but I just don't want to see you do something you'll regret."

"Dude, all I did was say hi."

"Cutie! You said cutie."

"So what?"

"I could probably chalk it up to you just showing off if it was some other girl, but it wasn't. It was Jasmin. And I know you still like her."

"Yeah, but that can't happen. Pete, I'm glad you know my secret and everything, but you don't think I think about the danger you're in sometimes, just because you *know*? And I didn't even really mean to tell you."

I didn't. I'd been attacked and subconsciously teleported into Pete's room one night, trying to get away from the fight, and save my life. That's how my best friend found out I was a sidekick. But if I could take it back, I totally would. Not because I don't trust Pete, but because I don't want him to be in any danger. If anything happened to

Jasmin simply because she knew my secret, that'd be the end of me.

Pete doesn't say anything, instead taking another bite of his sandwich, shaking his head.

"It's fine, okay?" I try to reassure him. "It was a one-time thing. I saw her and I was so hyped up because of the fight, I just couldn't help myself. Plus, like I said, it isn't even a big deal. I just said hi."

"Okay ..." he responds, not the least bit convinced.

All I did was say hi.

No big deal.

Things are still pretty quiet around the city, so after a quick training session with Doc, I meet up with Pete at the mall over the weekend. We agree to grab a burger before checking out a movie, after which I've decided I'll surprise him with finally taking him back to Alliance headquarters. After seeing how giddy he got when Daniel and I stopped the Turbo Trio, I figure I should be a good best friend and take him back.

"I don't think my mom's gonna let me use the car for homecoming," I say, taking a bite of my burger.

"How come?" he asks.

"I still don't have my license, just my stupid learner's permit. I was so busy last year that I never went down for my driver's test. So now, even though I'm sixteen and teleport around the city helping people, she won't let me take the car because I only have a permit."

Pete takes a swig from his soda. "Well, are you even going?"

"What do you mean?"

"The last time you were telling me about the dance you said you were gonna ask Mighty. Did you? And is she cool with me knowing her secret identity? It's not like Robbie Garcia can show up at our high school homecoming dance with Mighty Miss."

I can't help but flash a wide smile, taking another bite of my burger. "Dude, but wouldn't that be awesome?"

He agrees, laughing. "That would be pretty cool."

"I haven't been able to bring it up. I was going to today, but she wasn't at headquarters when I had my training session. I think she's gonna be okay with it though."

"That's cool. Just have her drive then." Pete tilts his head, his expression one of confusion. "How old is she again? I always forget she's an alien like Ms. Majestic. She looks young, but then again, so does Majestic, and she's pretty ancient."

"She's only seventeen, a year older than us. Well, in Earth years anyway."

"Cool. Speaking of Majestic, any word from them?"

"No, not really," I answer, grabbing a couple of fries. "They told us they'd be gone for a few weeks at least. I'm not too worried though. It's Mimic, Majestic, and Supron. The greatest of the greats."

"True."

Finishing off the last of my fries, I take a drink of my soda. "You know what I was thinking? After the movie, if you want to ..." I trail off, trying to build the suspense, but he just stares at me, confused.

"What?"

"Well, maybe we could ..." I pause again, trying to excite him. He has no clue.

"What are you talking about?"

"Dude." I shoot him an exasperated look. "Justice

Trial By Fire

Alliance headquarters. You up for a new tour? I got Doc to grant me clearance with you for a little more behind-the-scenes stuff."

His face lights up like a light bulb. *There's the excitement I was waiting for.* "Are you serious?"

"Yup." I smile, proudly.

"That'd be awesome!"

"I thought you'd like that."

"Let's just go now." He crumples up his food wrappers, standing from the table.

"Wait, what?"

"Yeah, forget the movie!"

"Aw." I frown. "I was kinda looking forward to *Bionic Commander 3*. It's the end of the trilogy."

"Come on, Robbie, please! Please-please-please!"

I've never seen Pete grovel so much. Not even when I used to spend the night over at his house and he begged his mom to let us eat ice cream for breakfast.

"Fine," I submit. "But we're definitely watching *Bionic Commander* next weekend."

"For sure," he says, wildly grabbing his wrappers, tossing them into the trash bin next to us.

I begin to scan the area, looking for a good spot to teleport us out of the mall, when my phone vibrates. Doc is calling.

"Hold up," I tell Pete, answering the phone. "What's up, Doc?" I chuckle to myself. No matter how many times I say it, it still makes me laugh.

"Worm, we've got a slight situation."

"Okay, what is it?" I look over at Pete, who's impatiently waiting for me.

"I need you to head back down to the harbor. There's been another sighting of a fire guy. Mighty is on control panel duty, and Hydro is assisting Forge over in Mercury City. It's really just a recon, but if we can get a location on one of them, it'll help us out a lot."

I let out a small sigh, knowing Pete is gonna be bummed. "All right, sure."

"If you do see something, don't intercede. Trail and locate. We don't know what these guys are capable of yet." I can hear the beeping of the machines in the background.

"Okay, no problem."

Ending the call, I look over at Pete, whose excitement has started to wane. "Pete, sorry, man. I just got called in."

"Aw, man." His shoulders slump and he hangs his head.

"I'm sorry. I promise, we'll take a tour next time."

"Yeah, it's cool." He tries to smile, but I can see how disappointed he is.

"You gonna be okay getting home?" I ask.

"Yeah, it's fine." He keeps his half-hearted smile on his face, raising his fist.

I bump my knuckles to his. "Thanks. Sorry again."

Finding a nearby corridor, I teleport away, first to my bunker at headquarters to change into my uniform, and then to the harbor. The sun's setting over a new containment ship, and the water shimmers, with nothing looking out of the ordinary. I tap the side button on my helmet.

"Worm, checking in to HQ."

"HQ here," Melissa responds.

"All good so far."

"The sighting was near the end, by Pier Fifty-five."

"Got it."

Teleporting over to the end of Pier 55, I scour the area, but everything still seems normal. A few people are around, but most of the public have left the area for the day. Off in the distance, I see a guy looking around cautiously, almost as if he's hiding from something.

I press my comm button. "Stand by."

Jumping atop a neighboring container, I stare down at the guy. He's wearing jeans and a dark gray hoodie, and seems to be on edge. His head jerks back and forth, scanning the area for anyone around him. Keeping a distance, I watch from above, and trail him. He reaches into his back pocket and pulls something out, but I can't tell what it is. Then, ahead of him, I see someone wearing a nice suit and tie, who also glances around nervously.

"You've got to be kidding me," I whisper to myself.

"What is it? Did you find him?" she asks.

"No. There's a stupid drug deal going down right now."

The two guys meet down below, and the one in the blazer reaches into his suit pocket and pulls out a wad of cash. As soon as the guy in the hoodie reaches for the money, I teleport down between them, sending them both falling to the ground in shock.

The drug dealer reaches for his waistband and pulls out a gun, but I quickly teleport behind him, grabbing him by the shoulders, and teleport him over the water, letting him fall with a loud splash. The guy in the suit stays on the ground, tears welling up in his eyes. He appears to be in his thirties, but right now he's acting like he's eight years old and was just caught trying to shoplift a candy bar.

"Please, oh God. Please!" The tears start falling down his cheeks. "Please, I can't go to jail. Please, Worm."

I cross my arms over my chest, letting out an annoyed sigh. "Are you serious, man?"

"Please, it was just ... it wasn't even a lot. Please, I can't go to prison!"

Clenching my teeth, I try not to laugh at how scared he

is. I'm not trying to be a jerk, but seriously, the guy is so scared of going to prison, when in reality he'd probably be booked overnight, bailed out, and then have to pay a fine.

"Get the hell outta here," I grumble.

"Thank you! Thank you!" He turns and scrambles away.

"You let him go?" Melissa asks in my headset.

"Yeah, I think he might've been scared straight." I chuckle. "Is KCPD on their way for the dealer?"

"Already in route."

I teleport up to a nearby roof and continue to look around, but there's no sign of anyone else.

"I don't know, Mighty." I sigh. "There's nothing else out here."

"Roger that. Head on back."

"Copy."

The split second it takes right before I'm about to teleport away, a searing heart scorches my back, and a huge fireball engulfs me.

5

The hot air rushes against my face, and then I feel weightless, falling off of the side of the building. Able to get my bearings, I teleport, but I'm not able to counteract the gravity in time and come down hard on a neighboring building's roof. My face smacks the roof, and I grab the back of my neck, feeling the singe of pain across my skin. Like a sunburn, only a thousand times worse.

Getting up, I turn around, trying to figure out what happened. I see what looks like a man engulfed in flames, flying through the air. He waves his hand in the air, bringing it down in a chopping motion toward me, sending another fireball through the air. With enough distance between us, and the fact I'm actually facing my attacker this time, I teleport to another building.

The fire guy scans the area, searching for me. I use the time to press my comm button on my helmet, but all I hear is static. Then silence. The heat must've singed all of the electrical components in my helmet, so there's no way to radio back to headquarters.

The fire guy finally finds me and flies over, leaving a trail of embers floating behind him. The closer he gets, it looks like his skin is glowing a bright orange, the yellow flames dancing over his body.

He propels himself faster, and I back up, holding up my hands.

"Okay, buddy," I shout. "Let's just hold on a second. Who are you?"

He flies closer but doesn't raise his hands to attack. He cocks his head to the side, as if he's trying to understand me.

"Who are you?" I repeat. "Why are you doing this?"

I inch closer to the edge of the roof, as he floats in the air. I'm about to ask again when he looks off to the side, almost as if he's listening to something.

I can see that he has a face; eyes, nose, a mouth. But any identifiable features all vanish under the orange glow. Lowering his chin, he scowls, and his eyes begin to glow a bright yellow. His mouth opens as if he's going to scream, but instead of a yell, a huge burst of flames shoots out. I teleport to the other side of the building just in time.

"Are you serious?" I scream at him.

Still not in any mood to conversate, he flies closer, hovering above the roof, and lets loose another round of fire breath. I teleport again, this time directly behind him, and can feel the heat coming off of his body. Unsure what to expect, I grab his leg as he's hovering, hoping the flames aren't hot enough to burn me, since they dance over his body.

I feel the heat coming from him, but my hand over his ankle feels normal. He jerks away and out of my grasp, spinning around, then lands on the roof.

Pulling back his arm, he throws a punch, but he stops halfway through his swing, and a fireball shoots out of his fist toward me. I roll out of the way quickly and look up, just in time to see him opening his mouth to release another fire scream. I teleport away behind him, and bring both fists down over his shoulders, sending him down to the ground.

On one knee, he peers up at me, only this time he doesn't scream; his face is twisted in anger. He raises both of his hands at me, hurling out fire. I teleport to the other side of the building, but the heat coming from his hands is unlike before. It's darker. Almost red. And it feels hotter, too.

He doesn't stop. Turning back to face me, instead of shooting fire again, this time his entire body explodes, heat and flames spraying out from him. I teleport to another building over, and he spins around, searching for me. When he spots me, he flies over, hovering in the sky, and releases another flaming scream.

Rolling off to the side, steam and smoke encompass us and I ready my fists, unsure what his next move is going to be. I know I have to take him down and de-power him some way, but don't have the first clue as how to do that. He lands on his feet and stares at me, as if he's about to take another shot.

Unexpectedly, he drops to a knee. "Ugh," he groans out, grabbing his temple. "Get out of my head!"

The flames that are covering his body begin to die out, but instead of revealing his skin underneath, he starts to smoke. Falling down on his knees, he raises his hands. Staring at his palms, confusion racks his face, which is now darkening, along with the rest of his body. Doubling over, he starts coughing, spewing out grime and dust.

I run over to him, dropping to my knees. "What's happening? Who are you?"

He doesn't respond. He brings his hands up again, and when his mouth opens, smoke starts to fly out. Choking, he spits out more ash. His body morphs into burnt charcoals, and starts scratching and creaking, as his joints rub together.

Collapsing onto his back, he gags. Every piece of him is covered in blackened charcoal, except for his eyes. They glow a soft yellow, and finally find me. Through the darkness, I can see the fear in them. He reaches up and grabs my hand.

"Please—" He chokes.

"What?" I ask, now on my knees right next to him. "What is this?"

"Please," he repeats, his voice hoarse. "He wants to burn you all."

"Who? Did someone do this to you?"

"H-he ..." Another cough.

More ash and dust spew from his mouth. His grip on my hand loosens, as his yellow eyes roll in the back of his skull. Then the glow vanishes. Just like the rest of his body, they're pitch-black, and charred beyond recognition.

"But there were no identifiable marks on him at all?" Doc questions, sitting across from me in one of the conference rooms at Alliance headquarters. We've been sitting in the room for over an hour.

After the fire guy died or extinguished or whatever he did, I teleported back to headquarters, and let Doc and the rest know what had just happened. At first, he was upset that I hadn't immediately called for backup, but once he saw that my comms were toasted, literally, he understood.

Doc wasn't sure if his body would just turn to ash if we tried moving it, but after inspecting him, his body remained in a sort of charcoal rigor mortis. Bringing his body back to headquarters, Doc placed it in one of his laboratories. After running a quick analysis, his body seems to be completely charred all of the way through. All vital organs are shriveled up as if they were burnt on the inside.

"None," I answer. "But, Doc, I think he was taking orders."

"He was talking to someone?"

"Not until the very end. He seemed like he was fighting against something. He said, 'get out of my head.' But the confusing part is, right before he died, he told me 'he wants to burn you all.'"

"You all?"

"Yeah. I don't know what he meant. Even though he was all burnt up, he looked terrified."

Doc strokes his gray beard, as he usually does when he's trying to piece together a problem. My first instinct when I sat down at the table with him was to ask if we should contact Mimic or the others. If for nothing else, to get their advice. But I don't bring it up. They left us in charge, and what initiative and responsibility would I be showing if I immediately called my mentor at the first sign of a problem? Plus, Doc may be the medical and science specialist for the Alliance, but he's been a member of the Justice Alliance for nearly thirty years.

"We'll have to keep a strict lookout over the city," Doc finally responds. "There isn't a whole lot we can do from here, especially since we don't have the reports back on the body. You're assigned weekend watch-duty, are you still up for it?"

I reach behind my neck. My skin still feels tender, but Doc attached a bandage when I got back, so the burning is starting to heal. "Yeah, I should be fine."

"Okay, go ahead and take over for Mighty." Getting up to

exit the room, he stops me as I reach the doorway. "And, Worm, remember, we still need another sample of your blood."

I nod before heading down to the control room, and see Melissa sitting behind the main desk, keeping tabs on the monitors. She taps her fingers over the keyboard in front of her, as she switches camera angles on the screens above.

"Hey," I say softly.

"Robbie!" Jumping out of her seat, she rushes over and wraps her arms around my neck. I immediately cringe in pain. "Oh no, are you okay? Is it bad?"

"It's all right," I reply, trying to play it off. "So, I guess I've got watch duty for the rest of the night."

She sticks her bottom lip out, giving a pouty expression. "I know. Ever since Majestic and the others left, we haven't been able to spend as much time together." She leans in closer, whispering in my ear, "We really need one of our scary movie nights."

A smirk crosses my lips.

Being from a different planet, she's never gotten into the pop culture of Earth, much less little things like going out on dates. Since we've been going out, I tried to introduce a few different things, and one of them was scary movies, in a very selfish attempt to get her to cling to me in fear. I should've known it wouldn't work. She's from another planet, with all kinds of different life-threatening dangers. Plus, she's been training with Ms. Majestic for years, so she's seen her fair share of scary things.

"Why are we watching this?" she asked, the first night I tried to implement the scary movie tactic, as we watched in my Alliance bunker. We got nearly two-thirds of the way through the movie, and she just watched in boredom. It was a good zombie one, too.

"Well, I just thought ..." I remember trailing off, unable to think of a good excuse.

She hit the pause button, right in the middle of an attack —a zombie biting the leg of a screaming girl. Paying no attention to one of the best parts, she looked at me, confused. "What?"

I hung my head in embarrassment. "Okay, this is so stupid." Taking a deep breath, I started to explain myself, fully expecting her to get upset and walk out on me. "So, on this world, scary movies are kind of ... well, it doesn't happen all of the time, but I mean, sometimes the girl gets scared, and then, you know ..." I was tripping over my words, but unable to stop myself.

She looked at me, shaking her head. "No. What?"

"Oh my God." I could feel my face getting red. "Sometimes the girl gets scared and they grab the guy and then ... you know ... start to make out or whatever ..." *I sound like an idiot.*

Her eyes popped open. "Oh. Wait, so you wanted me to get scared?"

"Well, no. I mean, I did, but I didn't want you actually frightened for your life or anything. I just thought you'd jump or something, and we could, I don't know ..." I took a deep breath, feeling really stupid. "Sorry, let's just forget it."

"No," she said playfully, pulling at my arm. "Robbie, if you want to get close to me, you don't have to put on a scary movie."

Shocked, my eyes widened. "That was direct."

"Not as direct as this." She flashed a coy smile and then leaned over, kissing me. We made out for the rest of the night.

We were only going out for about a month at that point. Ever since then, the "scary movie night" was kind of our code for make-out night. We still got a scary movie to play but paid no attention to it.

It was definitely a plus dating an older woman, even if it was just by one year. Wrapping my arms around her waist, I smiled back at her.

"We *do* really need one of those scary movie nights," I reply, before taking a seat at the desk.

As she walks through the doorway, she turns and casts a sultry glance my way. I curse under my breath at my responsibilities for the rest of the night.

6

After the weekend, I'm back in school, still feeling the effects from the fire guy trying to roast me. I mentioned to Pete that it was a long weekend after I left the mall but haven't gotten into specifics yet. After my watch duty, I tried to get some sleep and recover from the burns, but the next day I had to meet up with Daniel and get in some training, so I was thoroughly spent.

On top of all of that, weighing on me most, is the fire guy's ominous message. There's someone out there, able to control a flame-powered rogue, and they want to take me and my friends down. I can't get the fire guy's last words out of my head.

He wants to burn you all.

Meeting up with Pete at lunch, I eat in silence, still mulling over the encounter. Pete breaks through my mood with a deliberate cough.

I glance over to him. "What?"

"Dude, are you okay? You seem pretty out of it today." His head is cocked to the side as he studies me, his expression one of concern.

"Yeah." I sound anything but. "This weekend was rough."

Glancing to see who's around, Pete lowers his voice. "Does it have anything to do with that dude on fire this weekend?" I nod, taking a drink of my water. "The news reported some guy going crazy on the roofs with some kind of pyro weapons or something, but it never said someone from the Alliance was there."

"It didn't last long. He died."

Pete's eyes widen. "He what? Wait, you didn't …"

My eyes shoot open with the realization of what he's asking me. "No! Seriously, dude?"

"I don't know," he defends himself. "I know you're not a killer, Robbie, but what you do? Things can get life-threatening in a hurry."

"I know." I roll my eyes, more at myself than him. I love being a sidekick, and working with the Alliance, but it is extremely dangerous. "But, no, I didn't. He kind of just, like, extinguished or something. Doc is still running tests."

"Wow, that's crazy. Sorry."

I shrug my shoulders. "It is what it is. The fight isn't what's on my mind though. We think he was being controlled or was talking to someone, but we don't have any leads."

"Really?"

"Yeah," I say, getting up from the table. "Hey, I think I'm gonna head back to headquarters."

"What about the last two periods of school?"

"My parents and Mimic got it cleared through the liaison committee, so I'm cleared for missing certain times. They put that I have a blood disorder." I finally grin, Pete staring at me jealously. "Sometimes being a sidekick is crazy scary, but it does have its perks."

"You suck." He scowls while I keep a smile splashed across my face.

"Hit me up later. We still need to work on a homecoming date for you."

Pete rolls his eyes at my comment and I walk out of the cafeteria.

I head down the hallway toward a janitor's closet, somewhere I use as a backup teleportation spot. Deciding to drop my books at my locker first, I hear a giggle from behind and instantly know it's Jasmin. I glance back and see her facing away, talking to Maria.

"I still can't believe he said that," Maria says.

I feel slightly bad for eavesdropping, but curiosity gets the better of me, wondering who they're talking about.

"I know, right?" Jasmin replies. "He couldn't have been serious though."

"Jas, couldn't have been serious? You're kidding, right? First off all, he's an idiot if he wasn't serious. I mean, look at you."

"Maria," Jasmin scolds her, but I can tell she's a little embarrassed.

They're talking about a guy. Did someone ask Jasmin out?

"I'm serious," Maria says. "But more importantly, *he* was serious. Did you see him talk to any other girl out there? No. He singled you out."

"You think?" Though it's a question, more confidence laces her words and I'm gutted.

Some guy singled her out and she couldn't be happier. Of course she should be happy, and of course some guy would try talking to her. She's beautiful. But it's Jasmin. My Jasmin. She's supposed to be with me.

I shake my head at myself, feeling embarrassed and a

little pathetic. What am I talking about? I broke up with her. I'm with Melissa now. I can't be thinking like this.

"Jas, if he pops up again, you better say something."

"As if I'll ever see him again. It was a one-time thing. There was a group of supervillains flying by the school, and he showed up."

Wait, what?

"This may be King City, where superheroes and sidekicks are seen every day, but that doesn't mean I'll see him again. Worm's a sidekick, so I'm sure I'm the last thing on his mind."

WAIT, WHAT?

Holy crap, she isn't talking about some guy. She's talking about me. Well, not *me* me, but me!

"I wonder what he looks like under that helmet," Maria muses, as she shuts her locker.

"He does have cute lips," Jasmin says, letting out a playful growl, then laughs with Maria.

"See, there you go!" Maria says, their voices starting to fade into the background as they walk away. "Next time you better check him out a little more. See what else is cute on him."

They walk down the hall and I stand by the lockers, flabbergasted. I was so sure it was just a harmless comment. Sure, I did it because she's cute, but I didn't think I was flirting. I mean, it was just a comment, right? But now Jasmin thinks Worm is cute. She thinks I'm cute. I feel excited and heartbroken and guilty all at the same time. Stepping into the janitor's closet, I teleport to headquarters.

As soon as I get to the control room, I'm expecting to find Daniel there, but with him is also Doc and Melissa. Doc turns around as soon as he sees me.

"Worm, we were just about to call you."

I look at them, unsure. "What's up?"

"We received word from Supron," Melissa replies, smiling at me.

Her smile shoots a secondary round of guilt through me, though I smile back.

Why am I feeling so guilty? I didn't do anything. I just said hi. Sure, I added cutie, but so what?

Doc hits a button on the large control panel, and one of the large screens comes to life, Supron appearing on it.

"Greetings, sidekicks," he starts his message. He always refers to us as sidekicks, the same way an army general refers to others as soldiers. It's not a demeaning act, but I've never liked it much. Mimic will use either our real names or our codenames. "We hope everything is well. We've received the reports from Doc that say you three are working well together, so I commend you for that, and keeping King City safe."

The three of us all exchanges smiles.

"Our time here has been tumultuous to say the least. The first wave of attackers was worse than expected. We're holding up fine, but we're definitely going to be longer than we anticipated. We've decided to send you this pre-recorded message as a show of faith. There's no need to review your progress as a single unit from here on out. None of us need to debate anything, we know King City is in good hands. We likely won't be back on Earth for a number of months."

Daniel turns to me, his eyes wide, then asks Doc, "Did he just say months?"

"We're proud of you all," Supron's message continues. "We've sent personal messages to each of you, but I felt I needed to address one thing to all three of you, openly."

The tension in the room heightens.

"Hydro, we didn't place you in charge, but I'm expecting

a lot from you. You have the knowledge, and the drive. Be safe, son. Mighty Miss, your time with Ms. Majestic has been invaluable. Keep the team unified. Worm, with your powerset you have more at your disposal than not only your fellow sidekicks, but many superheroes in the Alliance."

I know teleporting is extremely rare, but his praise and commendation takes me aback. Melissa looks over at me, smiling. Daniel gives me a quick nod.

"You're only beginning to realize the power you possess. Even if you haven't reached your full potential yet, you must realize the seriousness of it. You have to work as a team, and if you do, I have no doubt that King City will thrive under all three of you as protectors until we come back. Thank you, and we'll speak again soon."

The screen goes black. We all stand there in shock, motionless. A loud clap echoes through the silent room—Doc slapping his hands together. "All right, you heard the man. Keep up the good work. Worm, a word?"

He walks past me, and I turn to follow him, but first glance at Daniel and Melissa. Daniel takes back over at the control desk, while Melissa gives me a small shrug. I was hoping to talk to her and finally ask her about homecoming. Maybe that's what I need.

We've been together for a few months now, but we haven't really had a real date. Like an actual confirmation of being official boyfriend and girlfriend. Perhaps homecoming will cement that down and I can get these straying thoughts of Jasmin out of my head. *But I guess I'll have to wait to ask about the dance*, I muse as I follow Doc out.

Arriving at one of his labs, he goes to stand at his desk. Papers are stacked neatly atop it, but vials and different serums are scattered over it. His desks always make me think he's some kind of mad scientist that looks like your loving grandpa.

"Have a seat." He motions over to a metal chair. "Any questions about what Supron said?"

Sitting, I shake my head. "Not really. I don't think there will be a problem with any of us. We're working really well together."

"No, not about that," he replies, not making eye contact with me. Instead, he opens a cabinet off to the side and pulls out a small, leather case.

"Oh. I mean ... I guess not. I know I'm a teleporter, Doc, and that there haven't been many of us."

Running his fingers over the case, his eyes finally find mine. He nods in thought, tapping a finger to his lips. "It's more than that, Robbie."

Unzipping the leather case, he pulls out a long syringe, and my eyes immediately double in size. "Whoa, Doc. What are you doing with that?"

He lets out an amused chuckle. "I had a small discussion with both Mimic and Supron about you ever since your first outing last year. Remember?"

"Of course." I roll my eyes. "I don't think I'll ever live down that embarrassment."

"Robbie, don't you remember what I told you later?"

I shake my head in confusion. "What?"

"When you teleported, you didn't just jump back to headquarters. You teleported back two seconds."

"Oh, right." I nod. "But I thought we've been over that. It was a freak accident or something. It was only two seconds. I'm a teleporter, plain and simple."

"No"—Doc shakes his head—"not plain and simple. Not even close." Pulling out a cotton swab, he dips it in a small dish of alcohol, and motions for me to roll up my sleeve.

"Hold still," he instructs, and inserts the syringe into my arm, drawing out blood.

With a slight cringe, I close one eye and look away with the other. You'd think after my training and being involved with fighting supervillains, getting a little blood taken from me wouldn't be such a big deal, but it still makes me queasy. Doc finishes and eyes the vial of the crimson liquid carefully.

"After I analyzed your blood last year, I found a very unique strand of platelets in your body," Doc continues. "There is a fraction of the plasma in your blood that is unlike almost any other I've seen before."

Okay, now he has my attention. "What are you talking about?"

"The platelets in your blood regenerate at an unparalleled level, which in turn causes your body to stay healthy longer. You don't heal faster, but once healed, your body returns to a state in which it's as if nothing ever happened to you. Why do you think you don't have any scars since you've become a sidekick?"

"I ..." I trail off. "I never thought about it."

"I've only seen these platelets in one other person, who ages at a decreased rate. Ten times slower than a normal human."

The shock from his words hits me across the face. I know exactly who he's talking about. "Supron? You're telling me I've got the same type of blood as Supron?"

"Sort of."

"What do you mean sort of, Doc? People look at Supron, his strength, the lightning, how long he's been around. He's looked at as a god sometimes. I'm not that. I can't do any of what he can do."

"Exactly," Doc replies calmly, raising a hand to my

shoulder. "Which is why I said sort of. The platelets are one part of what I've been researching. The other part is the plasma in your blood. A unique strain of plasma I've only seen one time."

"In who?" I ask, wanting to get to the bottom of this.

"I don't know."

I jump out of the chair, starting to get freaked out. "You don't know? How is that possible? And what's so unique about the plasma in my blood?"

"Robbie, this is why I've been trying to talk to you about this. It is serious, but please calm down. You're not dying. As a matter of fact, with the Supron blood, it's quite the opposite."

He smiles, and I know he's trying to put me at ease, but it's not working. "What about the plasma, Doc?"

"Robbie, I'm going to say these next words, but I need you to understand that we still have to run multiple tests to know what we're dealing with. Okay?"

His eyes bore into mine, while I slowly nod.

"The plasma in your blood we have on record has only been seen in one other person. We don't know who he is. He was hurt many years ago, and Supron helped save him. Once he healed, he disappeared. Since then, I've looked everywhere, searched for any clue as to who he was."

Doc stops talking just long enough to exhale deeply. He seems nervous, which does not help my anxiousness at all.

"I have eight confirmed sightings of him, in places throughout history. Our facial recognition scanners confirm it's the same person. All sightings are linked to different names though."

Pulling out a small tablet, he begins sliding his finger through the pictures. They're grainy, almost as if they were published in a black-and-white newspaper. One shows a guy with a fedora, and appears to be in the 1920s. Another picture shows him with dark hair, slicked back, as he stands in a dance club in the seventies.

"So ... what? As time goes on, he ages so slowly that he changes his identity every few decades?"

"No, that's the thing. Facial recognitions all confirm he's either older or younger in the scans. The sightings are spread out over two hundred years. All of the way back to the late eighteenth century, and then to the time Supron helped him almost two decades ago."

I don't know if it's the revelation that I have blood similar to one of the greatest superheroes in the world, or I'm getting mixed up in this ageless man, but I narrow my eyes, confused. "I don't get it."

"He ages at a normal rate."

"Then how can he live for so long?"

Staring back at me, he places a reassuring hand on my shoulder, keeping his gaze locked on mine. "He's not living for so long. He pops up at different moments in time. He's a time traveler."

7

The next week is a blur. I can't think about anything, not even about the second fire guy that's been spotted out in the city but then vanishes, or even Melissa and homecoming, which is rapidly approaching.

Nothing gets past what Doc told me at headquarters. There's a time traveler out there in the world. And the same type of DNA running through him, is running through me. How is that not earth-shattering news?

After Doc finished telling me that, I zoned out. He tried to keep me at ease, telling me he hadn't found any sign of the time traveler for years, ever since he and Supron had met him nearly twenty years ago. But they had the blood sample on file still. He'd gone over it with Supron and Mr. Mimic, trying to analyze it, to see if some latent powers in my system might manifest later, but all of his tests were inconclusive.

Sending me home, he told me to take the week off and rest. I'm not sure if that helped or not. Without visiting headquarters, I've just been aimlessly going through school days, dwelling on all of this information. Once the shock wore off, aggravations started setting in.

I can see Supron wanting to keep this news from me—he's very by-the-book and likes to keep everything close to the vest—but Doc should've told me. Mimic could have at least mentioned something. I even teleported back to headquarters during the middle of the week, when I knew Doc was on watch duty, and vented my frustration. His response only made me feel worse.

Mimic didn't want to concern me with something that I might never deal with or even have to know about. And after my time jump last year, Doc had been trying to get me in to see him and give him more blood to do testing, but I blew him off time and time again. He was trying to help me the whole time, and I just kept thinking he was being overcautious, or wanted to over-analyze things because he's Doctor Grandside.

I've kept in contact with Melissa, but I haven't told her yet. She's met my parents and offered to even swing by my home, but I can't do it. Although nothing has happened with me, it could. How do you tell someone that you might possibly have some latent time-traveling power kick in? Or not. So, I told her that I was getting behind in schoolwork. It's a weak excuse, since she knows I can be excused from missing some classes for almost anything, but she didn't protest.

Even though I've seen Pete all week at school, our conversations have been dull at best. He's hounded me about what's going on, but I've continued to tell him it's Alliance stuff. Of anyone, I should be able to talk to him about it, but I haven't. Wednesday, he asked if we could hang out this weekend and I said maybe, though I'd have to check my Alliance schedule. Then I didn't even show up to school the last two days.

There's a knock at my window as I'm lying in my bed, aimlessly playing a video game.

"Robbie, I know you're in there," Pete yells, and I can see his shadow through the closed curtains hanging in front of my window. I pause the game. "I heard your PlayStation!"

I glance back at my television, unsure if he's bluffing.

"Damn it, Robbie! I know something is going on, open up!"

I stay motionless. I feel bad for ignoring him, but he already knows my secret identity and that alone is a huge danger. This news could be life-altering.

I lie still, watching the window, and see his shadow fade and disappear. Leaning up, I move the curtains to the side and peek through, only to be knocked back in surprise as he plants his face against the window, yelling at me.

"Ha! I knew you were in there! Open up, you freak!"

I shake my head, unable to stop the chuckle from escaping. Nodding to my door, I get up, grab a red T-shirt, and head to my foyer to let him in. My dad is at work, and my mom went shopping with my abuela, so the house is quiet. After throwing the shirt on, I unlock the door for him.

"What the hell is your problem?" he yells, walking past me. "Why are you ignoring me?" Before I can answer, he spins on his heels, his face dropping. "Oh crap! Are you sick? Did you catch some alien virus or something?" He gasps, dropping his jaw. "Or is it worse? You didn't get discharged from the Alliance, did you? Like, for real this time?"

Shaking my head, I roll my eyes, and head back to my bedroom, hearing his footsteps behind. "No, it's nothing like that. It's ... it's just stuff, man."

"Ohmygod." He places both hands over his mouth, leaning against my desk, and I flop down over my bed. "You didn't ... You and Mighty didn't break up, did you?"

I let out another sigh. "No. We're still together."

"You don't sound very happy about it."

"Pete!" I groan out, pressing my head against my down pillows. "It doesn't have anything to do with Mighty."

"Well, I don't know!" he yells, taking a seat next to me on my bed. "You've practically been a ghost at school, only speaking when spoken to. And where have you been the last two days? Plus"—he holds up a finger—"no one's seen Worm out patrolling King City with Hydro or Mighty Miss. What am I supposed to think?"

He's right. And maybe more than that, I need to vent. I have to talk about this. With my best friend. Getting up from my bed, I head out to my kitchen. "Come on."

"Where are we going?"

"Oreos and peanut butter."

"Oh boy."

Pete and I have a long-standing ritual of dipping Oreo cookies into peanut butter while discussing our problems.

It started in third grade when I confessed to Pete I liked Becky Cooper and asked her to be my princess during recess. She said yes, and then proceeded to dump me the next day. Her reason? I wasn't her prince, but the gross frog. In sixth grade Pete broke his arm after we were playing around, jumping off of his couch acting like Supron and another superhero named Galaxium. After both events, we broke out the cookies and peanut butter.

Neither of our parents were big fans of the ritual, but after breaking his arm, they let us spend the week together and provided us with unlimited supplies. So, when either one of us bring it up, we know it's serious.

I grab the first cookie, dipping it into a jar of peanut butter, and take a delicious bite. Letting out a sigh of relief, Pete grabs a cookie and does the same.

"Dude, this week has been so crazy," I finally say.

"What happened?" he asks, already taking another cookie.

"Well, I guess I shouldn't say this week, it all started after I left you at the mall last weekend."

"You see, you should've blown off sidekick duties." He chuckles.

I can't help but do the same. "You're probably right. You know that fire guy I told you about that died?"

"Yeah."

"Well, right before he died, he left me with a completely freaky and ominous message. We think he was being controlled by someone else, like he was taking orders or something. And he said whoever was controlling him wanted to burn us all."

"Are you serious?" Pete looks shocked. "Like, you and the other sidekicks?"

"That's the thing, we don't know. That's why I was so out of it that day I left early. I couldn't stop thinking about it."

We both dip another cookie into the peanut butter. "And that's what's kept you so freaked out all week?" he asks.

"No, it gets worse. I took off to headquarters, and right when I got there, there was a message from Supron. The big three are gonna be off-world a lot longer than any of us thought. Probably for, like, months."

I stare down at the peanut butter jar, shaking my head.

"After Supron's message, he said some weird stuff. Doc pulled me aside and told me ... It's about my blood." Pete gazes at me, listening intently. "So, I guess, I kind of ... sort of ... have blood like Supron."

His mouth drops, little cookie crumbles falling out. "Are you serious?"

I nod. "We don't know what it means, and Doc still has a lot of tests to do, but yeah. My blood platelets are like Supron's, but that's not what's freaked me out the most."

"There's more? How can there be more?"

"There's a weird strain of plasma in my blood that Doc has only seen one other time." I take a deep breath, realizing I'm about to say it out loud to someone other than Doc for the first time. "The only other time he's seen it, it came from someone who can travel through time."

"What?" he deadpans.

"A time traveler."

Pete stands there, motionless. For a moment I think he's about to freak out, or possibly even faint. Then a huge smile spreads ear to ear.

"That. Is. Awesome!"

I chuckle in disbelief. "What?"

"You just said time traveler, right?"

"Yeah, how is that awesome?"

"Robbie!" he shouts, jumping up and down. "Are you kidding? You can travel through time! That's amazing! Not only can you teleport to, like, Egypt or something, but you can teleport to when the pyramids were actually being built. How are you not super stoked about this?"

I twist a cookie in my hand, staring at it. "Pete, this isn't a movie. I never even thought time travel was real, much less a power someone could have. I've already time traveled before and it was on total accident, so what if I accidentally do it again and—"

"Wait, what?" he shouts. "You've time traveled before?"

Oh crap. "Well, yeah, kind of."

"How do you *kind of* time travel?"

Leaning against the counter, I hang my head, and then dip another cookie. "Okay, so remember last year, before you knew I was Worm?" He nods. "When Worm first made his appearance, and teleported out of the fight, after that huge explosion nearly killed me? That's when I time traveled. I jumped back in time somehow by two seconds, but not only back in time, I teleported to a different location."

"Whoa, that's crazy."

"Yeah." I take another bite of my cookie. "Doc said it was an anomaly because, since I did jump back in time, I should've gone back to where I was, but instead I went to headquarters. He's been trying to figure it out. This whole time I just thought it was some kind of mistake, or maybe the wormhole I teleported through was messed up somehow. I don't know. But now, knowing there's an actual time traveler out there, and I have the same type of blood he does? It's really freaking me out, man."

Pete nods his head, dipping another cookie. "Wow. Sorry." I shrug. "But, Robbie, you guys don't know anything yet? Doc is saying it's just in your blood, right?"

"Yeah."

"Dormancy."

I stare at him, lifting a brow. "Huh?"

"Dormancy. We've been learning about plant life in biology and how some plants are dormant in winters. There are even some plants that look like they're dead for years but are actually alive. And then, there's a strain of plant life that causes certain flowers to bloom different colors, like blue instead of red, but it never actually happens. It *could* happen, but it doesn't. That strain in the plant just lies dormant for its entire life."

"Okay?" I'm still not getting it.

"Whatever's in your blood, maybe it'll stay dormant. Nothing will ever happen."

"But it already did happen. The two-second thing."

Pete grabs another cookie, excitedly dipping it into the peanut butter. "But you don't know. You said it could've been a number of things. Doc might even be wrong. I'm a huge fan of Doctor Grandside, you know that, but he has made mistakes in the past. And it's not like wormholes are an exact science. For as much as we know about them, there's still tons that we don't know."

I gaze at him, cracking a smile. Maybe he's right. Perhaps I am thinking about this too much. Who knows if it will ever come to anything. "You know what, you could be right."

"Pft, of course I'm right. Out of the two of us, who's always helping who with their science homework?"

I laugh. "Okay, who are you and where's Pete? You have way too much of an ego to be my best friend."

"I'm just coming into my own now, Robbie." He bumps his elbow against mine. "And this Pete knows a thing or two."

I chuckle again. "Fair enough. Anyway, sorry for bailing on you those last couple of days. And pretty much ignoring you this entire week."

He shrugs. "Eh, it's all good, except ..." His confident demeanor he had just seconds ago fades and he looks away.

"What?"

"Okay, don't be mad, but I kinda became friends with Jasmin again."

He stares at me; I'm sure trying to measure how I'm going to react. As much as I've always liked her, Jasmin and Maria were friends with Pete, too. Since we broke up, I know it's been awkward for him on some level.

"Oh. Yeah." I try to act as calm as I can. "Don't even

worry about it. I mean, it's kind of stupid, right? Just because we broke up, doesn't mean you can't talk to her or Maria."

"Cool. Yeah, that's what I said," he responds, but sounds anything but sure.

"So, um ..." I dip another cookie. "How'd that happen?"

"When you weren't there on Thursday, Jasmin and Maria saw me sitting by myself and came over and sat with me." A pang of guilt shoots through me. "It was weird at first, but then we started talking and it felt like old times. Yesterday, they came and sat with me again. We discussed it further, and ... yeah. We're cool now."

I nod, still trying to play it cool. "All right, cool."

Pete still cringes. "And I'm kind of meeting up with them at the mall tomorrow. Just to hang."

"Oh," I reply, sounding a bit more shocked than I mean to. "Right. I mean, yeah. That makes sense. Friends hang out."

His cringing persists, and he almost appears to be in pain, then looks away. "And I kinda ... sorta ... invited you along, too."

"You what?" I ask a little louder than expected.

8

Taking the package of cookies back to my room, I scrape off the frosting of one with my teeth, eyeing Pete suspiciously for a moment, before handing him a PlayStation controller. Pulling my gaming chairs out, we take our seats, and Pete sneaks little glances at me, I'm sure trying to measure how annoyed I am at what he's done.

He begins to explain to me that it was just a little comment. Something he didn't even mean, and that when Jasmin invited him to the mall, he said sure and threw my name out almost on instinct.

"I can't believe you, Pete," I grumble. "What am I supposed to do now? If I don't show up, it'll make it weird, and if I do show up, how's that any better?"

Selecting our favorite video game, I start it up, and he takes a seat in his chair before grabbing another cookie. "Robbie, I think you're freaking out about this too much. I know it'll be weird at first, but seriously, you can't go throughout all of high school without talking to her."

"It's not like I don't want to talk to her, but you know the deal."

"Yeah, but that's the other thing." He casts his eyes over to me, before looking back at the TV. "Um, I'm not exactly sure how to say this ..."

"What?"

"Well, see, she's ..."

"Pete?"

He drops his head back, eyes cast at the ceiling. "Okay, before I say this, you're cool with Mighty, right?" I nod. "You're into her, right? Like, it's not just a rebound or something?"

"Are you serious?" My mouth falls open and I gape at him. "Pete, we've been together for a couple of months now. It's not a rebound. I like her."

"Okay, okay. Cool, that's what I wanted to know. Like, for sure."

"You're not making any sense."

"I told Jasmin and Maria you were going out with her."

"You what?" I yell.

"No, no." He drops his controller, shaking his hands. "I don't mean like that. What I mean is, on Thursday Maria just blurted out asking if you were seeing anyone. I think Jasmin was wondering but didn't want to ask."

"Okay?" I give him a suspicious glare.

"I know you're dating Mighty Miss, but I couldn't say that. So, I made this face. We've both known Jasmin and Maria for years, and she obviously knew I was hiding something. So, I said you were kind of seeing some girl, and that she went to a different school.

"Oh." *Actually, that's a perfect cover.* "All right, that's not bad."

"Well, there's more."

"More?"

"After I said that, it's like the tension was broken. Jasmin looked a little sad, but then Maria whispered something to her. I couldn't hear what it was, so I was all like, 'what's that about?' and they both giggled."

"Giggled?"

"Yeah. Then Jasmin got kind of red. Before she could say anything, Maria told me Jasmin's seeing someone, too."

Just like before, I shouldn't feel anything over this. I told Pete I'm going out with Melissa, and it's going good. Jasmin and I can't happen, I know that. So why do I feel deflated that she's seeing someone?

"She's going out with someone?"

"Well, not really."

"But you just said—"

"Maria said that, and then Jasmin stopped her. Jas said she's not seeing anyone, but there was this cute guy she saw the other day. He doesn't go to our school, so she's hoping to see him again."

My eyes shoot open. She couldn't be talking about Worm, could she? No way. I shake my head, trying to get rid of the thoughts, because in the end it doesn't mean anything anyway.

"Then, today at lunch they said they were gonna go to the mall this weekend and invited me. Since you're going out with Mighty Miss, Jasmin likes some other guy now, and that encounter you two had the other day trying to get out all of the awkwardness, I don't know ..." He stares at his video game controller. "I said maybe you could come, too. They both nodded." He pauses and finally meets my eyes again. "I just want us all to be cool again. You know?"

I nod, starting to feel the guilt for the uncomfortableness I inadvertently put between Pete and them. He has a point. And who knows, maybe if I hang out a little more with them, I can start to think of her as just a friend. Because she is. That's all she can be.

We don't talk about it anymore, instead opting for a few rounds of our favorite first-person shooter game. It feels good to finally kick back with my best friend, and be a normal teenager for once, not worrying about getting called out to fight off some supervillain. And I try not to think about meeting back up with him and the girls the next day, but the awkwardness follows me anyway.

It's fine at first.

Pete and I arrive at the same time, and we meet up with Jasmin and Maria in the food court. She looks beautiful, with slight curls in her brown hair, wearing a lavender crop top that shows off her tan arms, and capri pants. But I don't notice it. Nope, not at all.

Walking over to a coffee stand, we get in line and I think about ordering her her favorite mocha caramel latte but decide against it. Would that be weird, me ordering her a drink?

After getting the drinks, we walk along the second story of the galleria, mostly window shopping, with none of us talking very much. King City Galleria is one of the nicer places to shop with five levels of stores, a twenty-screen theater attached to the mall, and two different food courts. Jasmin and Maria stop and stare at a display, whispering back and forth, pointing at homecoming dresses, before disappearing inside. While we wait outside for them, I'm reminded about Pete's situation.

"So, about your date?" I casually say, taking another sip of my caramel iced coffee.

He glares at me. "Dude, you won't stop with that, will you?"

"Pete, you said yourself you're a new man." He rolls his eyes. "Look, honestly, tell me to shut up if I *am* getting annoying. I want you to go with us and have a good time, but if you're not comfortable coming out yet, I totally get it."

I do. Yes, I've been harping on homecoming for a while, but I truthfully would never want Pete to feel uncomfortable. However, even before this weekend, I have noticed more pep in his step, if that's a thing. I have no idea what he's going through, but he does seem surer and more confident. If he's ready to go public, I'll be there for him. And if not, that's cool, too.

He chuckles, biting his straw. "I don't know ... There are times I feel like I want to come out already. I mean, my mom and you know, and that's all that really matter to me." He gives me a sincere smile, one I return. "But it's freaking terrifying at the same time."

I nod. "It's cool, dude."

"What about you? You ask her yet?"

"Ask who what?" Maria jumps in, as they exit the store.

Pete and I exchange worried glances. "Oh," I start, swallowing my nerves. "It's nothing. Just about homecoming, that's all."

Jasmin eyes me carefully. "Are you going?" she asks.

"Um ... I think so. You?"

"I'm not sure."

Her answer pains me on two levels. One, that she's not going is a crime just in itself. She should definitely be the gorgeous girl that everyone at the dance is looking at, with every guy jealous of her date. And secondly, I wish I could be that guy.

Damn it, Robbie. Get that out of your head. You're with Melissa.

Trial By Fire

Breaking up my traitorous thoughts, Maria interjects, "Where would you go, Robbie?"

I stare at her, confused. "What do you mean?"

Her eyes jump to Pete briefly, before landing on mine. "Pete said you were seeing someone."

"Maria," Jasmin scolds her, slapping her arm.

"Oh my God, you guys. We're sixteen. We can't act like little kids," Maria says, leaning on her hip, keeping her gaze locked on me.

She has a point. This is what we both probably need, right?

"You know what? You're right." I can't let Maria show me up as being more mature. I'm a sidekick after all. If that doesn't show maturity, what does? "I am seeing someone. She goes to Edgewater High." I think up the lie quickly. "I'm not sure if we'll be going to hers or ours. Maybe we'll do both."

Pete looks over at me with a surprised expression.

Jasmin stares at me, expressionless. I can't tell if she's interested, jealous, or indifferent. She just has a blank look.

"What about you guys?" I ask them both, but keep my eyes locked on Jasmin.

"Um, I don't know. Maybe."

Her stoic expression begins to morph. She casts her eyes down to the ground. Hoping to keep the mood pleasant, I nudge her arm. "Jas, I'm sure Maria could find one of those jocks she's always fawning over for you."

"Oh, you're so funny, Robbie." Maria scowls.

"Some things never change." I laugh.

Seeming to get more comfortable, Jasmin takes another sip of her drink, giggling. "Well, there is this one guy, but he doesn't go to our school either."

"Oh?" I raise my brows.

"Yeah, I just met him once. Um, Maria, where were we again?"

I bite my lip, trying to hold back the smirk.

"Oh, yeah. We were, um ... in Shadow Ridge. Yeah, that's it."

I eye them both suspiciously. "Shadow Ridge? Over by Five Points?"

"Yep, Five Points. That's it." Maria half chuckles, then looks away, taking a large drink from her iced tea.

Maybe I should drop it ... should move on past this subject. But I don't. I know she's talking about Worm and want to dig deeper. "So, what's his name?"

"His name?" Jasmin repeats and I nod, smiling. "It's W —" Her eyes glance at Maria, before looking back at me. "W-Will. William. Yeah, it's William." She giggles, nervously.

Deciding to finally back off, I give her a friendly smile as we walk along the shops.

"Cool. Well, he's a lucky guy."

My words are so casual, so voluntary and honest, that I immediately cringe after saying them. Jasmin's head snaps to the side and I can feel her eyes on me. I broke up with her. I told her I didn't like her anymore. Why in the world would I then say her date is a lucky guy? I'm such an idiot.

Thankfully, my phone buzzes and I step slower, letting them walk ahead of me, while I answer it.

It's an encrypted message from Daniel, asking me if I'm up for a distress call. After being on the bench for an entire week, and especially after my last comment, I'm now itching to get out of this situation. Pete glances back over his shoulder and I wave my phone to him, nodding to the side that I have to leave. The girls walk into the next store and he comes over to me.

Trial By Fire

"You get an alert?" he whispers.

"Yeah. Sorry, man. Hydro just messaged me and—"

"Hydro?"

"Yeah. Wants me to help out with something. Would you hate me if I bailed right now?"

"Go for it. Just remember, we're still supposed to take that tour of headquarters."

I laugh and we bump fists. "I know, I know. What will you tell the girls?"

Pete looks over at the store and a smile floats across his face. "So, you're not gonna like this, but Thursday I told them I thought you caught a bad case of diarrhea."

"You what?" My eyes almost fall out of their sockets.

"Sorry, it was the first thing that came to mind."

"Are you serious? *That* was the first thing? I told you my excuse with the school is a blood disorder."

"I know." He sounds apologetic but is still smiling. "But that sounds so serious. I figured this was an easy one. I'll say something else this time."

Dropping my head back, between my shoulders, I let out a sigh. "Fine. Whatever."

Taking off toward the exit, I have to walk in front of the store that Pete goes into to meet the girls. Still within earshot of them, I hear them talking.

"Robbie's leaving?" Maria asks.

"Uh, yeah," Pete responds. "Something came up."

I should be grateful he says that and doesn't resort to the excuse from previously in the week. But I don't feel grateful. A slight wave of shame washes over me from Jasmin's words.

"So, he still has his disappearing acts, huh?"

I try to shake off the pathetic feeling, remember that this is exactly why we aren't together now. Why we couldn't be together last year, and why it can't work in the future. As a sidekick, and hopefully a superhero one day, I'm always on call. And even worse than that, my world is dangerous. I can't put her in the way of that.

None of those valid reasons does anything to quell the feeling of guilt in the pit of my stomach.

9

I find Melissa and Daniel across town, at King City Zoo. Teleporting atop of a huge orangutan cage, I look around and see people running in every direction. Then, three elephants stampede through the cement walkway, causing the animals in neighboring cages to go hysterical. Daniel glides overhead and lands next to me.

"What's happening?" I ask.

"Lioness! She's at the eastern part of the park, near the owl tower." He jumps up and skids away on a sheet of water and I follow, teleporting to the east side of the park.

Now, you might think in a zoo that's being overrun with animals, when someone yells out the word lioness, the logical conclusion is that a lioness has escaped her cage. Normally, you'd probably be right. But Lioness in King City is a B-level supervillain.

She has the senses and reflexes of a lion and can also communicate with feline animals. She's made it her personal mission to cause as much chaos and pandemonium as she can, all in the name of freeing animals. She wants to set animals free all over the world. It's not a horrible mission, but in her case, she wants them to overrun everything, and of course she'd be in charge of the animals.

Two large tigers, a mountain lion, and a panther all circle around Lioness. They pace back and forth, guarding her, awaiting her mental instructions to attack anyone that comes near.

If I'm being honest, Lioness is really hot. With an hourglass figure, her entire body is covered in shimmering, golden fur, and her orange mane of hair sways as she stalks. Her emerald cat eyes dart back and forth, then lock on Melissa, who flies in and lands in front of her. I land directly next to her, and Daniel slides to a stop on my other side.

"That's far enough, Lioness!" Melissa demands.

She flips her hair, rolling her eyes, and lets out a demeaning chuckle. "It's the children again." The large cats tense up, ready to pounce. "If I didn't know any better, I'd say all of the adults in the Alliance decided to take a vacation."

I send an anxious glance over at Daniel, who returns the look. Mimic and the others didn't announce to King City they were leaving. But since they've been gone, there's been more and more chatter. Doc told us he'd send out a press release soon, informing the city of their whereabouts and that we'd have backup from neighboring superheroes, but this is the first time we're being called out on it.

Melissa ignores the insult. "This ends now!"

"You're right. It does." Letting out a large growl, she points her finger at us and the cats attack, all of them running directly at Melissa.

Grabbing her hand, I teleport her out of the way, and Daniel springs into action, erecting a huge water barrier between him and the cats.

"Hydro, form a capsule!" I yell out, and he nods.

Grabbing more water out of the air, he encloses the cats among themselves, creating a huge orb of water, locking the cats inside of it. They flail around, their paws paddling in the cold water, and I look to the side, seeing an enclosed amphitheater with no other animals inside. Teleporting down, I run and dive at the waterball. As soon as I touch it, I teleport it and the cats into the amphitheater. A huge splash sounds, and the cats scatter, shaking their paws and fur.

"She's running!" Melissa yells out.

I turn around and see Lioness taking off in the opposite direction.

"Worm!" Melissa calls out, and I look back at her, our timing perfectly in sync.

She jumps and I grab her arm, teleporting her in front of Lioness, who doesn't have enough time to react, and Melissa smashes her across the face with a forearm, knocking her down.

With Lioness dazed, Melissa kneels over and handcuffs her, then puts a mental power dampener around her forehead, so she can't communicate with the animals anymore.

"Have you guys practiced that before?" Daniel asks, a surprised smirk over his face.

"I guess we just know each other," she answers, giving me a smile.

Moments later, the police show up and haul Lioness away, while more emergency personnel work to get all of the animals of the zoo back in order.

"Media is waiting outside of the zoo," Doc radios to our headsets. "I think one of you should be the one to let them know the big three are off-world."

The three of us look at one another, trepidation across our faces.

"Are you sure, Doc?" I ask, putting a finger to the side of my helmet.

"I think coming from you it'll be better. You just helped take down Lioness, and in great fashion, might I add. Nice work. Stay calm and confident. The city trusts you three."

We all exchange glances once again.

"I'll do it," Melissa speaks up.

"Are you sure?" I ask.

Grabbing my hand, she gives me a smiling nod. "You guys head back."

"Are we sure we're ready for this?" Daniel asks. "I mean, we know what we're doing, but this makes it *official*. Who knows what other supervillains out there are going to want to take a shot at us, once we tell them Supron, Majestic, and Mimic are off-world?"

Melissa gives me a timid glance, but I smile back, confidently. "We got this, you guys."

A moment of silence floats between all three of us, and then Daniel nods. "Okay."

Exchanging smiles with Melissa, I grab Daniel's shoulder and teleport us back to headquarters, leaving Melissa to talk to the reporters. As soon as we enter the control room, Doc greets us.

"Excellent work out there. Supron and Mimic would be proud."

"Thanks," I reply.

"Hydro, can you take over on the control desk? I need to go over some information with Worm."

"No problem," he answers, taking a seat at the desk.

Following Doc out of the room, we head down to one of his labs. "I hope the light workload helped you this week, Robbie?"

"It was okay," I answer. "To be honest, getting back out

there today helped me focus more than this entire week of doing nothing."

"Good." He nods and we enter his lab.

"Have you found any new results from analyzing my blood?" I lean against a large mahogany desk, lined with half a dozen different microscopes, all various sizes, and containers with different specimens of whatever he's working on.

"Unfortunately, no." He grabs three large cotton swab sticks, and motions to my face. "Neck back."

I do as he orders, and he wipes one swab down my neck.

"Mouth open." Again, I follow his instructions, and he swabs the other two sticks in my mouth, one sliding along the roof of my mouth and the other over my tongue. "I'll probably ask for a few more samples. I want to continually monitory your DNA and see if there are any fluctuations at different times of the day or as time goes on."

"Okay." I nod, unsure what else to say. He's still running tests, so there's not much I can even think to ask. "Am I good to go?"

"Yes." His eyes soften, giving me a smile, and then he turns around, sliding the cotton sticks into three separate vials.

Leaving the lab, I venture down the hallway where a large window sits, with a gorgeous view of the heart of King City.

King City Tower is off to the right, the business district a mile to the west. I love King City. Yes, it's all I've ever known, and yes, it's been home to the greatest superheroes in the world, but this place has always been *my* home. They call the city a beacon of hope to other places out there. An example of what can truly be accomplished if everyone works together.

With the sun setting, the orange and yellow glow from the dusk simmers over the skyscraper windows, a sense of hope instills in me. Everything that could be going on with me is nothing compared to what is *actually* happening. I'm a sidekick. I'm doing what I've wanted to do since I was five years old. And that instills a sense of pride and determination in me, blocking out any apprehensions over Doc's tests.

Turning a corner, I'm promptly met by Melissa, who stands right in front of my bunker door with her tiara mask off. She gives me a tight hug, and a soft kiss, and then opens my door, pulling me inside where we fall onto the small couch in my room.

"How'd the press conference go?" I ask, brushing a strand of hair away from her face.

"As good as expected. Some reporters were shocked about the news, but most nodded and just started asking about Lioness."

I laugh. "See, people know we're awesome."

She giggles, rolling her eyes, and then sits up and reaches under the couch. "I got us something."

"Oh yeah?"

Watching as she pulls out a plastic bag, I lift a brow, unsure what it is. A quick round of laughter follows, as she shows me the cover of two DVD movies; *My Bloody Axe* and *Die, Zombie, Die*.

"I thought these sounded the scariest." She smirks. "What do you think?"

"Well, we watched *Die, Zombie, Die* already."

"We did?"

I laugh again. "Yeah. It's the one where you showed me that very sexy thing you can do with your tongue."

She blushes. It doesn't happen much, but I love it when it does. It never escapes me that she's from a different planet. Not only her culture, but her entire world, is different than mine. But when she gets embarrassed, she's just a cute girl who's my girlfriend.

I'm reminded that we haven't been around each other for a week. She nervously picks at the edge of the DVD, and I lean closer, kissing her cheek.

See, this is exactly what I need. To remember I'm with Melissa. She's my girlfriend. There's no need to get all freaked out about lingering feelings over Jasmin, because that's all they are. Lingering feelings from liking her for so long. Melissa's who I'm with now. Then I remember about homecoming.

"So, I've been meaning to ask you something."

"Okay."

As if we haven't already made out a hundred times, nervous butterflies bubble around inside. "See ..." I take a deep breath.

She puts a hand to my cheek. "What's wrong?"

"No, nothing." I shake my head, letting out a nervous laugh. "Okay, the thing is, on this planet we have high school dances. We have one coming up in a few weeks, called homecoming."

"Okay?" She stares at me, unsure.

"And when we go to them, we usually invite a date. Most of the time it's a girlfriend/boyfriend thing, or at least someone you like. So ... I was wondering if maybe you'd want to go?"

"Oh." She sounds surprised. "I think I'd like that. On our planet we have functions where people get together. Do they have music?"

I laugh, finally feeling more at ease. "Yeah, of course. You can't dance without music."

Smiling, she leans closer to kiss me, but I stop her.

"There's just one more thing. It's not like I can go as Worm and you as Mighty Miss. I want you to go, but as Melissa Caspian. Is that okay?"

Her eyes light up. "Of course, it's okay."

"But you remember my best friend? Pete? If you go under your real identity, he'll know who you are."

"I trust you, Robbie," she answers without hesitation. "And if you trust Pete, then I do too."

That was a lot easier than I thought it was going to be. "Wow, um, okay. Great."

Raising the movies in her hands, she waves them back and forth. "Which one's it going to be?"

I point at *My Bloody Axe*. "As much as I loved *Die, Zombie, Die*, let's try something new."

"My thoughts exactly."

Going over to the small TV, she inserts the DVD and then walks back over, kissing me again, as the movie plays in the background.

10

The next week passes by surprisingly trouble free. There haven't been any sightings of the fire guys anywhere. Doc's taken a couple more samples of my blood, but everything is normal. I've had a few training sessions with Daniel, and the homecoming dance is right around the corner. Maria and Jasmin have even started eating lunch with Pete and me again. The first day it was a little weird, but that passed quickly.

The highlight is finally telling Pete that Melissa agreed to not only be my date but share her secret identity with him.

After school, I stop Pete before we head home. "Since you're going to meet her at homecoming, I think it's time."

"Time for what?"

A Cheshire smile crosses my lips. "For your tour." He stops walking and his jaw drops. "I'll take you to Alliance headquarters, and then I'll introduce you to her, informally this time."

Grabbing my shoulders, he stares intently at me, completely focused. "Are you serious right now? Don't play with me, Robbie. I can't be held responsible if you're messing with me."

I laugh. "I'm totally serious."

"Right now? Tonight?" He clenches his fists together, trying to contain himself.

"Whoa, no. Not right now." He scowls at me. "Pete, we can't go this second. I still have to get official clearance on your pass and everything. We can go this weekend."

"I have to wait until the weekend? Do you know how difficult that's gonna be?"

I laugh it off and head home, only to meet up with him the next two days at school, to watch him try to contain his excitement. Every time we're alone in the hallways, or at our lunch table before the girls join us, he whispers about how excited he is.

Hey, I love superheroes. I've wanted to be one since forever. But his excitement borders on crazy. I constantly have to remind him to calm down. It's a little confusing, since between the two of us, I was always the one gushing about how awesome superheroes are. He mentions Doc, and I know he looks up to him since Doc is the official "science guy" for the Alliance, and Pete loves science. He asks what he should wear, and I tell him just his normal clothes are fine, but he frowns at my response. It's ... strange.

When Saturday rolls around, we finally head over to headquarters, and to keep everything official I walk us through the visitor entrance, getting his pass from the front desk. He holds the pass in his hands in awe, mesmerized.

"Thanks, Julie," I say, giving the front desk associate a smile. She has to hold back her giggle at Pete's reaction.

Motioning for him to follow me, we walk through the first floor. There are small tours held for civilians, and Pete's already seen all of the common things on the first floor, so we bypass the legacy room, and instead of heading to the second floor, I decide to go directly to the fifth level. It's not high security, but it's a level civilians almost never go.

Before the elevator doors open, a voice sounds through the speakers.

"Warning, heat signatures and DNA scans are not cleared for visitor five-six-eight-zero. Requesting fingerprints and voice authority, please."

Pete looks over at me, one part scared, one part in awe.

"Authority code one-eleven. Codename: Worm."

"Acknowledged." A small screen slides out from the wall, with a glowing outline of a hand. "Fingerprint scan, please."

Removing a glove, I place my hand over the screen, and a confirming beep sounds.

"This is so cool," Pete whispers with glee.

"Welcome, Worm," the voice says as the doors open. "By authorization of Doctor Grandside, you've been allowed one guest, eligible for visitation rights up to level ten. Please have your guest say aloud their name, for vocal recognition and confirmation."

I look over at Pete and nod.

"Um, Peter Malory."

"Welcome, Mr. Malory."

"All right, let's go." I clap my hands and walk through blue laser beams in the doorway. Pete doesn't move, his eyes carefully scanning the lights. "Come on, it's fine. It's the body scan."

Taking a small step, he squints one eye, and hurries through the blue lights, biting his lip. I let out a laugh, slapping his shoulder. "Good job, freak."

"What?" He scowls at me. "I didn't know I was gonna get a body scan."

"Dude, it's the Justice Alliance, not an art museum."

"Whatever." He rolls his eyes and I laugh again.

His head is on a swivel, as he looks any and everywhere. There are two minor control rooms with computers and large maps he can see into, and then we pass a large lab when he practically drools over the window, peering inside.

"Is Hydro on duty today?"

"I think he's in our main control room right now. Why?"

"Oh, no reason." His gaze meets mine for moment before he looks back into the lab. "What about Doctor Grandside?"

That's who I thought he'd ask about first. "Check it out," I call out to him, opening a door and nodding for him to go inside.

Pete's jaw drops when he enters the laboratory. I've seen Doc's labs hundreds of times, but I take it in with new eyes, watching Pete inspect everything. White walls, marble floors, and his lab tables are set up with half a dozen experiments he's working on, all off-world plants and species. Doc turns around from examining a microscope, and delivers his grandfather-like smile, extending his hand to Pete.

"Ah, Mr. Malory, a pleasure to see you again."

With his mouth still hanging open, Pete nods.

"Thanks again for the pass, Doc," I say. Pete's still shaking his hand. "Okay, Pete, he's gonna need that hand back."

Pete lets out an embarrassed chuckle. "Right, right. Sorry. I know I told you last time I was here, but I'm just … I'm a huge fan, Doctor Grandside. You're a real inspiration."

"Thank you, young man."

Pete's attention is caught by something on the table behind Doc. "Holy crap, is that a D-Ray microtube?"

"Nice," Doc replies. "You know your physiology tools."

Trial By Fire

"Oh, absolutely. I'm a bit of a science nerd, I may have told you that before."

"Well, the world can always use more of us nerds." Giving him another smile, Doc looks over at me with a bit more trepidation. "Not to be the bearer of responsibility, but I hope Robbie has conveyed to you the seriousness of your visitation here."

"Oh, yes, sir." Pete stands up straight, seeming to finally calm his giddiness. "I absolutely take this very serious. I'm well aware that knowing anyone's secret identity, even if he is my best friend, is a massive responsibility. I promise I won't let you down, sir."

We've been best friends for years. I'm older than him by only six weeks. But the way he's conducting himself, and his total respect and reverence for Doc, instills in me a sense of pride over him.

Doc must realize it, too, as his demeanor morphs back into a natural and friendly ally. "Excellent. I know you won't, Pete. Why don't you guys head out and check out level six?"

"Level six?" Pete asks.

"Inter-dimensional utility room."

"Oh, awesome!"

After checking out level six, we venture over to one of our training rooms, and I show Pete the cool voice and neural activation protocols the room has. It can read our vital signs and neurological pathways, which in turn can adapt to our training situations so we're always kept on our toes. It's a bit technical, but I figure Pete would love it since it's the kind of stuff he loves. After we're in the training room for a couple of minutes, he looks around.

"Hey, do you think we could check out the main control room?"

"The control room?" I ask, and he nods casually. "Yeah, I

guess so. I mean, Hydro's on watch duty right now, and it's the middle of the day, so there's probably not a lot of stuff to see. Honestly, the control room is the most boring room in the entire building."

He shrugs, averting his eyes. "Yeah, I guess ... but visitors don't usually get to see it, right?"

"That's true," I answer. "Yeah, sure."

Melissa's out on a patrol right now, but my nerves are amped up because that's the other reason for the visit. He's supposed to meet her and finally learn her secret identity. So, I try to stay calm, and just enjoy Pete's enthusiasm over the tour.

"So, it's pretty cool, right?"

"Mm-hm." He nods, seeming a little more on the nervous side.

We walk into the control room, and since I told Daniel that I was bringing in Pete as a visitor, he's still powered up as Hydro. Sitting at a desk, the blue sheen of water covers his head, masking his identity, while his dry hands tap away at a keyboard.

"Hey, Hydro. This is Pete. I think you guys met once."

He throws a quick glance back and then returns his attention to the computer monitor. "Hey."

I roll my eyes at Pete, silently apologizing for the abruptness. "Anyway, has Mighty radioed in?"

"Yeah," he replies, still staring at the monitor. "She was helping King City Police with a situation, but they're almost done now. She should be back soon." Swiveling the chair around, Daniel stands up and leans against the desk. "So, Pete, how's the tour been?"

I expect him to gush all over the place, and act like a kid in a candy store, telling him about everything we've seen.

Instead, Pete looks down at his shoes, shrugging. "Uh, yeah. It's been cool."

Through the sheen of water over his face, I can see Daniel smirk. Pete lifts his gaze and they make eye contact, only to have Pete look away again.

"Excuse us." I grab Pete's arm, ushering him quickly out of the room, and stab a finger into his chest. "You jerk!"

"What?"

"'It's been cool.' You've got to be kidding me! You haven't been excited to come and take a tour, you ... you ... I can't believe you."

"Robbie, I have no idea what you're talking about."

"Oh, you so know what I'm talking about. You've got the hots for Hydro."

"Dude!" Pete cringes, his eyes scanning the area. He doesn't deny it. And he turns a bright red. "Not so loud."

"That's it, isn't it? That's why you've wanted to come back here so bad."

"No," he answers, looking anywhere but at me. "Not totally."

"What do you mean 'not totally'? It's *totally* totally. Why didn't you just tell me?"

He folds his arms, his embarrassment fading, and he glares at me. "Seriously, Robbie?"

"What?"

"You're my best friend, but you're also a sidekick. I didn't want to be like 'Oh, hey, can I come to the Alliance headquarters with you so I can check out and hopefully flirt with someone you work with?' This isn't like school, where I can ask you to ask him something. Besides, it's more than just that."

I flinch. "What's that supposed to mean?"

"It means—" His words cut off and his attention diverts

from me to over my shoulder. "Uh, dude? Is that your girlfriend?" He wrinkles his nose.

Turning around, Melissa walks toward us, completely covered in what looks like green goo. It drips from her mask and hair, leaving little splotches on the ground. Her feet leave a trail of sludge.

I hurry over to her. "Whoa, what happened—"

"Don't get close to me!" She throws up her hands.

"What is this?"

She scowls. "Evidently, King City Police don't train their rookies to inspect all gamma ray toxin pockets with greylon adapters before initiating a cleanup protocol. It's Klactian bacteria."

I cringe. "Ew."

"Yeah." She rolls her eyes, the green slime continuing to drip. "I'm gonna go wash this off, but ..." Trailing off, she drops her head. "I need some help."

"With what?"

As she slowly turns around, I realize a creature the size of a softball is sticking to her left shoulder. The tangerine and marigold colors of it swirl around, with little turquoise spikes covering it. No discernible eyes or nose, but two claws dig into her shoulder and a suction cup mouth is stuck to her skin. *Disgusting*.

"Gah!" Pete jumps back. "What the hell is that?"

"It's a Klactin." She wipes the lime green sludge off of her forehead. "They aren't fatal, but they latch on like leaches. The only way to get them off is by administering a toxin in three different parts of their body. Unfortunately, since it's behind me, I can't reach."

"I better go help her." I start following her as she heads to her room, but quickly turn and point a finger at Pete.

"We're not done talking about this. Keep your hands to yourself in that control room."

Pete stares at me, cocking an eyebrow.

I've studied about Klactins and the different bacteria they possess. They affect different species in various ways, but I know they can make humans especially sick. I wait outside of her bathroom as she rinses off, and search through her tools, grabbing a set of pliers and gloves from her supply shelf. I really need to stock up my room with Alliance necessities. All I have are empty potato chip bags lying around.

"Robbie?" she calls out.

"Yeah?"

"I got it all rinsed off. Can I get your help now?"

"Sure."

Walking into the bathroom, the steam from the shower still floats in the air. She stands in front of the bathroom counter, a towel wrapped around her torso, leaving her shoulders bare. Her wet hair falls over her right shoulder, leaving the left one exposed with the alien creature.

"Whoa."

"I know, it's disgusting." She frowns, glancing behind at her shoulder.

"Well, yeah." I rub the back of my head and look away, embarrassed. "But, uh, I was talking about the view."

Snapping her head around, her mouth drops. "Seriously?"

"Mel, I definitely need to see you in a towel more."

"You Earth boys," she replies, rolling her eyes.

I feign a hurt look. "I thought you said I was the first Earth boy you dated."

"You are. Doesn't mean you're not like all of the others."

"Well, in that case ..." I turn around. "I might as well call Daniel in here. He'd be just as much help."

She giggles, grabbing my arm. "No, come on. Help get this thing off."

Pulling out a small silver canister from a cabinet, she hands it to me, along with an eyedropper. "All you need to do is place three drops of that on it."

"Then what?" I ask, taking a look at the little bugger. "I got these pliers if we need them." I wave them at her.

"No. The toxins from the ointment will shrivel it up. We should be able to just pull it off after that."

Setting the pliers down, I lift my brows. "Sounds easy enough."

Taking the eyedropper, I fill it with the ointment from the canister, and squirt the drops over the alien. Immediately it starts to shiver, then begins shrinking in size. Getting smaller, almost to the size of a grape, it seems like it's completely dehydrated, but keeps shrinking. Finally, the shrinking stops, and it's about the size of a small Band-Aid, crinkled up like a piece of weathered, orange paper.

"Okay, now just pull it off." She looks at me through the reflection of the mirror we stand in front of.

My face cringes, but I grab the edge of it and pull. Peeling it off of her skin, it's crispy, but not dry enough to where it will start to break apart. Her skin underneath has little blotches of orange and red, almost like a rash, and I hold up the Klactin.

"What do we do with it?"

"Just throw it in the garbage."

"We don't need to decontaminate it or something?"

"Nope, that's it." Before I can throw it away, she turns around and wraps her arms around me, planting her lips on mine. "Thank you."

"I'd be much more into this kiss if I wasn't holding some gross little orange thing with my other hand."

She laughs, then ushers me out of the bathroom. "Why don't you go back to the control room? I'll be there in a couple of minutes."

"Okay."

Throwing the shriveled-up critter into her wastebasket, I leave her room and head back to the control room, only to be shocked once again.

Hydro is depowered. He's leaning against the control desk, Pete leaning into him, both of their arms around one another, in a full-blown make-out session. I clear my throat, loudly, causing them to immediately jump away from one another, red slashing across both of their faces.

Pete finally meets my eyes, then shrugs.

11

All four of us—Pete, Daniel, Melissa, and me—all sit around the large conference desk usually held for Supron, Majestic, and Mimic. If a sidekick is in this room, it's because we're either being coached on our latest mission or going over review policies that we've screwed up on. And, I guess, in a way we're doing that again.

Daniel sits next to Pete, still depowered, which means Pete can see his true identity. Pete stares at me as if he's just been called into the principal's office. Melissa's eyes bounce everywhere, first to Daniel and Pete, then over to me, as she stays silent. She's also without her mask, but the bombshell of Pete and Daniel making out has completely derailed my original purpose today of introducing Pete to her properly, revealing her secret identity.

We sit there as minutes roll by, none of us saying anything. Finally, I explode. "What the hell, you guys?"

"Dude, calm down." Daniel lifts his hands.

"Calm down? Daniel, you just completely blow your cover as Hydro to make out with my best friend?" I turn to Pete. "And you. This is not why I brought you here today. All of this time I thought you just wanted to hang out when you really just wanted to *make* out."

"Robbie, it's not that big of a deal," Daniel protests again.

"Seriously? Last year all you talked to me about was 'keeping proper protocol' this and 'making sure we remain professional' that. Now you're revealing your identity and making out with my best friend?"

"Of all people, I thought you'd be the coolest about this."

My jaw drops, and I start shaking my head. "What are you talking about?"

Daniel looks over at Pete. "Wait, you didn't tell him?"

Glancing at Melissa, I realize she's as confused as I am. My eyes meet Pete's. "Tell me what?"

Pete scratches the back of his neck nervously, looking down at the table. "I was going to, and then Melissa walked in covered in slime."

"It's actually Klactian bacteria," Melissa corrects him. "It's similar to—"

"Is that really important right now?"

She stops, with Pete and Daniel exchanging glances. "I was meaning to tell you," Pete starts. "The thing is ... we've kind of been together for ... a while?"

"A while?"

"A month."

"*What*?" I shout, jumping to me feet.

Daniel responds by getting to his. "Robbie, when you brought Pete over last year, we kind of exchanged looks."

"Oh my God." I pinch the bridge of my nose.

"I waited for you to bring him back to maybe get to spend some more time with him, but then you never did."

"Yeah, because Mimic and everyone else was telling me how dangerous it was. You were one of those people!"

"Yeah, but I didn't think you'd actually listen to me,"

Daniel protests. "Anyway, my point is I looked him up in the database, and a few months ago I paid him a visit. I didn't reveal my secret identity at first, but ... yeah. Eventually, I did. Last month actually."

I slump back in my chair. "This is crazy. Pete, why didn't you ever say anything?"

Fidgeting with his fingers, he avoids eye contact. When I glance back at Melissa, she seems sympathetic to him, and it isn't like I'm not. But I just don't get it. I've been trying to hook him up with someone for homecoming, so I would've been stoked to find out he's actually dating. Shocked, sure, but excited for him, nonetheless.

I'm about to tell Pete that it's okay, that he can talk to me, when Daniel reaches over and gives his hand a comforting squeeze. They exchange smiles, and for the first time I don't see Pete as someone who has been crushing on a sidekick I work with. I see my best friend, nervous, and getting strength from his boyfriend.

"I was scared," he finally speaks up. "I didn't want you to think I was keeping secrets from you. I was gonna tell you, but then Mimic and the others left, so you guys had all of this extra responsibility on your shoulders. Then the whole time travel stuff was freaking you out."

"What time travel stuff?" Melissa looks over at me.

Pete cringes. "Sorry."

I shake my head. "It's nothing."

"Robbie." Pete gives me one of our nonverbal looks, urging me to tell her the truth. I shake my head, grinding my teeth. Pete nods again, but I twitch my head to the side, trying to tell him to be quiet. Melissa and Daniel are watching us and our silent conversation.

"What's going on?" Daniel asks.

"It's nothing," I urge.

"You should tell them." Pete taps his fingers on the table.

"Pete, would you be quiet?"

"What's going on?" Melissa repeats, sternly.

Boyfriends, girlfriends, secrets, high school dances, and time travel. How did my life get so confusing?

"Doc has been running tests on my blood."

"Why?" she asks. I can hear the concern in her voice.

"It's nothing ... I have similar blood platelets as Supron. And the plasma in my blood has the same DNA code as one Doc has on file. One from a time traveler."

Daniel's mouth falls open in shock.

"By the gods, Robbie. Why didn't you say anything?"

"Because it's nothing." I look at Pete, a silent pleading shooting across to him, hoping he doesn't say anything about the two-second time jump. "Doc has been running tests and that's it. He found similarities, but nothing more. No mutations or alterations. I'm fine."

"Still, dude, you should've told us," Daniel says.

Suddenly, every set of eyes is on me and I feel like I'm being scolded by Mimic. Or my parents.

"Wait, no. No, this isn't about me. This is about you two." I point to Daniel and Pete. "We have to tell Doc now."

Daniel stands up, crossing his arms. "Uh, we will do no such thing."

"Daniel, this is serious," Melissa agrees with me.

Pete stands next to him. His face softens to a hurt expression. "You don't ... you don't want him to know?"

"Not because of you, Pete." Glancing back at Mel and me, he turns to face Pete. "It has nothing do with him knowing. Of course, we'll tell him, but not before the dance."

I shoot up from the table. "Whoa! The dance? You're Pete's date to homecoming?"

Pete bites his lip. "Yeah. It was actually gonna be a

surprise. You know, like 'Surprise, your best friend came to the dance with your sidekick partner.'" He scratches the back of his head. "Looking back on it, it might not have been the best idea."

"It would've been awesome," Daniel assures him, holding his hand. "I will tell Doc, but after the dance." His gaze bounces between Melissa and me. "You two know what he'll do. He'll bench me for sure. Supron expects so much of me. I love the man, he's like my father, but his standards? I might get suspended longer than you were. They'll both tell me I'm being reckless and putting Pete's life in danger."

Silence cuts through the air in the room. Melissa and I exchange glances, and Daniel waits on us. Mimic warned me about having a girlfriend last year, but all three sat me down when I broke rank and went after Vacuus. And Supron above them all takes these matters extremely seriously.

"All right," I agree.

"Thank you, Robbie," Pete says, giving me a grateful smile.

"So, are you two, like, official now?"

A crimson veil splashes over Pete's face and I have to hold back from laughing.

"Yeah," he answers, looking down at the table. "We are. Right?"

Daniel returns his smile, nodding, and for the first time I don't see Daniel as a rival, like I did last year. I don't see him as another sidekick or someone I work with. I just see a guy my best friend likes.

The following week at school, Jasmin and Maria are quick

to pick up on Pete's obvious good mood. Maria is the first to bring up that Pete might be seeing someone and asks if there's a special girl in his life. It reminds me that Pete has kept his biggest secret from everyone, sharing with only me and now Melissa. A light chuckle escapes me, thinking that Daniel means enough to Pete that he's coming out to the entire school with Daniel as his date.

"What?" Maria asks me.

"Oh, nothing."

Pete side-eyes me, but I shake him off.

Ignoring my straying laugh, Maria continues. "Are you going to ask her to homecoming?"

Jasmin's eyes dart toward me. I immediately look away, not wanting to make it uncomfortable.

"Maybe," Pete says, and I give him a mischievous smile.

He really *is* going to come out to our friends by bringing Daniel to the dance. I have to hand it to him; Pete has more courage than I do.

"So, are you still seeing that girl from Edgewater?" Jasmin inquires, taking a drink of her soda.

"Oh, uh, yeah."

The fun and lighthearted attitude of being in on the secret for once vanishes, and I can't meet Jasmin's eyes. I've settled the dance situation with Melissa, and now Pete knows who she is, but knowing Jasmin will either be going alone or going with someone else twists my insides. And it shouldn't. It absolutely shouldn't because I'm with Mel.

"Uh, what about you?" I ask.

"I think—"

"Oh, she's got a hot date!" Maria cuts her off. Jasmin throws her a scowling stare, to which she shrugs. "Anyway, what's your girlfriend's name?"

"Her name?"

I glance over at Pete, unsure what to say. It's not a secret, since she'll have no idea Melissa is Mighty Miss, but it's ... weird.

"She does have a name, right, Robbie?" Maria jabs after my prolonged silence.

"It's, uh ..."

"You forgot her name?"

"No, of course not." They wait silently. Pete's eyes widen, and I swallow the nerves I didn't know I had. "It's Melk—" I cough. "Mel. Melissa. It's Melissa."

Pete lets out a soft laugh, shaking his head. I'd like to feel a little more at ease, but Jasmin stares at the table, slowly turning around her can of soda. Maria immediately picks up on it and points one of her chips at me.

"Well, goody for you, Robbie. I'm sure she's okay, or whatever, but Jasmin's going with Jared McMann."

"Jared McMann?" My eyes pop open. Jasmin doesn't move. "Wait, what happened to that guy, William?"

"William's the past. Jared's the future," Maria says, proudly.

"Jasmin, that's awesome," Pete speaks up, casting me a sideways glance. "Jared's the captain of our varsity wrestling team. And he's a junior."

She finally releases a little giggle but doesn't look back at me. "It's not official or anything. But we've talked a couple times during homeroom."

Before I know what I'm doing, I roll my eyes. "That guy's a douche."

"Excuse you." Jasmin shoots me a dirty look. "He's nice."

"Careful, Robbie," Maria butts in, looking at me with a roguish smile. "You're starting to sound like a jealous ex."

"Maria!" Jasmin snaps.

I glance over at Pete. He's nodding in agreement. "What?

No, no," I say, looking down at our lunch table. "No, it's ... cool. Seriously, whatever." I search for the right cover. "I've just heard some stuff. That's all."

"Those are just rumors," Maria counters. "Besides, like Pete said, he's a junior. And because of wrestling I've heard he's rocking a six-pack." She leans closer and whispers to Jasmin, making her blush. "Probably like a certain you-know-who."

"Whoa, who are you talking about now?" Pete asks, leaning closer to them.

"That's for us to know and you to find out, Petey."

The bell sounds, ending our lunch, and as Pete and I walk to our next classes, he tugs at my arm.

"Hey, not to make this weird or anything but ... you're not ..."

"What?" I lift a brow.

"You're not still into her, right?"

"Pete—"

"Because I thought we were past that whole 'hey, cutie' comment you made. But now you're acting like you're seriously jealous of Jared being her date."

I scoff. "Pete, you're being ridiculous."

"Am I?"

Stepping off to the side, I lower my voice. "Of course you are. I'm with Melissa. That comment was just that ... a comment. I'm not jealous of Jared, I just think he's a douche." Before Pete can respond, I turn and start walking away. "I'll see you later."

12

Leading up to the homecoming dance, Pete's happy mood doesn't fade.

Daniel and I end up contacting Granite—a superhero who can control the dirt, stone, and all of the mixtures that create Earth—and ask him to cover for us. He's older than us, but only by a few years, and became an official superhero two years ago. Letting him in on the secret, he took it well, and said he knows a thing or two about trying to have fun with your alter ego. Granite will cover Daniel's watch duty shift, and he'll tell Doc that he's not feeling good. Our only concern is whether we'll be called away to stop some lame supervillain doing something stupid, but that's a chance we're willing to take.

Pete and I get ready at my house, and then I teleport us to headquarters where we meet up with Daniel and Melissa, who are hiding in my bunker. Both Pete and Daniel opt for matching suits and ties: dark navy blue. If I thought Pete was giddy leading up to the dance, he's downright ecstatic when he sees Daniel all dressed up. My breath catches when I see Melissa.

She's wearing a shimmering gold and silver sequin dress, which comes down to her knees, and has spaghetti straps. Her dark hair has a few curls in it, is slightly pulled back, and hangs over her right shoulder.

"Wow." I let out a breath.

"You clean up pretty good yourself," she replies, straightening my silver bow tie that matches her dress.

"Melissa, you look amazing."

"Thank you. Is it too much for a high school dance?"

"Definitely not."

"I got a rental car and parked it over on Fifth Avenue," Daniel says. "You guys ready?"

Smiling over at Pete, he nods, and then I take in Melissa one more time. "Let's do it."

Walking to the rental car, we get a few onlookers taking in our more formal attire, but it does nothing to dampen the mood, as we all smile and laugh. Pete takes the front seat, next to Daniel who drives. I open the door for Melissa and we get into the back seat, listening to Daniel's "Party Mix" playlist he made, and I take a couple of selfies as we travel.

The school gym is loud with bass music thumping away, and strobe lights piercing through the doorway as we arrive. Inside, balloons are everywhere along glittering streamers hanging from the rafters, and spinning spotlights swirling in the air, while a DJ booth sits off to the side. It makes me think we're in some nightclub, even though I've never actually been to one.

Waving to a couple of friends, I glance over at Pete, who now wears a timid expression. His pace slows down, and we all pause as he comes to a stop.

"You okay?" I ask him.

His eyes never break away from the crowd, from where we stand in the gym doorway. "Uh ... yeah."

"Pete, you don't have to do this," Daniel tells him. I want to add something, but I don't know what. For the first time, I realize this isn't something I can understand as his best friend. "We can go in separate if you want."

Melissa glances over at me, concern across her face.

"No." Pete shakes his head. His timidity fades, and he looks back at Daniel with a determined smile. "No, I want to do this."

"Are you sure?" I ask.

He nods to me, before looking back at Daniel. "You'll be there, right?"

"All night. I'm your own personal sidekick tonight."

Pete laughs, breaking the fearful tension. I elbow his side. "Hey, what about me?"

Melissa chuckles, rolling her eyes. "Earth boys."

After another round of laughs between us, and a deep breath from Pete, we enter the gym.

Eyes jump to us, and I feel a sense of pride, knowing Melissa looks gorgeous. My ego immediately deflates, and embarrassment sinks in as Jerry Jenkins, a guy in the Spanish class Pete and I have, comes over. Raising his fist up, I go to bump his knuckles, but he walks right past me and exchanges the greeting with Pete.

"All right, Pete. Way to go!"

A deep red slides across his face, and Daniel swells with the pride I had seconds ago.

"Uh, thanks," Pete responds, gazing at the ground.

After grabbing a quick drink, we split up, and decide to take in a few dances. I continue to notice everyone in school excitedly coming over to Pete, who takes in the admiration, smiling ear to ear.

"You okay?" Melissa asks, noticing my distraction.

"Yeah," I answer with a chuckle. "I'm just happy for him.

He's been my best friend forever, but tonight he finally seems like the same ol' Pete I've known for years. Having fun and being carefree. I don't think I realized how much this was weighing on him until just right now."

We dance to a couple more songs, and though she dances fine, she continues to look around almost in marvel. After pausing for a minute to grab a drink from the refreshment table, I whisper over to her, "Is this completely different than your world?"

"A little." She nods. "It's very formal on Kratoa. Royal affairs and such. It's nice, but very strict."

"Sounds like a blast," I tease.

Leaning over, she kisses my cheek. "This is much better. Come on, I want to dance again."

She pulls me out on the dance floor with the next song playing. Pete waves at me from the other side of the room, still smiling. Dropping my hand, I accidentally bump into someone.

"Sorry." I turn to apologize, and come face-to-face with Maria.

With a curt smile, her eyes flash to Melissa and she freezes, her jaw dropping. "Whoa."

Melissa, still moving her legs to the rhythm, smiles at her. "Hello."

"What the hell?" Maria's eyes jump back to mine. "Robbie, is this ..."

I let out a chuckle. "Yeah. Sorry, Melissa, this is Maria. Maria, Melissa."

"*This* is Melissa?" Maria asks, shock smothering her voice. "Are you a senior?"

"Oh, yeah, sorry," I jump in. "Did I forget to mention that? She's a senior at Edgewater."

Maria's stare doesn't break. "Sorry. You're just, like ... *really* pretty."

"Thank you," Melissa replies, sincerely.

Maria spins around and grabs her date's arm, dragging him away. Watching her, she heads to the other side of the gym.

"That was weird," I mutter, still shuffling my feet.

When Melissa asks what I meant about Edgewater, I laugh and explain to her what I told Maria and Jasmin was her cover story. Pete and Daniel dance over to us.

"Dude, what was that?" Pete whispers to me.

"What?" My brows pinch in confusion.

"Why'd Maria just bolt like that?"

I shrug my shoulders. "I don't know."

"All right, all right," a voice rings out over the speakers as the music dies down. "I think it's time for us to slow it down a bit."

The fast, bass-filled music fades out, and a slow rhythm circles the air. Some people get off of the dance floor, leaving the couples remaining wrapping their arms around one another. Sliding my hands over her waist, Melissa wraps hers over my shoulders.

"You do any slow dancing at those regal events?" I grin.

She nods, smiling, and then leans closer. Laying her head on my shoulder, we sway to the rhythm. "Robbie, this night's been amazing."

"It has. Thank you for coming. Thank you for everything, really. Being so cool with Pete, being there for me after I was hurt last year."

With the music encompassing us, her fingers skim over my hair. Her whispering words drift up to my ear. "I think ... I think I'm in love with you."

I hear her words, but as she's saying them my eyes find

Jasmin. Standing off to the side, her gaze meets mine. She doesn't look mad. She doesn't look sad or hurt. She just seems lost. Her eyes jump to Melissa, whose back is to her, before landing on me again. A soft, but hurt, smile crosses her lips. There's no Jared by her side. No one at all. I can't see the tears, but I know she's crying because her hand rises and she wipes her eyes with a napkin. She lets out another broken smile, then finally turns around.

That jealousy I've felt around her when she's talking about other guys? Calling Jared a major douche? It's all minuscule compared to how much of a lousy, rotten dirtbag I feel like holding Melissa, hearing her words, but staring at Jasmin.

"I love you, too."

13

For the rest of the dance I attempt to put on a smile, but as much as I try not to think about her, I keep looking over at Jasmin. Every once in a while, I'll catch her glancing my direction, before quickly averting her eyes. I don't know if I've been trying to ignore my feelings, pretend I didn't have them anymore, or I'm just an idiot. Probably the last one. Because I'm one hundred percent sure I'm not over her now.

Pete and Daniel want to head to an after-party some friends are having, but I tell everyone I'm not feeling well. Melissa asks if I'm okay, so I make up an excuse that I ate a bad appetizer. After telling them they should go and have fun, which they do, I teleport home and go to sleep.

The next week at school, it's obvious that Maria and Jasmin have decided to not eat lunch with us anymore. Wanting to forget a night I should be trying to remember, and hoping things will return to normal, I ask Pete if he's talked to Jasmin or Maria. Instead of answering, his eyes are locked on his phone.

"Hey." I nudge his shoulder.
"What?"

"Have you talked to the girls?"

Again, no answer.

"Dude, stop texting him so much," I growl.

"Sorry. Danny was just texting a funny meme."

"Oh my God, you're calling him Danny now?"

Pete scowls at me. "Yeah. It's his name."

"Daniel is his name."

He scoffs. "What crawled up your butt?"

Letting out a sigh, I drop my head, staring at my bagged lunch that I haven't even touched. "Nothing. Sorry."

"What's up?" Pete asks, putting his phone away. "You've been acting weird ever since you left the dance."

"I'm an idiot." I let my forehead fall to the table.

"Why? What happened?"

Turning, so my cheek is on the table, I glance up at him, letting out a disgruntled breath. "Pete, what I'm about to tell you is top secret. Seriously. Like, top of the top of the top of secrets. Even more than my secret identity." Sitting up, I glance around and lower my voice. "You cannot tell Daniel. I'm serious. You can't tell anyone."

A solemn expression falls over his face. "What's wrong?"

Staring back at my lunch bag, I swallow the nerves and that despicable feeling I've had since the dance. The feeling of being the biggest douchebag in the history of douchebags. "I think I still like Jasmin."

"What?" Pete asks, completely monotone.

"No." My weak voice trembles. "It's worse than that. I think I'm still in love with her."

"Robbie." He grits hits teeth. "Are you crazy? How is that even possible? You guys broke up. You're going out with Melissa."

"I know! That's why I'm an idiot. I mean, she's hot, right?"

"Who?"

"Melissa." I look at him like he's crazy.

"Of course she is. And she's into you."

"She loves me."

"What?" His mouth drops.

"She told me at the dance. And I said it back. But ... I don't think I meant those words for her."

"Are you serious? Robbie, that's beyond low."

"Yeah." My defeated posture returns. "I'm such a scumbag."

"Yeah, you are."

I look up at him, rolling my eyes. "Thank you."

"Listen to me, you broke up with Jasmin for a good reason. Your world is too dangerous. I know you still like her, but you've got to get over it, man. You should've seen how giddy Melissa was at the after-party."

"Kick me while I'm down, why don't you."

"I'm serious. Look, I'm gonna be real. Jasmin is my friend; I think you should be with Melissa. It's better for you, and it's safer for Jasmin."

His words hang in the air, and I know he's right. Without a shadow of a doubt, he's right. It's better for me. Jasmin won't be in danger. I don't have to worry about collateral damage. Melissa not only gets my world, but she's a part of it already. Everything about it makes sense. So why am I hung up on this so much?

When the end of the weekend rolls around, I'm up for patrol duty and get to headquarters early to suit up. Melissa's called and texted me a few times, but I've kept our encounters brief. I don't know how to handle this. I should be with her. Everything about it is logical and the safest thing to do. Nevertheless, I can't keep that moment at the dance out of my head. And it just makes me feel worse when I see her.

Daniel's manning the control desk when I walk in. "How's it look out there tonight?" I ask.

"Another quiet one," he responds.

"Cool. I think I'm gonna go hit the west side. Get an early jump on patrols."

Activating my helmet, I'm about to teleport away when he grabs my arm. "Hey, I wanted to talk before you go."

"Okay, what's up?"

Looking away, he awkwardly picks at the corner of a book on the desk. "Um, I'm not sure how to bring this up, but ... are you and Melissa cool?"

"Aw, crap. Did Pete talk to you? I told him not to say anything."

He stares at me, confused. "No, Melissa did."

"She did?"

"Yeah. It wasn't anything serious, it was just ... She said you've been acting weird this past week." He seems to wait for me to reply, but I don't have the first clue of what to say. "Robbie, she really likes you. If you've just been messing around, not taking it serious, you should probably tell her."

"It's not that, it's just ..." *I'm a bottom-feeding douchebag.* "I just got this stuff going on, that's all. Thanks for the heads-up." I let out a deep breath and teleport away.

Landing on the King City Arena, where the city's basketball team plays, I look out over the large parking lot. The King City Tigers have a game tonight against the Edgewater Eagles. It's just before tip-off, and down below, fans are entering the building. Everyone looks happy. I can't stop seeing different couples walking hand in hand into the arena. I roll my eyes at my pathetic mindset and teleport away.

After a few more jumps, I've teleported over ten blocks in thirty minutes, and find the city quiet and calm. A few sirens sound off in the distance, but radioing back to Daniel, they are all normal occurrences. Nothing a superhero or sidekick would need to get involved in. With nothing going on, I could head back to headquarters and teleport out again later tonight for another patrol, but I don't want to head back yet. Maybe I should and get everything out in the open with Mel. But I don't.

Teleporting over to the cineplex, it looks like a movie just let out. Patrons walk down below, into the parking lot or down the street toward the train station. Just like everywhere else tonight, everything is quiet. Walking along the edge of the building, a familiar voice sounds below. Jasmin and Maria are exiting the movie theater.

"Oh crap," Maria says, grabbing her pockets. "I think I left my phone in the bathroom. I'll be right back."

"Okay," Jasmin replies.

Maria runs back inside, and I see Jasmin waiting at the crosswalk of an intersection. The screeching of tires sounds through the air, and as the lights change colors, a car that should be stopping at the red light slams into the crossing traffic. The car T-bones another, which sends it spinning, directly toward Jasmin.

In a snap, I teleport and grab her around the waist, then teleport us to the other side of the street. The car that was twirling comes to a sudden stop, crashing into the light signal post.

Jasmin's face, drained of color, stares at the car, then at me.

"Are you okay?" I ask.

Trial By Fire

"Oh-ohmygod. Holy crap." She embraces me in a tight bear hug. "Ohmygod. Thank you!"

I let out a chuckle. "Wait right here."

Jumping over to the driver who hit the light post, I check on him. He looks dazed, with blood dripping from his forehead. Then I jump to the offending driver, and I smell the booze on his breath as I reach the door. He's passed-out drunk.

"Hydro," I call out, putting a finger to my helmet. "We've got a DUI. West side, near the cineplex. Sixth and Kirby. Two minor injuries. We need ambulance support."

"On it," he radios back.

Jumping back to Jasmin, I look her up and down. "Are you okay?"

A shocked and surprised smile crosses her lips. "You saved me."

"All in a day's work," I reply with a smile.

An adorable blush creeps over her face. "Thank you. You probably don't remember this, but a few weeks ago you stopped the Turbo Trio by my high school."

"I remember."

"You do?"

I lean in closer. "Of course. Who could forget a cutie like you?"

I haven't stood this close to her since we broke up last year. I can smell the same sweet-scented rose perfume she always wears. There's a shine from the moon over her hazel eyes. My voice modifier is working, my helmet and visor concealing my identity, but there's a small part of me that wants her to see past all of it.

She leans closer. "All of the tabloids, and even The Cape Zone, say you're with Mighty Miss. I don't know if she'd appreciate you calling another girl cute."

That should bring reality crashing down around me. It should wake me up from the delusion I'm having, thinking I'm in love with her, and remind me that I'm with Melissa and that's what's best for me. But it doesn't. Instead, I wrap an arm around her. "Don't believe everything you read."

"Oh. My. God." The voice is unmistakable. Glancing back, I see Maria standing across the street.

"I think your friend might be jealous," I joke with a coy smile.

To my surprise, Jasmin returns the flirtatious tone. "I think you're right."

My ear comm beeps. "Worm, we got something."

Backing up, I place a finger to my helmet. "What's up?"

"110th and Slott. East side. Someone called in reports of a guy on fire flying in the air."

"I'm on it."

"Stay at a distance," Daniel warns. "Doc's coordinating with Mighty to meet you there."

"Copy that," I answer, then look over at Jasmin. "Well, cutie, looks like I gotta run."

She smiles, but it fades a little with regret. "Oh, okay."

Before I teleport away, I glance around the scene; an ambulance is pulling up near the wrecked cars. Maria waits across the street still, and Jasmin keeps her eyes on me. "You know, I have this patrol route on Sunday night. Same time."

Flashing another smile, I teleport away, but not before she smiles back.

14

It's wrong. I know it's wrong. I should not be flirting with another girl while I'm going out with Melissa, even if that girl and I have history. Probably, especially so.

Trying to block out those thoughts, I get to the other side of the city and stand atop a building near Slott Avenue, completely forgetting Daniel's warning to stay back until Doc and Melissa show up.

I scan the area on the street, but don't see anything out of the ordinary. Looking across the rooftops, the night air is quiet. Then I spot it. A light flickers from inside of a building, a block away. It isn't the normal fluorescent glow you see from ceiling lights. It sways back and forth, as if a huge candle burns in the room.

I teleport into the building, on the other end of the room, and hear what sounds like a stifled yell. Creeping behind a large, metal filing cabinet, I peek out; the room looks like a huge office area, with two rows of desks lined up. A spark of brightness shines, before dimming to a glow, and then I hear another yell.

"Where is it?" the fire guy screams.

"Anything?" Daniel asks into my comms, catching me off guard. I can't answer him and risk the fire guy hearing me, so I ignore the question. "Worm?" he repeats. I tap my helmet, turning the communication off.

"Damn it!" the fire guy screams.

Another burst of light shines, and I edge closer to him, ducking below a desk. Tiny sparks dance among the carpet before dying out. He crumples up a paper, torching it, and the ashes fall over a desk. The closer I get, the hotter the temperature becomes. Sweats drips under my helmet, and then he moves, walking across the room.

Crawling to where he was, I look over the burnt paper, but can't make out anything. It's burnt to a crisp. I feel the heat worsening as I edge closer behind him. He's wearing what looks like a wetsuit, but it's crackling, almost like it's made of charcoal. It leaves his arms and head bare, with smoke drifting up from him. His light brown, shaggy hair waves around his ears, as he holds another file.

"Yes. This is it." He chuckles.

Standing up, I know it's now or never. Plus, if he has whatever it is he's searching for, that might help us if I get it from him.

"What's it?"

Spinning around, his orange eyes lock on to mine. I see his face only for a second, before his entire body engulfs into flames, and he starts to float in the air.

"You!"

I raise my hands, taking a step back. "Okay, just calm down a second."

Before I can say anything else, he opens his mouth to yell at me, but instead of a scream, a huge stream of fire shoots out. Diving to the side, the fire-scream crashes into the desks behind me, setting them ablaze. I teleport to the other side of the room and run into a side office.

Through a frosted glass partition, I can see him walking, still covered in flames, and he approaches the door. I teleport behind him, trying to ready myself.

"Okay, calm down," I yell out. "Why are you attacking me? What's this about?"

He doesn't answer. Instead, he raises his hands, and shoots another stream of fire at me, this time coming from his hands. Again, I teleport away. Behind him, I run into another room, filled with more desks, filing cabinets, and computers. The heat circles me. Eventually the fire sprinklers are going to turn on, but they aren't going to be able to quell this guy's attacks. I have to lure him away from the building.

When I jump back into the room he's in, he doesn't see me behind him. Instead of trying to attack, my sight catches the folder he was looking at. Fire dances around the desk, but maybe if I can grab that file, it will give us some intel on these guys finally. I let him continue searching for me, and I sneak over to the desk.

The edges are burnt, but I read through the top sheet. A lot of redacted information, with multiple lines blacked out, but there's information about biological testing. A corporation named Daedalus is listed, but almost everything about it is blackened out.

The next page lists test subjects, all with different serial numbers. There are almost fifty subjects listed, but again, most of the information is deleted. Flipping another page, I find something called Project Ignis. Then a dossier on a former CIA agent named Gunther Ledias. Skipping through the edited information, I see another name listed; Dean Macall.

Before I can search for anything else, a huge fireball explodes the desk in front of me, and I feel the scorch of the flames cover the exposed part of my face. I teleport away, but as soon as I land, I'm hit with a massive fireball to my back, sending me down to the carpet.

I can feel pieces of my suit burning me, then a cold draft, and know a large portion has melted away. I start to crawl, trying to duck under a desk, when I'm encircled in a ring of fire. Choking on the fire and the smoke, I grab a breathing tube from my jacket, but before I can use it, I'm nailed across the face with a flaming fist. I feel my skin burn and the breathing tube falls on the ground.

"I can't believe Gunther burned out to you," the fire guy yells. "Then again, he was never a team player. Always trying to fight Macall."

Raising his hand, he swings it through the air, sending a line of flames down at me, but I teleport away just in time. On my feet, I ready my fists, throwing the file I'm holding to the ground.

The sprinkler system finally activates, and a small sliver of hope sparks in me. Feeling the cool sting of the water hitting my burns, I direct my attention at the man in flames. Through his orangish-yellow glow, I can see an evil smile cross his lips—almost as if he's flexing every muscles in his body, he lets out a scream, and a wave of heat emanates from him. Suddenly the sprinklers stop, and steam drifts around us. He evaporated the entire water system.

I gape at him in shock. "How?"

"You ain't seen nothing yet, kid."

He releases another fire scream, but I teleport across the room, and watch the fire engulf my previous location. Spotting me, he throws fireball after fireball, while I try to dodge his attack. More fire and smoke fill the room.

Choking on the smoke, I drop to a knee to gather my bearings. I need to teleport out of here. If I can get outside and have him follow me, I'll have a better chance. Trying to muster up the concentration to enact my plan, I'm hit with a fireball, which scorches the front of my uniform, knocking me back into a filing cabinet.

If I can't focus, I can't create a wormhole. And if I can't do that, I can't teleport. I don't know if he knows that's how teleporters work, but it doesn't matter, because the searing heat keeps me from getting to my feet, as I choke on more smoke. I feel his scorching hand grab a part of my uniform that isn't singed, and then he slams a flaming fist across my face.

"Macall was given the lead," he starts. "Gunther always tried to fight it. But me? I'm with Macall. We escaped Daedalus and we have no intention of ever going back. But that doesn't mean we can't take the power they wanted to use us for anyway. And you all deserve to die."

The tears from the smoke leak from my eyes and I gag, cracking my eyes open just enough to see he's resumed his pre-fire appearance. His orange eyes glow, and he raises his fist, unleashing a new round of flames over his hand.

Instead of a punch, he picks me up. Knocked out on my feet, he takes both hands and slams his palms into my chest, sending a massive fireball out, hurling me across the room. I can't do anything to stop myself from crashing through the high-rise window, and out into the night air.

In all of the time I've been training and working as a sidekick, I've never been in a situation that I thought I was going to die. Even last year, when Vacuus had me at his mercy, there was that hope I had inside. Supron and the others were out there. Plus, I blacked out, so I had no recollection of what happened those last few minutes. This is nothing like that.

Free-falling out of a thirty-story building, the pain from the burns is excruciating. My arms and hands flail. I can't catch my breath, probably because of the fear, the pain, and the smoke. I can't concentrate to teleport. I'm going to die.

Then I'm hit hard. I feel my ribs crack, and suddenly I'm not falling to the ground, but I'm flying away. Coughing, I look over and see Doc carrying me, zooming us through the night air with a jetpack strapped to his back.

"What's up, Doc?" I cough again, then pass out.

15

Blinking my eyes, the first thing I notice is that I'm lying on my stomach. I'm inside of the medic bay of Alliance headquarters, there's a plastic mask over my mouth, and I'm looking down at the floor. My pillow has a hole in the middle, and my eyes shoot back and forth along the tiled floor, trying to figure out what's happened.

I push up on one side of the bed and roll myself over, instantly cringing in pain, as my back touches the sheets. I flop back to my previous position, staying on my stomach.

"You've been out for hours. It's almost three a.m." The voice is faint, like a whisper, but I can tell it's Melissa.

Looking over, I see she's sitting in a chair next to my bed, still in her uniform. "What happened?"

"You tell me." The softness in her voice is gone. A hard line crosses her brow. "Robbie, you were supposed to wait for backup. We didn't have any idea what this fire guy was up to."

I close my eyes, still feeling the pain from the burns, but feeling worse about not following proper protocol. "I know. I'm sorry."

"Daniel said you turned off your communication device. Why?"

I stare back down at the floor. "I was already in the building. I was just trying to talk to him. I was hoping that if I could reason with him, it might end up better than the last one I met."

"Instead, it ended up a whole lot worse. You could've died."

"I know, okay? I screwed up. I'm sorry." When nothing follows, I look back over at her. Her eyes stay locked on me, searching for something. "What?"

"What is going on with you?"

"What are you talking about?"

"You haven't been the same since the dance. You've been distant. Like you're in your own little world. And tonight, you nearly got yourself killed."

I swallow nervously, unsure what to say.

My mind races, trying to think of how to say what I know I need to. I can't stay with her when my feelings are still so strong for Jasmin. I have to break up with her. But how? How do you tell someone who just confessed their love for you, that you do have feelings for them, and they are real? They just aren't enough.

Knowing that's where my mind is at, almost makes me wish I suffered these burns all over again. Anything is better than the feelings running through me, knowing how she feels and how I should feel, but don't.

I look around, face down in my donut pillow, unable to say it.

Coward.

She lets out a long sigh, and I hear her get up and leave the room. When the door shuts, I hear another set of footsteps walking toward me. Looking up, I find Doc. Not following orders, leading a girl on, and now I have to deal with him telling me I screwed up. I can't do this.

"Look, I'm sorry, okay? I screwed up."

"Well, you certainly did that. Can you sit up?"

Taking a deep breath, I nod and gather my strength. Pushing myself upright, I sit on the edge of the bed, cringing as my skin moves. Doc lifts a syringe with a six-inch-long needle, flicking the tube, squirting out air bubbles.

"What's that for?"

"I applied ointment to your burns. Your chest first, followed by a speed-healing paste. I needed to make sure the heat didn't damage any vital organs. However, your back seems to have taken the worst of it. Even though by tomorrow they should be downgraded to first-degree burns, I want to give you this extra serum and then draw more blood."

He takes out an empty syringe.

Shaking my head, I extend my arm. "Fine." He's quiet while he injects me and then draws the blood, leaving questions about the fire guy swirling. "Were you guys able to find anything on that floor?"

"No." He shakes his head, applying gauze and tape to my arm. "Police and fire were on the scene quickly, but by the time the fire was put out, anything that could've been evidence was burnt to a crisp. Robbie, what happened?"

I gaze down at the tiles, trying to remember. "I was inside, and he was looking for something. A file. I thought I could talk to him. After the first guy, I wanted to help him."

"Did he say anything?"

"Gunther. Gunther Ledias. That was the first fire guy's name. He said Gunther didn't want to do what they wanted to do. This one found a file, but a lot of the info had been scrubbed."

I try to focus, remembering what I found.

"Dean Macall. I guess that's another fire guy. Supposedly the person this one is working with or for, I'm not sure."

Doc strokes his gray beard, taking in the information. "Get some rest, Robbie. We'll go over this in the morning. I'll need a full debriefing … and then I'm suspending you from this case."

"What?" I hop out of the bed, cringing once again. "Doc, come on, you can't do that. Look, I'm sorry, okay? I know I should've waited, but you can't suspend me."

"Robbie, this is the second time."

"The first time my comms got fried!"

"It doesn't matter. You knew you were to wait for backup. What if we hadn't gotten there in time … Please, don't make this harder than it has to be."

"But it's just us watching over King City right now. You need me."

"I'm well aware of our situation, and I'll deal with it. Right now, I can't take another chance of this happening. You'll still run patrols, and assist at the control desk, but anything that pertains to these individuals is completely off-limits."

Grinding my teeth, I seethe as he heads back to the door. My fists clench and I know I only have myself to blame, but I should still be out there helping them catch these guys. I'm the only one who's faced them. I'm the one with the one-on-one intel.

"Get some rest. We'll debrief in the morning."

Waking up the next morning, I instantly feel a hundred times better. I jump to my bunker and change out of the medical scrubs, throwing on some jeans. When I zip up my hoodie, I feel a slight twinge on my back, but nothing worse than a minor sunburn.

Grabbing my phone, I have three text messages from Pete. I open them, positive that they're worried messages over me, then scoff as I read them.

Pete: Hey, Danny just asked what I know about you and Mel?
Pete: Did you tell him something???
Pete: TEXT ME BACK!!!

Sliding my phone into my pocket, I roll my eyes. That'll have to wait until later. I'm not as frustrated as last night, but the aggravation still lingers knowing that I'm about to debrief Doc on everything that went done with the fire guy, and then I'm off this case. Walking into a conference room, I stop in the doorway. Melissa, Daniel, and Doc are all sitting at a table. Along with Forge, a superhero from Mercury City. And everyone is in uniform.

"Robbie, come in," Doc calls out, waving me over.

"Uh, okay."

Forge doesn't make eye contact with me; instead, he scans a file filled with paperwork. He shouldn't be here. Other superheroes aren't called in for debriefings, unless ...

"Why's Forge here?"

"Well, that was direct," Daniel whispers, but loud enough for me to hear.

"Robbie," Doc calls out again. "Please. Sit."

Slowly, I approach the table and sit across from them—a mentor, a superhero I've interacted with a few times, a friend who I work with, and my girlfriend. All people I should feel comfortable around. But I suddenly feel on edge and defensive.

Forge still reads over the papers in front of him.

"As we discussed yesterday," Doc begins, and I roll my eyes, "you are being taken off of this case. Forge is going to help further the investigation. His superpower is fire control and manipulation, so he's a natural fit."

He finally looks at me. He's the same age as Granite, so only a few years older than me. "It's all good, Worm. We got this."

"Right," I respond, my voice flat.

"So," Doc speaks up again. "Please elaborate on everything you mentioned yesterday. We have the names listed, but anything else would be extremely helpful."

My eyes dance between Forge and Doc, eyeing them both suspiciously. "Okay ..." They all wait for me to start. Daniel seems indifferent, and Melissa still watches me like she's trying to figure out an equation. Forge has returned to reading his file. "Um, what do you want me to say?"

Doc clears his throat. "Well, last night you mentioned the names of the individuals."

"Sure. So, Gunther Ledias was mentioned. And someone named Dean Macall."

"Good," Doc encourages. "What else?"

I sit there, staring at them all. Forge lifts his head back up, catching my sight.

He's a little taller than me, and his uniform is black with red flames coming up his right leg and crossing over his chest. Around his back, he has a small chamber from where he draws up the fire he uses. He can't create it, but he can control it and manipulate it in different ways. Covering his face is a mask with red goggles. I have no reason to dislike him, but right now he's coming off as a veteran quarterback being called on to take over for the rookie who's made a mistake. Or maybe that's just my ego talking.

"Robbie?" Melissa calls out, breaking my thoughts. A new, insecure frustration hits me. *Why is she going along with this?*

Looking over at Daniel, I see he's waiting, too. Neither of them are arguing to keep me on the team, as it were.

"That's it," I reply, standing up from my chair, sliding my hands into the front pockets of my hoodie.

Doc narrows his eyes. "That's it?"

"Yup."

Under his goggles, Forge cocks his head sideways. Daniel gives me a side eye. Melissa still searches my expression.

"Last night you mentioned something about a file," Doc says.

I nod. "Yeah, but I just saw the names in there. Like I said, everything was blacked out, except for something about a fire experiment. I put one and one together."

Lying's becoming second nature now. *That's great.*

Doc leans forward and furrows his brow, lacing his fingers in front of his beard.

"Am I done now?" I spit out.

None of them move. Maybe if I can find some information on my own, about whatever Project Ignis is or what Daedalus is, I can finally figure out why the fire guys want us dead. Besides, those are corporation names. I'm sure they'll be able to search for it in the Alliance databank servers. This is the only lead I have and I'm keeping it.

My eyes stay locked on Doc's, and after a minute of silence, he nods. One final glance at Melissa and I can see it on her face. She knows I'm lying.

"If you think of anything else, let us know," Doc says as I turn around.

"Sure."

The door slides open, and as I walk out of the room, I hear Forge in the background. "Well, that wasn't awkward at all."

16

Getting home, I immediately go to my room ... which is where I stay all weekend. Pete sends me a couple more text messages, but I don't want to talk to him, or anyone for that matter. Melissa messaged me when I left, and again a few hours later. I still haven't replied to her. By Sunday the burns feel all but gone, but I still do nothing.

After my parents visit my abuela, my mom knocks on my door, checking on me. "Roberto, we brought some of Abuela's albondigas soup."

"Thanks, Ma. I'm not hungry right now."

Frowning, she walks in and sits next to me on my bed. When I first became a sidekick, she worried like crazy. In the last year, her fears have eased, but I can see the concern on her face right now.

"Mijo, what's wrong?"

"Nothing." I shake my head, trying to smile. "I'm just tired. You know, it's been a lot of work since Mimic and the others have been gone."

"You do too much." I shrug off her comment, and she

leans over, kissing my forehead. "If you want to stay home from school tomorrow, that's fine."

"Thanks."

She walks over to the door, then turns around and points a finger at me. "But only one day."

I laugh. "Okay."

Lying in bed, I flip open my laptop, plugging in my Alliance USB decoder. I scan the internet for anything related to Project Ignis, but find nothing. Searching for Daedalus, a cached webpage pops up linking to a site covering DNA and biophysics. It's only a small paragraph, on a website for a corporation called Hadrix Industries. Never hearing about it before, I scan the internet for the company, but nothing is found. Deciding to call it quits on the search for the night, I suit up and head to headquarters for patrol duty, unsure how tense it'll be since I haven't talked to anyone since the meeting.

Getting to headquarters, I make my way to the control room, and find Melissa sitting behind the desk ... and curse myself for forgetting she's watching the monitors tonight.

"Hey," I mutter.

Spinning in the chair, her face drops. "Robbie, where have you been? Are you okay? You haven't replied to any of my messages."

"Yeah, I'm fine. I've just had ... family stuff going on, that's all."

She's eyes me carefully, and I don't know if she believes me or not. "Well, are you okay for patrol tonight? We can call in Hydro or Forge to—"

"Ugh." Rolling my eyes, I cross my arms over my chest. "You don't need to call in Forge. I'm fine. My burns are practically healed."

"The attack was only a few days ago. Doc just wanted to—"

"I said, I'm fine," I snap and instantly feel horrible. "Sorry."

She doesn't look hurt. She seems upset. "I'm just trying to help. We all are."

"Yeah, right. Way to help me out in that meeting."

"What's that supposed to mean?"

Leaning over the control desk, I stare down at the metal and feel the frustration rising again. "It means I walked into an ambush. Look, I get Doc's reasoning. I don't agree with it, but I understand it. But what really sucked was having you guys there and not even backing me up, just letting Doc replace me."

"Robbie, he's not replacing you."

"He is. He thinks I'm reckless or can't handle it, or whatever. So now I'm relegated to patrol duties instead of going after those guys, who, by the way, I'm the only one who's faced them and has any kind of knowledge of how they fight. But no, let's bring in a superhero and kick Robbie to the curb. You know, I thought you might have at least said *something*."

"Excuse me?" She gets to her feet, her face morphing from annoyed to insulted.

"Melissa, you're my girlfriend and you just sat there. You could've had my back."

"Oh, am I your girlfriend, Robbie?" She steps to me, jabbing a finger into my shoulder. "You could've fooled me this last week. You've been practically ignoring me."

I open my mouth to counter her, but I can't. She's right.

"You know what? Let's just keep this strictly business tonight. We have work to do."

"Fine."

"Fine," she shouts back.

Hitting the button on my earpiece, my helmet comes alive and wraps over me. My annoyance over my sidekick life mixes with my embarrassment over my personal relationship. I tap a button on the side of my helmet.

"I'm going in stealth mode tonight," I say, and she narrows her eyes. "I think that's for the best. I'll radio in case of an emergency."

Clenching her fists, she stamps the ground and then sits in her chair. "Fine. Whatever. Let's get to work, *Worm*."

"Fine, *Mighty Miss*."

I teleport out of the room, trying to leave all of the tension behind.

The first hour I teleport around the east side, and find things calm for the most part. There is a high-speed car chase going down highway one-eleven, so I jump ahead of the path the car is heading down, and when it gets closer, teleport into their back seat. The driver flips out and skids the car off of the road, sliding it to a stop in the dirt along the highway.

Teleporting the driver into the trunk of the car, I sit on the hood, as the police cars arrive and let them haul him away. Other than that, the night goes by slowly. There's not much action for a Sunday night, and I make my way over toward the west side, when I hear a lady screaming down below.

She runs out of a convenience store, and I teleport down below, to see an armed robber and an accomplice pointing guns at the store clerk.

"Put the money in a bag!" one of the guys yells.

"No masks?" I call out, leaning in the doorway. "Aren't you worried about cameras?"

Both of them spin around, staring at me in shock. The

first one keeps his gun on the man at the register, while the other points his gun at me. "Get the hell out of here, sidekick!"

"Aw, come on." I feign a sad face. "It's been a slow night. I could use a little action."

"Fine. You want action?" Raising his other hand, he grips the gun. Teleporting in front of him before he can pull the trigger, I grab the barrel of the gun and teleport next to the second gunman, delivering a swift kick to the back of his knee, sending him down to the ground.

"Hold this for me." I hand the gun to the clerk, who stares at it like it's a rattlesnake about to bite him.

Reaching down, I grab the other gunman's weapon and teleport it into a locked liquor case. The first one takes off running through the doorway, and I teleport outside, tripping him to the ground. "Now, now. You can't leave until the police get all of your information. You know, things like prior offenses, outstanding warrants, stuff like that."

"Screw you!" He kicks at me, but I jump out of the way, just in time to see the second criminal making a break for it in the opposite direction.

I stare down at the first guy. "Don't move, buddy. That'll only make this worse."

Teleporting over to the runner, I grab his arm and then teleport him back into the store, the clerk behind the counter jumping in fear. "You call the cops?" I ask him, and he nods. "Good."

"Oh, the guy! He's running!" The clerk points out through the window.

"Man, these guys are annoying." I point down at the criminal on the ground. "If I have to chase you again, it's gonna get ugly."

Jumping back outside, the first one is halfway down the

block, and I teleport in front of him, tripping him to the ground. "Dude, come on. Just because I don't have hyper speed, doesn't mean I can't catch you."

Grabbing his arm, I teleport back into the store, his accomplice still on the ground. "Hey, look at you. You get a gold star for finally listening."

"Go to hell, you stupid sidekick."

I chuckle to myself, and turn my attention to the clerk, who's now calmed down and holding back a laugh of his own. Sirens ring out and two police cruisers skid to a stop outside, the officers rushing in.

After handing them the weapons, and giving the officers all of the information they need, I'm gifted a footlong, sub sandwich from the store clerk, and since I haven't eaten all day, I take it and thank him. I teleport back over to the east side, sitting on the edge of a building, and let the night pass with no more disturbances happening.

After another hour, I end up at the top of King City Tower. I love being atop this building. The tallest in the city, you get a spectacular view of the city skyline at night, with all of the lights shining off of the glass. And during the sunrises and sunsets, it's beautiful. And calming.

Sitting on the edge of it, thoughts of everything start to comb through my mind once again. Not only did Melissa not have my back, but Daniel didn't either. We've grown a lot closer since our rivalry last year, and especially with him dating Pete now, I feel like he should've at least said something. And then there's Forge himself, just walking into headquarters like he's big man on campus.

I scoff, feeling the annoyance building up once again. Maybe I should've told Doc I couldn't do a patrol tonight. That I was still too hurt and hung out with Pete. I still want to see that movie and—

Jasmin. I forgot I told her about my patrol route.

Teleporting over to the cineplex, I scan the area, but don't see her anywhere. Checking the time, I see it's about thirty minutes later than when I was here last time. Maybe I missed her. Or she didn't even show up. Dropping my head, I let out a long sigh, both at the possibility of missing her and trying to meet up with her again.

I shouldn't talk to her until I've spoken with Melissa. That should be the first thing I do.

Strolling along the top of the building, I'm about to teleport away, when I see someone walking away from the theater. From behind, the hair kind of looks like Jasmin's, but I can't tell, so I jump over to the neighboring building. She crosses the street, heading toward the subway station and stops, looking at her phone. The light from the screen tells me it's her, and she seems to be sad.

"Hey," she answers her phone. "No, he didn't show. Yeah, I know. It was stupid anyway, right? I mean, he's a sidekick, Maria. He's probably like that with girls everywhere. I just thought ... nothing. Forget it."

The light turns green at the crosswalk she's waiting at, and she heads across the street. I teleport to the next building, still eavesdropping.

"No, I'm fine. Yeah, I'm gonna take the M Train. Okay, talk to you tomorrow."

She nears the steps to the station entrance, and I teleport down to her, leaning against a light post. "I'm late. Sorry about that."

She whips around and her eyes widen. "Oh ... yeah. It's okay." An adorable blush crosses her face. "I thought ..." Swallowing her nerves, she bites her lip. "Well, I mean, I know you're probably pretty busy."

Lifting my shoulders, I walk over to her. "A little. Just a

high-speed chase, and a couple guys trying to knock over a convenient store."

Her face drops. "Really?"

"Yeah, nothing serious."

She lets out a soft laugh, shaking her head. I love her laugh. "Only a superhero would describe something like that as 'nothing serious.'"

"Well, technically I'm not a superhero."

It appears her nerves have eased as she steps closer. "Oh, excuse me. Sidekick. You seem to handle yourself pretty well nonetheless."

"I do, don't I?" I smile, feeling more confident than usual.

The street isn't very busy, but there are a few bystanders who've stopped and are watching the interaction. I look around and give a friendly wave, as someone else pulls out their phone.

"So ..." She bites her lip again, leaning against the rail of the steps, the only barrier between us now.

"So," I reply, flashing another confident smile.

"Can I ask you something?"

"You can ask me anything," I answer, and I completely mean it.

Being under the mask in front of her, I have this confidence I don't usually feel. And at the same time, I'm completely at ease, forgetting the world. She could ask me who I am, and I wouldn't hesitate to take off my helmet, revealing myself to her.

"I was just wondering ..." Still biting her lip nervously, her eyes stay locked on my visor. "What is this? Why did you come here tonight?"

Why *did* I come here? Reality creeps back into my mind and I know I shouldn't be here. I shouldn't be pining after this girl, no matter how long I've liked her for, when I'm going out with someone else. I should just man up, confront Mel, and end things before it gets out of hand and I do real damage.

But I can't. Because this is Jasmin, and not only did I never get over her when we broke up last year, I don't know if I'll ever get over her.

"You ..." The confidence and bravado vanish. I stare back at her, the tint of my dark visor discoloring her, but it does nothing to erase what I know she really looks like. What she really feels like. "I guess you feel like someone I can talk to. A friend."

"Oh." She deflates. "A friend."

Knowing what she thinks I mean, I reach over and hold her hand. "An incredibly gorgeous friend."

Her face lights up, which in turn puts a smile on my face. I wish I could be this close, this honest with her as Robbie and not as Worm. But I can't. This'll have to do for now.

"Do you need a friend?" she asks, her words honest and sympathetic.

My thoughts now race over recent memories. Where the hell were my friends these past few days? They let me hang out to dry while a superhero came in and took my spot.

"Yeah, I guess I do."

"What about the other sidekicks?"

Biting my lip, my gaze finally breaks away, and I stare down at the sidewalk. "Things are ... weird right now."

Catching me off guard, she raises a hand to my chin and brings my vision back to hers. "Are you okay?"

My basic instincts take over and I wrap my arm around her, keeping us as close as we can be with the guardrail between us. My thumb runs over her cheek, and I push a strand of hair behind her ear. "I am now."

Time slows down. I lean forward, wanting to kiss her,

but somewhere in the back of my mind I know I shouldn't. I wait there, inches from her lips, my mind waring with itself. I can smell the sweet, floral perfume she always wears.

It's intoxicating.

Then she kisses me. Wrapping her arms around my neck, her lips crash into mine, and it's all I need to let go of any and every thought. Everything I used to feel for her comes roaring back, ten times over.

Finally breaking away, her lips are swollen, and that adorable blush has now turned into a crimson splash. Smirking, she looks around, biting her bottom lip, and I can't keep the grin off of my face.

"I'm sorry," she says, avoiding eye contact.

"Don't be," I reply. It's in that moment I realize a small crowd has gathered, and they're all standing around. Some of them have phones out, taking pictures. "Looks like we've drawn a crowd."

She giggles. "More like *you've* drawn a crowd."

"Well, can you blame them? A sidekick with a cutie as beautiful as you."

She snorts, shaking her head. "Jasmin."

"What?"

"As much as I like it when you call me cutie, my name's Jasmin."

My smile widens. "Jasmin. I love that name. But if you don't mind, since you like it so much, I'll keep the cutie reference."

She bites her lip again. "I don't mind."

"I guess I should be going." Her face drops, slightly defeated. "Can I see you again?"

The defeat vanishes. "Of course. Should I, I don't know …" She pulls out her phone.

I let out a light chuckle. "No, it's okay. I'll find you." I take in another breath of her scent and then teleport away, up to the top of the building, and out of sight.

Leaning over the edge, I watch as the crowd begins to disperse, and Jasmin shakes her head, starting to jump up and down. Pulling out her phone, I catch the start of her conversation as she heads down into the subway station.

"Maria! Oh my God, you won't believe what just happened!"

17

Just after midnight, I finally teleport back to headquarters, unsure what I'm going to find. I stayed in stealth mode all night, and while that's not usually a problem, I probably should've radioed to check in at least once.

I walk down the hallway toward the control room. Doc's the first person I pass. We haven't spoken since the meeting, so I'm not sure how awkward our interaction will be, but he doesn't bring it up. What he does do is raise his eyebrows, shaking his head. Not in a disappointed way. More in a way that says, "*now you did it*."

I narrow my eyes at him, confused.

"When it's over, meet me in my lab please."

He doesn't stop to explain his statement. I pause, watching him continue on, unsure what he's talking about.

Entering the control room, Daniel stands next to Melissa, who's sitting in a chair, her back to me. His hand is on her shoulder.

"Hey, what's going on?" I ask.

She spins around and her eyes are red and puffy. Daniel scowls at me, shaking his head.

Trial By Fire

"What happened?" I ask again.

Jumping from her seat, it takes her two steps to get to me, and then she slams her fist across my face, knocking me down to the ground. "You asshole!"

Grabbing my face in pain, she stomps away, and out of the room.

Daniel stands over me, his arms crossed, with not even a hint of helping me off of the ground. "It's all over the internet."

"What is?" I shout, getting to my feet.

He turns around and pulls up The Cape Zone website on a monitor. As soon as my eyes see the screen, my faces drops. "Oh, shit."

Someone took a picture of Jasmin and me, our arms wrapped around one another, kissing. From the angle, you can't see her face, but I stick out like a sore thumb.

"Yeah." Daniel nods. "What were you thinking?"

"I wasn't ... I mean, I didn't ..." I have no words. What can I say? Instead, I drop my head low and stare at the desk. "How many sites are running it?"

"How many?" he scoffs. "It'd be easier to find out which sites *aren't* running it. TCZ was the first to break the story." He looks at the monitor, reading it. "'*Mr. Mimic's sidekick caught in late night rendezvous.*' You're trending on every site. You broke the internet, dude. This is the biggest story since Frost revealed her secret identity."

My face cringes from pain, stupidity, but mostly embarrassment. *How could I have been so stupid?* I was so caught up being with Jasmin, I knew the crowd was there but didn't even think about the consequences.

Daniel puts his hand on my shoulder, and I glance over at him. "You're not mad?"

"Honestly? Yeah, I'm pissed off at you. She's my friend,

Robbie. She's like a sister." I nod, feeling the embarrassment grow. "But you're my friend, too. You screwed up, man. There's no doubt about that."

"Yeah."

"I don't know how or when she'll get over this, but she will. You're not her first boyfriend. You're lucky she was holding back when she hit you, otherwise your skull would probably be cracked."

"Daniel, you have to believe me, this all just got out of hand. I didn't mean to—"

He cuts me off, raising his hands. "It's none of my business. But, you and me? We're good."

He takes a seat at the desk, and closes the websites running the story. I wait there, in silence, appalled at myself and feeling disgraced. I can't believe I did what I did. Nodding to myself, I leave the room and head to Doc's lab, unsure what exactly to expect, since he obviously knows, too.

Walking to the lab feels like the longest walk of my life. The side of my face she hit hurts more now, and I can feel it starting to swell up. As painful as it is, I have a feeling Doc's about to add on to my discomfort, and I totally deserve it.

"Have a seat." He motions over to the chair I've been accustomed to sitting in when I visit his lab. He pulls out two long syringes. "The analysis of your blood when you received the healing ointment came back with some interesting results. Nothing outlandish, but it seems your blood was reacting strange to it. I'd like to do some more tests."

I nod, waiting for the other shoe to drop. That being my monumental screwup I just had. "Okay."

Injecting the first needle, he finally brings it up. "So, what happened tonight?"

I let out a long breath. "Doc, I just ... I screwed up."

Trial By Fire

Without thinking, I start purging my mind of everything that's been going on, dating all the way back to last year. Breaking up with Jasmin to keep her safe, and the tug-of-war I've had with those emotions ever since. How I really do like Melissa, but when I saw Jasmin at the dance, I realized it wasn't the same. Then I transition to Forge and feeling like the outcast of the group and being replaced. It all comes gushing out like a waterfall.

Filling up his second syringe with blood, he listens intently. When he's done, and I'm through with the verbal vomit, he strokes his beard in thought.

"I'm not going to pretend to know what you're feeling. I don't have powers, Robbie. When I first came to the Justice Alliance, I was part of a science research team, and over the years I've earned my place. I was never in the spotlight like the superheroes. Like you."

I nod.

"But I do know that this position you're in, and by that, I mean your status here with the Justice Alliance, it's dangerous. It can be life-altering. World-altering even. You have to realize that, yes?"

I nod again. "I know. I'm sorry, Doc."

"So am I." He stands up from the chair, casting a sympathetic look at me. "You're suspended from all patrols and missions."

"What?"

"I'm sorry, but it has to be done."

I jump to my feet. "Doc, you can't be serious."

"I am serious. Robbie, I warned you. After you went and faced the threat of the fire-enhanced suspect the other night without backup, I warned you. And now tonight? You deliberately ceased communications. Do you know how dangerous that is? And then you went and put a civilian's life in danger, engaging with them in public. We've scanned all known photos on the internet, and it doesn't look like she's recognizable. But what if a camera had caught her face? Do you know how many threats she'd be under just for being associated with you?"

"I didn't—"

"I know you didn't mean for it to happen, but it did. You've been far too reckless. You're suspended, end of discussion."

I stand there, shocked. I knew there'd be consequences, but I didn't think being completely suspended would be one of them. King City is already down the big three, with only us to protect it. And there are still the fire guys out there.

"You have access to headquarters and training facilities, but no missions, no patrols, no investigations whatsoever. You'll have control desk responsibilities on the weekend. Please, don't make me take those away, too."

"Doc, come on! You know I'm the best chance you have at finding and bringing the fire guys in."

"Not like this you aren't. Not until you can control your emotions and your thinking." He turns and reaches for the door handle. "I'm sorry, but you did this to yourself."

Pete, like every other person in the city, saw the pictures. When I get to school the following week, I fill him in. He first saw the story online and texted Daniel, who, to his credit, isn't giving him a lot of information, and told him he should talk to me when he saw me. It was the first thing he brought up.

Jasmin's become somewhat of a celebrity in our school. You can't see her face in the pictures, but anyone who knows her can see the resemblance. I've heard the gossip around school and some girls are jealous. Some girls want the details, and some are even fangirling over her, asking for her autograph. It's insane.

Unlike the previous week, Maria and Jasmin stroll casually to our lunch table, and take a seat. A senior in our school, who's captain of our varsity football team, Michael Peterson, stops by the table and asks her out. I scowl, listening to him try to convince her, telling her he's way stronger than Worm. She laughs, then lets him down politely, and returns to eating.

"Sorry," she tells us, giggling.

"This is too much." Maria laughs.

When I'm not rolling my eyes, I keep them locked on my lunch bag, unsure what to say or how to act. I can feel Pete's gaze on me, looking over every time someone walks over, or we hear someone talking about it in the cafeteria.

"Oh my God, you guys," Maria blurts out, slapping her hand on the table. Her eyes are locked on her phone. "The Justice Alliance just released a press release. Worm's been deactivated from all current ongoing missions or patrols."

Damn it. I completely forgot about Justice Alliance protocols.

Whenever a superhero or sidekick is injured—or otherwise incapacitated—they send out a press release so as to not cause concern in the public. Several years ago, a superhero had somehow lost his power during a battle. He wasn't seen in six months, but in the meantime, everyone assumed he died, and a panic spread throughout King City. Ever since then the Alliance sends out press releases to let the press and others know King City is still protected.

"Oh no!" Jasmin stares at Maria's phone. "You don't think … You don't think this is because of me, do you?"

Before I know what I'm doing, I roll my head back and let out an annoyed groan. "Ugh! Why is everyone so freaked out about Worm?" Pete shoots me an incredulous look. Maria and Jasmin both look at me the same. "Seriously, he's just a sidekick."

"Easy, man," Pete whispers.

"Robbie, weren't you the one freaking out about him last year?" Jasmin asks.

"Yeah, Robbie," Maria piles on. "You were like his number one fanboy. This wouldn't be another jealous ex thing, would it?"

"Whatever, I gotta go." I grab my backpack and leave the table.

Exiting the cafeteria, I'm surprised to feel a tug at my arm, and hear Jasmin's voice. "Hey, what's wrong with you?"

"Me?" I nearly shout, causing Jasmin to jump back a step. "Sorry, it's nothing."

Raising her hand, her fingers skim over the black eye I'm sporting. In my pathetic mood last night, I decided to not apply any special serums or ointments Doc has for the mark Melissa gave me. "It wouldn't have anything to do with this, would it?"

Her touch catches me off guard. Everything around me —the noise, people walking—it all vanishes. Then a split second later, the moment passes, and she jerks her hand back.

"Sorry," she whispers, looking away.

"It's okay. No. This"—I point to my eye—"is just me being stupid."

She smiles, then a more serious expression crosses her face. "I want to apologize."

"For what?"

"I know you saw me at homecoming, Robbie. I just—"

She pauses, taking a deep breath. "It just caught me off guard. Seeing you with another girl. I mean, I know we were talking about it before and everything, and that you mentioned her, but I just thought ..." She doesn't finish her sentence. I wait, hoping to know what she's thinking, but she shakes her head. Steadying her gaze, her eyes find mine again. "She's very pretty, your girlfriend."

Without thinking, I roll my eyes. "Oh yeah."

"What?"

"Well, we aren't exactly together anymore."

"You're not?"

Her concerned gaze does something to me. Of all of the reactions I could've hoped for when telling her I didn't have a girlfriend, I never thought I would've seen concern. Hopeful, sad, unsure? Okay. But concerned? I cringe, knowing that she seems to have moved on and getting back together with me is probably the furthest thing from her mind. Especially with Worm running around, making out with her.

"No." I try to sound relieved.

"Well, that's too bad."

"Mm." I raise my eyebrows. "But, enough about me," I try to change the subject. "Looks like you got yourself a new guy."

She gives me a skeptical glare. "Oh, *now* you want to talk about Worm."

"I know, I know." I shrug. "What can I say, maybe Maria's right?"

"About what?"

"Being jealous."

18

After a couple of days, the story about Worm making out with some girl on the street has died down. Mainly because a superhero was caught up in some drama over whether or not he was the father of a major Hollywood star's three-month-old baby. Baby mama drama usually isn't a huge deal, but superhero trumps sidekick every time.

I remain frustrated the rest of the week. My phone still receives the emergency alerts through the Justice Alliance app, and every time it pings, I let out an annoyed grumble, knowing I can't do anything about it.

Daniel checks in on me once to ask how I am, which is cool of him. It's been radio silence from Melissa, and deservedly so. My black eye has faded a bit, but as grumpy as I've been this week over not being able to contribute to Alliance functions, I've been doubly ashamed every time I see my reflection. I'm not sure when she's going to talk to me again, if ever. We're broken up, there's no doubt about that, but maybe we'll just never talk to one another again. I have no idea. I do want to at least apologize to her, face-to-face. It's the least I can do.

Trial By Fire

Since I don't have anything else to do, after school I immediately teleport home and try to search every nook and cranny of the internet, looking for anything related to Project Ignis or Daedalus. After not finding anything on either, I decide to search for Dean Macall, and actually find a few things on him.

He was a professor at King City University, and news outlets reported that he went missing over a year ago, right around the time I debuted as Mimic's sidekick. He taught molecular-biology and his record is squeaky clean. Then, he disappeared out of nowhere.

Police searched for traces of him in his office, at his home, and found nothing. Nothing was out of place, and all of his personal belonging were still accounted for. It's as if he vanished. His wife and daughter checked in with the police daily for three months straight. She even went on missing person talk shows, hoping for some kind of lead, only to never get any tips. A month after her appearance on the show, she and her daughter went missing, too. Police found a car registered to Macall a few weeks later, torched a few miles outside of city limits.

Other than that, there's nothing else on him.

The rest of the week goes by painstakingly slow. When Friday night rolls around, the nerves and tension mount. It'll be my first time back at headquarters, doing the only thing Doc's letting me do, manning the control desk. My apprehension doubles when I teleport to headquarters, knowing Melissa is supposed to be taking the patrol shift tonight.

Almost tiptoeing into the control room, I look around and don't see anyone else there. Walking over to the desk, I take a seat, and then nearly jump out of it as Daniel calls out to me from behind.

"Hey."

I take a couple breaths to calm myself down. "Crap, man. Don't sneak up on me like that."

He chuckles. "She's not here."

"Oh."

"How are you?"

Typing my password into the keyboard, I pull up a few different camera angles, then lift my shoulders. "I'm here. So ... whatever. You're taking the patrol tonight?"

"No, I just got in." I look over at him and he reads my nervous expression. "Don't worry, she got Forge to cover her shift tonight."

"Right." I nod.

She's avoiding me. I can't blame her, but it makes me feel worse than I already do, knowing that I hurt her that much.

Daniel leans against the desk. "In other news, Supron and the others are supposed to be transmitting a message next week."

"How's everything going over there?"

"Doc says they've started getting the upper hand, but the battle's been bloody."

"What's up, Worm?" Forge asks, walking into the control room.

"Hey."

He tightens his gloves and wristbands, both of which are connected to the ignition apparatus on his back, so he can draw up the fire he uses. "Sucks about you and Mighty."

I look over at him and scowl. Lifting his brow, he turns and heads back toward the door. "Anyway, I'll be out there. We on channel four tonight?"

"Yeah."

When he leaves, Daniel taps my shoulder. "I know it

stings, Robbie, but Forge is only helping. He's the only one who's dealt with that kind of heat and can withstand it."

"No, he's not. I've dealt with it. Twice. With the actual guys we're looking for, might I add." He doesn't respond, and I feel embarrassed all over again. "Sorry. I know what you're saying. It just ... sucks. That's all."

"Yeah."

"Forge checking in from Alliance Pod One," Forge says through his headset. I teleport, but for the heroes who can't fly, they use Alliance hover crafts we call pods to get around in the city for patrols.

"Roger that," I answer back.

"I'll check in when I hit the east side. Forge out."

Daniel waves as he leaves the room, and I settle in for a night that's probably gonna be filled with a lot of eye rolling, depending on how annoyed I get with Forge. Which isn't even his fault, I know that, but I can't shake the aggravation of being replaced.

It's a slow night, and as expected, he starts to talk. Not like he's trying to be buddy/buddy, but just passing the time. It's what we all usually do. I learn he prefers baseball over football, and he enrolled at Edgewater University, but never completed his last semester. He loves fettuccine Alfredo, but only if it's made with real butter. His last year as a sidekick, he was invited to the Oscar's as a date with one of Hollywood's hottest teen stars, but his superhero mentor told him he couldn't go, which he's still bitter over. And he loves hip-hop. Basically, I learned he likes to talk. A lot.

While I'm listening, I insert the casual "oh" and "mm-hmm" when he pauses, trying to make it seem like I'm paying attention. Since it's a quiet night, I use all of the time I can to search the databank servers for any new information on Macall, but the Alliance doesn't have anything on him either. A few more particulars for his education, but before disappearing he was a complete straight shooter. Nothing out of the ordinary.

Switching the search to Daedalus, I finally find something I can sink my teeth into.

For the last ten years, Daedalus has been the primary corporation to create, modify, and disperse cutting edge bio-molecular enhancements. The corporation has multiple contracts with different branches of the military to work with soldiers who are hurt in battle. There are a number of video files that show soldiers who are paralyzed, but after working with Daedalus, they're able to start walking again. It looks promising, and something that can help millions of people around the world.

The latest updated file is from two years ago, and after that there's nothing. All functions of the corporation seemingly cease. A high-ranking army general, Samuel Watkins, is listed as the primary point of contact for the business, which strikes me as kind of odd. He's in charge of the rehabilitation procedures.

Next, I search for Project Ignis, and once again find nothing, which now sends a ripple of concern through me. I can understand not finding anything when I searched from home, but I'm searching the Alliance servers. They have information on every superhero, every supervillain, and every black-market trade item. If it exists, it should be found on the servers. But there's nothing.

"So, I mean, is that true?" Forge asks while I type away still.

"Uh ... yeah," I answer.

"Dang, that's cold."

My eyes dart back to a different monitor, showing the

location of Forge. He's atop a building on the lower west side of King City. "Wait, what's cold?"

"What you did."

"What I did? What'd I do?"

"I just asked if you really cheated on Mighty Miss."

"Oh! Well, you know ... it's complicated."

Closing my search browsers, I decide to finish out the rest of my shift and try to pay more attention. It's not like there's a lot of information to dig through anyway. When my desk duty is over, I head back to my bunker, trying to decide if I want to stay here tonight, or go home. Plopping down on my bed, I pull out my phone to see a text message from Pete.

Pete: Hey, just wanted to give you a heads-up. Danny's meeting Maria and Jasmin tomorrow. We're going to the movies. Just didn't want it to be weird.

I let out a long sigh, thinking again about how I messed it all up. I'm not with Melissa, and it's still awkward to hang out with Jasmin. But not as Worm.

An idea hits me, and I head to a storage room, grabbing an Alliance burner phone that we keep on hand. I input Jasmin's number into it and head back to my room, typing out a text message. It's just a simple message, but my thumb hovers over the "send" button, and I nervously try to decide if I should send it. It's past midnight, so she might not even be awake. I hit the button.

Worm: Hey, u up?

I stare at the phone, waiting for a reply.

Jasmin: Who is this?

My smile is instant.

Worm: Cool, ur up! :)
Jasmin: I think u have the wrong number

I laugh.

Worm: No, I don't. Cutie :)
Jasmin: !!!!!!!
Jasmin: Worm?!?!!
Worm: At ur service
Jasmin: Is this really u? How do I know this isn't Maria, or someone else, messing around???

Pausing, I stare at the screen, unsure how to confirm my identity.

Worm: Ask me something? Anything from the times we've seen each other?
Jasmin: No good. I've told Maria everything.
Worm: Everything? Really? O_o
Jasmin: Yes, MARIA! I know it's you!

A mischievous smile spreads across my face. I've been to Jasmin's apartment before, so I know she lives in a condo on the upper west side. I also know her bedroom has a small fire escape. I activate my helmet.

Worm: Look out your window

Waiting for a reply, the anxiousness builds.

Jasmin: I'm looking. I don't see anything.

Trial By Fire

And that's my cue. I teleport to her fire escape, and she jumps back from her window, startled. Covering her mouth, her eyes are wide. I can't keep the grin from spreading across my lips. She does a double take, looking back at her phone, then at me. I raise my phone and show it to her.

She walks over to the window, sliding it open, her bottom lip seemingly stuck between her teeth. "You're ... here. You're actually here."

Smiling, I lean against the fire escape rail. "I am. And apparently you like to kiss and tell."

The cute blush I've started to grow accustomed to spreads across her face. "Sorry. It's just girl talk."

"It's cool." I scan her up and down and smirk. She's wearing emerald green, silk pajamas that are tiny boy shorts, along with a spaghetti-strapped top that shows off her stomach. "Love the pajamas, but the way."

"Ohmygod!" She jumps back, grabbing a sheet from her bed, wrapping herself in it. "I can't believe this."

Walking back to the window, she keeps the sheets around her.

"I know we haven't had the first snowfall yet, but how do you stay warm in something like that? Not that I'm complaining."

Her blush is now bloodred. "You-you-you ..." She scowls at me, a smile still across her face. "You are so not acting like a superhero right now."

I point to my face. "Sidekick."

Ignoring my comment, her eyes scan my body. "How do *you* stay warm in that?"

"Wouldn't you like to know." I laugh, and she narrows her eyes at me. "Electro-thermal lining." I tap the insignia on my chest. "It wraps around my torso, legs, and arms. It's also on the inside of my helmet. Comes in handy when it starts snowing and I'm out on patrol."

"How'd you get my number?" she asks, seeming more at ease. "And how'd you know where I live?"

"I know a guy," I joke.

"What, like a stalker?"

We both laugh and I lean closer, against her window. "No, not a stalker. A friend. A friend of a friend, really." Yeah, that sounds feasible.

The silence drifts between us and the night sky. As weird as everything has been in my life, as horrible as I've felt for how I've acted with Melissa, and as cheated as I've felt from Doc for suspending me, I forget everything. I always do when I'm with her.

She clears her throat. "So ..."

"So ..." I try to get a grip. I'm the sidekick, after all. "Hey, I want to apologize for everything that happened. That was really reckless of me. I hope it hasn't caused you too much trouble."

"Me?" She lets out an incredulous laugh. "I heard the Justice Alliance deactivated you for all future missions. I'm so sorry."

"Don't be." I wave her off. She sits on her window sill and I lean against the edge. "Everything that's happened to me is on me. No matter what, I know what my responsibilities are."

"But—"

"Jasmin. Nothing that happens to me is your fault. Okay?" She pauses, her eyes locked on to mine, though she can only see her reflection in my visor. It's a serious look I've seen on her. One where I know something's on her mind. "What?"

"The way you say my name. It's almost like you know me."

Whoops. I'd love for her to know it's me under my helmet, but I still have that little voice telling me it's too dangerous.

"I guess you're just easy to talk to," I reply, standing up straighter.

"Which reminds me, I'd love to talk to you more. But I can't kiss you again."

My eyes jump to anywhere but her, and I take a step back, nodding. "Oh, yeah. No, I get it."

She giggles. "Not unless you answer some questions."

Her flirtatious demeanor puts me at ease, and I lean back to where I was. "Is that right?"

"Number one: Who are you under that helmet?"

I let out a loud laugh. "Oh, come on. You know I can't answer that."

"It was worth a shot." She shrugs. "Number two: How old are you?"

I tap my chin. "Mm, under eighteen. I can't be too specific."

She narrows her eyes at me. "I'm guessing sixteen or seventeen. Which means you're most likely in high school, so ... What school do you go to?"

"Pass."

She scoffs, then slaps my arm. "You can't pass."

"Why not?" I ask with a chuckle. "You didn't tell me the rules."

"Well, that's a rule. No passing."

"Okay. Now I know." I smile widely, leaving her scowling.

"Fine. Last question." Her lighthearted vibe morphs and a skittish guise floats over her. "It ... it might sound stupid, but just be honest, okay?"

"Always. Well, except for the whole secret identity thing."

My joke doesn't break through her anxious mien. "Are you ... I mean, am I ..." Taking a deep breath, she closes her eyes and then spits out her question. "Am-I-just-another-girl-you-go-around-making-out-with-I-just-need-to-know."

I can't help it. A robust laugh breaks forth and her eyes shoot open, staring me down. Slapping my arm again, she frowns. "Stop laughing. I'm being serious."

"I know, I'm sorry." I finally calm the laughter. "No, I don't go around making out with girls. And no, you aren't just another one."

Her nerves seem to calm down, but she averts her eyes. "Really? Because, well, I heard you and Mighty Miss are a thing. And then, after our kiss, I wasn't sure if you were some sidekick Casanova or something."

Another round of laughter breaks out.

"Worm!"

"Sorry, sorry."

Casting a glance inside of her room, my eyes find her dresser. There's a picture of us. It's from our homecoming dance last year. I can't believe she still has it up. I let out a breath of relief and frustration. I'm thrilled she still has it when I would've thought she tore it up last year. But I can't really be with her. Can I?

Looking back at her, I discover her watching me, for me to confirm or deny my make-out habits. Her wide, hazel eyes wait for me.

"The truth is, I don't know that I've ever felt like I do when I'm around you."

"But you hardly know me."

I smile, lifting my shoulders. "Maybe it's like you said, I feel like I know you. When I'm around you, everything else fades away." I lean closer, sliding my thumb across her cheek. "It's only you." She offers a small smile. "Did I pass your test?"

She nods. "I just don't want to be another girl. I know your life is crazy, completely different from mine, and I don't know what this is, but—"

"Jasmin." Her words stop and she stares at me. "You aren't just another girl. You're the only girl."

"You pass," she whispers, and leans closer, smashing her lips into mine.

19

A knock at her door cuts our kiss way too short, and she spins around as the door creaks open. I teleport to the fire escape above hers and hear the conversation.

"Jasmin, is someone in here?"

"What? Of course not, Mom."

"I thought I heard something."

There's a pause. "Nope. Sorry, I was just opening my window for some cold air."

"Okay. It's late, honey, you should try and get some sleep."

"I will."

Another pause. Then the door shuts. Teleporting back down to her fire escape, she slaps her hands over her mouth, quieting a yelp. "Don't do that," she scolds me.

"Sorry." I peer past her, at her closed door. "I guess this means I don't get to meet your parents."

"It's just my mom. And no, you don't." She narrows her eyes, but smiles.

Leaning closer to her again, she follows suit, and I reach for her hand. "Maybe next time."

Her head drops, as she lets out a confused chuckle. "This is crazy."

"I know." I hold her gaze. "But I would like to see you again. It's just ... it can't be out in the open. If people learn who you are, that you're someone close to me, you could be in serious danger."

The apprehension fades from her face and she smiles. "I guess we'll have to figure something else out."

"I guess we will."

There's a faint midnight breeze, and she leans closer to me, our hands still interlocked. She's kissed me twice now, so I don't wait, and finally find her lips again.

It's odd and familiar at the same time. She doesn't know who I really am, but I know her. And as much as I ignored my feelings or tried to tell myself that I'd get over her, I now realize I was kidding myself. It's always been Jasmin.

She breaks away, wrapping her sheet around herself a little tighter. "Okay, sidekick, I guess I can't keep you to myself all night."

"I wouldn't mind."

"Plus"—she holds a finger up, trying to counter me—"it is getting a little cold."

A devilish smirk floats across my mouth. "I could help with that."

Smiling, her jaw drops. "If we aren't at the meeting-my-mom phase, then we definitely aren't ... I'm in trouble with you, aren't I?"

Raising my hands, I feign ignorance. "Whoa, what are you talking about? I was talking about teleporting us somewhere warm. It's nice in Australia right now. I'm sure it's not too cold in Hawaii. What were you— Oooh. Wow. It's always the quiet ones."

She playfully pushes me away. "Goodnight, Worm."

Holding her hands one last time before she breaks away, I lean against the rails and she closes her window. Silently, she offers me one last wave, and I wave back, then teleport across the street, to an adjacent rooftop. Closing her blinds, the only thing brighter than the smile on her face is the moon. And even that is a close call.

Getting home, I can't sleep at all. I should be concerned, or worried, or even irritated that all of this is happening as Worm and not as myself, but I can't be any of those things. Because even if she doesn't know who I really am, she does know me. When I'm not Worm, she knows me. And now she's getting to know this other side of me. In a weird way, it makes sense.

I know I'll tell her eventually. I have to. This time, I don't know how to go back. But I push those thoughts from my head, relishing in the fact that I get to be with her this way. At least, for now.

With only a few hours of sleep, I wake up the next morning feeling amazing. Making my way to the kitchen, I discover my mom has already cooked up some chorizo and egg burritos, her usual breakfast on the weekends. Turning the stove off, she sets her spatula down, when I walk over and give her a kiss on the cheek, before pulling out the orange juice.

"Good morning."

She eyes me suspiciously. "Look who's up before ten o'clock."

I scoff before taking a drink from the orange juice cartoon. "Mom, you know I do patrols on the weekend."

"Don't drink it like that." She takes the juice from me. "And why are you so happy?"

"I'm always happy."

Side-eyeing me, she looks over at my dad, who sits at the

dining room table, reading his tablet. "No. You always *act* like you're happy. Roberto, what's wrong with your son?"

"Seems okay to me," he mutters, never taking his eyes off of his screen.

"Mom, I'm fine."

Pointing her spatula at me, she narrows her eyes. "What did you do?"

"What?" I gape. "Nothing. I just had a good night, that's all."

"Ay dios mío," she swears, shaking her head. "You better not be out with girls."

"Mom!" My cheery mood vanishes and my jaw drops.

"I remember what boys were like at your age. Roberto, tell your son."

"Robbie, be safe," he says in a complete monotone.

"Oh my God! This is so not happening right now. I have to go."

"I'm serious!" my mom shouts as I return to my room to grab my jacket.

"Love you, too!" I shout back and teleport to headquarters.

Jumping to my bunker, I finish gearing up, and decide to hit the training facility, since patrols are off-limits now. Before my control desk shift tonight, I've decided to try another search, and see if I missed anything.

Turning a corner, I almost collide into Melissa. We stand there, staring at each other in silence. Well, I stare in silence. She delivers an apathetic glare.

"Worm," she says curtly, and walks past me.

I should let it go. Everything just happened and I'm sure she's either still hurt or mad. Probably both. But I run over and stop her. "Mel, please let me explain."

To my surprise, she waits. "Okay."

"I, uh ..." I rub the back of my neck, my mind going blank.

"Exactly," she spits out and continues walking.

"No." I run in front of her again. "Please. I'm sorry, okay? I'm really, really sorry."

Finally, her face breaks from the stoic glare. It softens with a hint of sadness, but only for a moment. It's immediately replaced with disgust.

"Robbie, if you didn't like me you could've just told me."

"It's not that. I like you, Melissa. A lot. It's just ..." I trail off again. This time I know the words, but there's no way I can say them. How can I? How do you tell someone you've been going out with—who confessed their love to you—that you liked them, but there was always someone else, even if you didn't consciously know it?

Instead of waiting, she jabs a finger into my chest. "You like me a lot? Really? So why were you out kissing girls on street corners, huh?" The anger and hate vanish. Her face softens once more and she looks away. "You ... that really hurt, Robbie."

"I'm sorry. I never meant to hurt you."

The few uncomfortable minutes standing in front of one another feels like hours. Suddenly, I realize how horrible I am at breakups, remembering breaking up with Jasmin last year. Lying to her face that I didn't like her. This time I didn't even bother to lie. I let news and gossip websites reveal the truth. I'm a horrible boyfriend.

"Whatever," she finally says, regaining a neutral composure. "We have to be professional. Especially right now, since it's just us." I nod. "I traded with Hydro tonight, but I'll be back on patrol duty next weekend while you run the control desk."

"Okay." I give her a faint smile, but it disappears with her next words.

"We aren't friends though. We aren't even acquaintances. We're work associates. I don't think I can be anything other than that with you right now."

I gulp, staring at her. "I understand."

"Good." Without another word, she proceeds down the hall.

Letting out a pathetic sigh, I nod to myself, and then continue on my way. Before reaching the training room door, Doc waves over to me, standing near one of his labs.

"Robbie, I'm glad you're here. Got a moment?"

"I was just about to hit the training room." I point to the door.

"I ran some more tests. I'd like to go over them with you first."

I nod. "All right."

"You can't be serious?"

"I'm afraid I am," Doc replies.

He has a tablet out and a large clipboard, reviewing all of the data about my latest blood test results. Isolating certain parts of the plasma in my blood, and the strand that is similar to Supron's, he tested the super-healing ointment he used on me when I got burned. Other than all of the scientific jargon he went over, half of which went over my head, breaking down the results for me in laymen's terms has me stunned. Shocked, actually.

The cells in my DNA regenerate at a higher efficiency rate when pressed beyond their limits. Once he found that out during the heat testing, he tested my DNA with multiple viruses he has on file, and found that my body reacted the same way. The disease attacked the blood sample, but then the platelets went into overdrive, after a momentary lull period. And once my blood healed itself, my DNA was as good as new.

"You can't die." Doc says it a second time, but I'm still dumbfounded. "Well, no, technically you can die. But your body will heal itself and you'll come back to life."

"Doc …" I stand there, my jaw on the floor. "Are you saying I'll live forever? That's impossible."

"That's not what I'm saying, Robbie. The properties in your DNA, they don't make you immortal. Supron only looks how he does because his platelets are spliced together with his super strength. You, on the other hand, will continue to grow and age. Your body advances just like any other person's, except when it's under attack."

I squint my eyes, rubbing my forehead. "I don't understand."

"Think of it like this: you're a battery. We're all batteries, right? We go through life, and by the time our life ends, that means our batteries have run out. The difference between you and other batteries is that if something unnatural happens to you, your body recognizes it, and you will recover from that."

"But still, Doc, that doesn't make any sense. Unnatural? How does my body know when something is unnatural? Or just an accident? Or something I did on purpose by making the wrong choice?"

Doc scratched his beard. "I don't know. It possibly might have something to do with the time anomaly. There is nothing I can do about testing for something like that. All I know is, from every single test I've run so far, they all point to your body, your DNA, healing itself."

I roll my eyes. "Great. So, I can heal myself back from death, but I'll still die in the meantime."

"Robbie, your body has the ability to resurrect itself. That's nothing to take lightly."

"I know, Doc, I just wish I knew what exactly is going on with me."

He puts a hand on my shoulder. "We're getting there."

20

After the training session, I stop by Doc's lab and ask for his clearance codes so I can dig deeper into the databank servers. I know I'm supposed to stay as far away from the fire guy investigations as possible, so when he asks me what I need them for, I lie and tell him I'm researching the species Mimic and the others are battling. He pauses for a moment, eying me suspiciously, but eventually gives me his clearance. Unfortunately, I have absolutely no idea what I'm looking for or where to start, so I wander aimlessly through the digital files.

Searching both Daedalus and Project Ignis, I finally happen across a page that's linked to Griffin Consortium, which is a conglomerate enterprise of Justin Griffin, a renowned genius and billionaire. A high-tech mogul who also happens to be locked away in Chromium Penitentiary.

Chromium is a supermax prison for supervillains. Griffin, though, doesn't have superpowers; he is locked away there because of his brain. He was at one time thought of as the smartest man in the world, and many still believe he is.

But he decided to use all of those smarts and try to take down the Justice Alliance five years ago.

He convinced nations around the world that in the decades since superheroes have shown up, they could no longer be trusted. Alien invasions, battles wrecking entire city blocks, and superheroes acting above the law; he argued that their power should not be left unchecked. Even though there are accords, treaties, and even certain protocols set in place, he wanted to get rid of superheroes. Plain and simple.

When the Alliance investigated further, they found out that Griffin's company wasn't only trying to depower superheroes. They were conducting human experiments, trying to replicate superpowers, and were also working on inventions that killed superheroes and sidekicks.

Griffin Consortium and all parties were investigated, brought up on charges, and found guilty on all of them. He was sentenced to a life in Chromium and all of his assets were frozen. At least, that's what I've always assumed.

The files I'm reading say that, while all of his assets and monetary gains were frozen, with an off-shore bank account, all of the research was sealed and transferred to a company called Winston Industries. It's random tunnel after random tunnel, and the maze of information spreads, but everything I look up for Winston Industries seems legit.

Either way, I've finally found a connection. It's my first lead in trying to find a clue, and I take note of the location of Winston Industries corporate headquarters, which is based in Lost Hills.

Finally, I head to the control room for my shift. Daniel walks over to the desk, leaning against it, and I look up to find him staring at me.

"Yes?"

"So ... Pete told me."

I cock an eyebrow. "Told you what?"

He lets out a sigh, folding his arms. "Before I tell you, you have to promise me you won't get mad at him. I was pushing it. I just wanted to know why you did it, especially since it seemed like things were going good between you and Mel."

"Great." I roll my eyes.

"I was being super annoying, and kept asking him, and he finally told me about your history. The one you have with that girl."

"Damn it, Pete," I grumble under my breath.

"It's not his fault. Look, I'm not saying you weren't wrong, because you totally were, but ... I kind of get it now. Still, you should've told her first."

Getting up out of my chair, I point a finger at him. "You think I don't know that? You don't think I wanted to say something? I didn't know how."

He shakes his head. "You just say it, man. It's called growing up."

"Oh, easy for you to say," I retort.

"Seriously?" Glaring at me, he looks like I slapped him across the face. "I'm a black guy, sidekicking for one of, if not *the* most powerful and famous superheroes in the world. A man people revere as an icon; a god. Oh, and on top of that, I'm gay. Yeah, things are *so* easy for me."

Regret and shame spread within. "Sorry, I didn't mean—"

His frustration turns to anger. "Yeah, you didn't mean because you didn't think. That's your problem. You never think about the consequences, which is why you're in this situation."

Waving his accusation off, I turn around, staring down at the keyboard on the desk. "I don't need this right now."

"I'm just trying—"

"I know what you're saying, okay?" I look back at him, putting a finger in his face. "You repeating to me that I'm suspended, ignored protocols, and cheated on my girlfriend is not helping. You think I wanted to do that to her? Hell no. She told me she loved me, and I repeated the words back to her, all while meaning them for someone else. You think that made me feel good? It didn't. I screwed up. I lied about it. I took the easy way out and was a coward. Thanks for shoving it all right back in my face."

Meeting his eye line, I notice he's not looking at me. Instead, he stares past me, and I turn around to see Melissa standing by the door, listening to everything I said.

"Crap." Tears run down her face, and she turns and runs out of the room. "Melissa—"

I start to go after her, but Daniel grabs my arm, holding me back. "Let her go."

"I can't just—"

"Robbie. Let her go." Taking a deep breath, he shakes his head. "It's probably the best thing for her to hear in the long run." Pulling my arm away, I sink back into my chair, thoroughly disgusted with myself. "You gonna be okay?"

"Yeah, peachy," I grumble. "Comms are on. You should get out there."

To say the rest of the night is tense would be an understatement. It's another slow night, and we barely talk to each other. There are two distress calls during my shift, and that's the only time I communicate with him. He tries talking early on, but I ignore him. After a couple of minutes, he asks if the comms are working, to which I reply, "They're fine."

The minute he gets back to headquarters and heads to the control desk to finish his shift, I teleport to my bunker. Throwing my jacket off, I lie across my bed and gaze up at the ceiling, still filled with shame. How did I screw everything up so badly? We were a solid unit when Mimic, Supron, and Majestic left on their mission. Now, we feel fractured. Like a broken vase, glued back together, with huge chunks still missing.

Pulling out my burner phone, I stare at Jasmin's number, then send her a text message.

Worm: U up?

Dropping it to my chest, I wait for a reply. Unfortunately, none comes. I know she's probably asleep, but I just feel like I need to talk to someone. Which doubly sucks because normally I might text Pete, but now I don't know what he'll tell Daniel.

Opening a news app, a new video starts playing.

"In other news," a reporter talks to the camera, "another sighting of the mysterious flying man on fire was seen again."

I perk up, curious as to why nothing popped up on the radars tonight during the patrol.

"Officials are saying King City residents have no cause for alarm, as the fiery man was seen flying over Parkfield City. Numerous eye witnesses reported seeing the strange glow from the sky, which seemed to touch down at Parkfield Center, but then disappeared."

The screen cuts to the superhero of Parkfield, Lazerbeam.

He's an experienced superhero, with twenty years of service under his belt, and has called Parkfield his home city for the entire time. Wearing a traditional superhero costume, with bright blue pants and top, edged with a bright red belt, cape, and blueish-silver eye goggles to mask his identity, he's well respected within the Alliance. He's called Lazerbeam because of the lasers he shoots from his eyes.

"There's no cause for concern," he says, talking to a reporter on the screen. "I've been in contact with Parkfield PD and Fire and Emergency. We don't know why he was here, but we do know that he's gone now."

Sitting back up in my bed, I grab my jacket. After throwing it on, I activate my helmet and open up my Alliance app, downloading the file I searched and found on Winston Industries. It's time to put some real work in, and not wait around for a team that's replaced me. I'm not sure what I'm going to find, but I know a spot I can start looking. And it's a good thing I have a contact in Lost Hills.

21

**I'm in Lost Hills.
Could use some intel.
Worm.
.
.
.
Sidekick to Mr. Mimic.**

That's the encrypted message I sent Shadow nearly twenty minutes ago. Since then, I've jumped from rooftop to rooftop, trying to think of my next move. I know the location of the Winston Industries building, but it's always good to get the okay—or at the very least to let another superhero know you're in their city—before you begin working on something. Even if it is Shadow, who hates to be called a superhero.

I've had limited interaction with Shadow, other than spending a training night with him last year. He's ... intimidating. And his superpower? Yikes.

Think of something that would truly terrify you. Not just

scare but haunt you. Literally. Now, try to imagine everything around you turning pitch-black so you can't see or hear anything. Then, that terrifying monster you thought of attacks you. No, not attack, it annihilates you. That's the closest thing I can think of to describe Shadow's power.

He calls it the Dark. He moves like I do when I teleport, only he's not jumping through wormholes. He's traveling through shadows. And in those shadows, he controls terrifying creatures. And he uses said terrifying creatures in his fight against the criminals who live in Lost Hills.

He's technically a member of the Justice Alliance, but he doesn't associate with anyone. Supron and Mimic call him a consultant.

As close as anyone can figure out, he uses an interdimensional travel process to travel within the Dark. The shadow doesn't have to be large either. Somehow, he can slip through them even if the opening is as thin as a ruler. The horrifying part comes in when he calls on what he's named the Feeders. The criminals who've been there and survived call them gremlins.

So, even though I sent him a message, I've secretly been hoping he doesn't answer. That means I won't have to shudder at the prospect of having to deal with his brand of justice. With thirty minutes passing, I decide to travel to the location I've mapped out on GPS.

Lost Hills is nothing like King City. It's dark and dreary, and even in the middle of the night, with the moon and stars above, there's an air of hopelessness. I feel bad for the citizens, but many different superheroes have offered assistance over the years to Shadow, and he rejects them every time. He says the city is his, and he'll clean it up his way.

Standing atop the building, I run a scan of the different rooms, trying to find a point where their servers might be located, and a room pings on the hologram showing from my wrist guard. I teleport into a large room with four towering servers. Pulling out a small flash drive from my jacket, I plug it into the first server.

Letting the flash drive download, I look around the small room, and find a filing cabinet. It's a long shot, but I might as well check on hard copy files since I'm here.

By all outward appearances, Winston Industries is as clean as they come. Peering through a small window that looks out into a wide-open office, the walls are laced with awards, plaques, and certificates for donations all over the world. There's even an award given to Winston's CEO for philanthropist of the year.

Continuing to flip through countless files, I find absolutely nothing. No mention of Daedalus or Project Ignis. As I shut the filing cabinet, my wrist guard beeps.

"SECURITY BREACH DETECTED" flashes across my wrist in large red letters.

Crap.

As soon as I unplug the flash drive, loud sirens ring out through the room, with flashing strobe lights. The worry and concern hit me first, followed closely by suspicion. Why would a company as clean as this one have security protocols and alarms in place for their computer systems?

Before I teleport out of the room, four heavily armed guards appear outside of the building, floating in the air, with jetpacks on their back.

Whoa. Okay, this is definitely not a normal company.

All four guards hover in the air, their guns raised. I offer an uncomfortable smile, waving at them, and then teleport to the top of the building, only to find four different flying guards with their guns drawn, too.

"Freeze!" one yells out.

I teleport behind them, to the next building over, and I'm cut off by a new set of guards. *Okay, this company definitely has some stuff going on if they have an entire squad of jetpack-flying, machine-gun-carrying soldiers at their disposal.*

Changing directions, I sprint across the rooftop.

"Don't move!" a different guard screams while I teleport to another building over.

Glancing behind, I discover I now have an entire fleet of soaring guards chasing me, and the panic starts to set in. Teleporting back to headquarters could be an option, but if the USB drive I used is tracked, then that's going to lead them back to the Alliance. I'll be busted for sure, if not by them, then most definitely Doc.

Two guards pop up in front of me, cutting me off at the edge of the building. Raising my hands, I take a step back. "Okay, I can explain."

"You're one of those sidekicks from King City."

"If you say so. You know, you guys are mighty equipped to be rent-a-cops."

"We take our orders from Mr. Winston," another speaks up. "And he doesn't take kindly to people hacking his systems."

"Who's hacking? I was just updating my InstaPic profile."

Teleporting again, I jump from rooftop to rooftop, drawing them away from the building. If the drive is tracked, it might also have a virus. And if that's the case, I might not be able to get any information off of it at all. But maybe if I can get back into the office, I can grab a laptop from one of the desks. There has to be something on one of those.

I'm about five blocks away from the building, still with the group of jetpack guards trailing me. It's now or never, so I teleport back into the server room, then sprint down the hall, looking for any office that might have a laptop. Finding an open office door, I run inside and grab a computer, only to turn around and stare right into the barrel of a gun.

"Freeze!"

I grab the gun and quickly teleport it to the other side of the room, leaving his hands bare. He swivels his head, looking for his weapon, and that gives me just enough time to see through the window of the office, finding an empty office room in the neighboring building.

Shots ring out as soon as I make the jump, and I dive to the floor, glass shattering around me. These guys aren't messing around. Crawling with the laptop in hand, I wait behind a desk, trying to figure out my next move.

When the shots finally stop, I slowly peer around the desk. Finding a shattered window, the night breeze blows papers around in the office. With no guards in sight, I slowly crawl forward, about to teleport to the Winston rooftop, when a dark orb gets thrown through the window.

Everything feels like slow motion. I'm staring at the object being thrown into the office, trying to figure out what it is, and by the time it hits the office carpet I finally realize, only it's too late. A loud bang rings out, followed by an immense burst of light, blinding me.

I squeeze my eyes shut, the brightness from the flash orb burning my eyes, and take a chance on teleporting off of memory, without looking through the wormhole for direction. Tripping, I feel cement under my knees, and try to open my eyes, but it's all still a haze. Blurry images of guards start to buzz around, and I scramble, trying to get up but falling back down.

One of the guards lands a swift kick to my ribs. Not only does it send a jolt of pain through me, but I completely lose focus, and gasp for air.

Trial By Fire

"We'll take that," one of the guards says.

Two more guards land, and I roll away, clutching the laptop. I block an attack merely from ducking my head, and finally gather enough focus to teleport to the other side of the building. Staring back at them, my vision clears a touch, but it's still blurry. With their jetpacks, my only chance is ground level.

I roll off to the side, leaning over the edge of the building, and peer down. Then I teleport. Looking back up from ground level, I can see the tiny guards looking down at me, then they fire up their packs and begin flying again.

I teleport across the street, then into a neighboring alley, and find a fire escape. Teleporting up to it, I see that the escape is attached to an abandoned room, and I break through the window with my elbow, crawling inside.

Pressing a button, I retract my helmet for a moment, rubbing my eyes, trying to get my vision back. Once it's good enough, I stumble through the empty room, and then down a hallway, not hearing anyone give way to chase. A small glimmer of hope kindles, hoping I've lost them, but as I begin to make my way down a stairwell, I hear their footsteps.

"Checking stairwell," someone says. "Keep your eyes on the sky. He can teleport and we can't lose him."

Heading back to where I was, across the street I see another building. This one has a department store on the ground level. I try to jump down to the street level as fast as I can, but it's not fast enough. A guard sees me, and shots ring out as I teleport into the store, and I dive to the ground, attempting to avoid more glass.

I crawl behind a small stand, then a mannequin, hearing the shots continue to ring out. I feel like a human pinball and these guys keep swatting me around. Searching the area, I see more clothing stands and mannequins. An idea hits me. If I can change into regular clothes, I can teleport a block away, and casually walk off under the guise.

Ducking behind a long rack of clothes, I hear footsteps crunching over shards of glass, and crawl between two large clothing stands. Picking out a hooded sweater, I retract my helmet, and slide the hoodie over me. Grabbing another to tie around my waist—hopefully to hide my gold pants—now I just have to find a spot to teleport out of here and hope they don't catch me.

"Visual?" I hear a radio go off.

"Not yet. He's in here somewhere."

"Just got the word; Lethal force approved. No leaks."

Crap! This is really not good. No matter how much trouble I may get it, my only option might be to call Doc and get some help out of this.

"Copy that."

Crawling farther into the store, I hide between a set of mannequins wearing active wear. Next to them sits a bin with basketballs. Grabbing one, I watch as the guard looks the other way, and I launch the ball across the store. Hearing it bounce once, a loud blast rings out. It's not bullets. They are definitely using some other type of ammunition now, and this is my only opening.

Getting up, I sprint across the store, and then teleport to the front of the building, landing outside on the sidewalk. Searching for the best place to jump to next, I don't have any time to think, as a blast explodes the window I'm in front of, shattering it, slamming me right in my shoulder. I fall to the ground, the laptop clanging on the cement, and I clutch my arm in pain.

Rocked by the blast, I reach over for the fallen laptop, but feel a gun pressed against my back. "Don't move."

Two guards pick me up, holding my hands behind my back. Twisting my arm, the shoulder that was shot stings in pain, before my arms are suddenly let go. Relief floods me, and I turn around to see why they let me go.

One guard stands next to me, his eyes darting everywhere.

"Damn it!" he yells out, before grabbing his radio. "Shadow's on the scene. Repeat, Shadow is here."

I don't think I've ever been happier to hear those words. The guard strikes me with the butt of his gun in the back, and I fall down in pain. Squinting, I see the laptop still lying on the ground, and grab it.

"Dillon, do you read me?" he radios, only to hear silence. "Thompson, can you confirm? Do you have a visual?"

Again, silence.

Then I see it. A hand comes out of nowhere. Literally. And just like that, the guard is pulled into the Dark. All I hear is the silence of the night, with the faint rumbling of traffic in the distance.

Getting to my feet, I'm grabbing my back and shoulder in pain, when a guard comes sprinting around a corner. I tense up, readying to teleport, but suddenly I realize he's not running toward me. He's running away from something. The terrified expression on his face tells me he knows what he's facing and wants no part of it.

Appearing through a shadow from a streetlight post, half of Shadow's body emerges. He grabs the guard and then disappears into the darkness.

I wait for a moment, unsure if Shadow is going to reappear, or if I won't see him again. After a minute passes, I figure it's the latter and dust myself off. That's when he decides to pop back up.

"You lost, sidekick?"

I flinch back, caught off guard. "Whoa! Did you ... get my message?"

"Yes." There's a hint of aggravation in his voice. Scowling at me, his black, full-face mask covers everything but his eyes and mouth. He narrows his eyes at me, as if his answer to my questions is a question of his own.

"Sorry. I was ... I just needed to look into something."

"Doctor Grandside didn't send any word."

"No, I ..." I look away, unsure how he'll respond to my reason. "I'm kind of working on my own on this one."

He adjusts his long, black leather trench coat, eyes me up and down without emotion, then looks down at the laptop I'm holding. "Is that Winston Industries hardware?" I nod. "They'll have safeguards on it."

"So I found out."

Studying my face one more time, he presses his palm against my chest. "Come with me."

It's not an invitation or even a request. It's a demand. I'm pressed back into the shadows and then we disappear.

22

Shadow's base of operation, the Cavern, looks more like a villain's lair than a superhero's headquarters. Since the last time I've been here, I've learned that it's somewhere deep underneath Lost Hills. He has a plethora of high-tech equipment, computers, hologram projections, and gadgets. But it's musty. It's damp. The walls are craggy, and the lights are low-hanging bulbs. I can slightly hear water dripping somewhere in the background, but I can't find it because other than the few desks he has set up for gadgets, and his long desk with his computer monitors, everything else is pitch-black.

Without a word, he yanks the laptop out of my arms, and sets it on his desk. I open my mouth to say something, but think better of it, and instead watch as he takes a small, metal disc, adhering to the top of the computer. Hitting a button, a red light starts blinking on the disc, and he plugs in a flash drive on the side.

Flipping it open, the laptop comes to life, but instead of opening to a normal startup screen, a large, upside-down triangle with a spiral in the middle appears. It's the same insignia Shadow wears on the forehead of his mask. For a moment the insignia on the screen blinks red, spinning, then it glows a bright green.

"You have to be careful when you're dealing with types like Ted Winston," he says, his voice low and grainy. "Hackers working for the CIA or NSA have stuff that can be hacked, but Winston? People like him, who have secrets on top of secrets, use the latest in technological advances for spyware and code breakers."

"Oh."

The last time I was with him, I only saw how in depth and thorough Shadow was with handling criminals, even if he did come off as a sociopath. Watching him in action now, breaking into the computer system, he appears much more precise and logical. I don't get any of the psycho-vibes I felt last time.

The insignia vanishes from the screen, and it turns to a black screen with a flashing zero. Shadow takes a seat at the desk, and starts tapping his fingers across the keyboard, entering an abundance of binary codes into the laptop. Rows and rows of numbers begin to scroll over the screen. He doesn't say anything to me, and the prolonged silence makes me survey the Cavern.

The next desk over is littered with different gadgets, and I reach for what appears to be some kind of grappling gun.

"Don't," he growls out.

Rolling my eyes, I turn back around and decide to just wait next to him while he does whatever he's doing. After a few more minutes, he stops typing.

"Okay, kid. We're in. What were you looking for?"

I lean over, inspecting the blank screen. A small line of code, with random numbers and letters, blinks at the top. "Anything related to Daedalus or Project Ignis."

He snaps his head to the side, staring at me. "What do you know about Daedalus?"

I shake my head. "Not much, except there are these fire dudes who have been attacking us. The last one I fought was rummaging through a file, and that's all I could find."

He squints through his mask. "Daedalus was a subdivision of Griffin's Hyperion Initiative."

"Justin Griffin?"

"Yes. As you're probably aware he was obsessed with ending superheroes, and he worked on a number of different projects and experiments under what he called Hyperion. I've been through all of the files, and the main works were filed under Daedalus, Cronos, and Jupiter. I've been looking for ties to the Cronos Corporation."

"Okay, well, what happened after Griffin went to prison?"

"Nothing. They all went dormant. Everything was transferred to Winston Industries and hasn't been activated since."

"No, that can't be right." I rub my forehead. "The file said Daedalus. Can you search for Project Ignis?"

He turns around and starts typing, hitting seemingly random keys, and the screen comes alive, scrolling a massive amount of info.

"Okay," he says, running his finger along the screen. "It says Project Ignis was an experiment under Daedalus Corp. They were testing on human subjects, trying to find compatible hosts for a biological, combustible serum." He hits a few more keys. "It supposedly would let the hosts produce, control, and manipulate fire."

"Well, they found their subjects. One of them died already."

"What about the other two?"

"I fought one, but he almost killed me and got away. I don't know his name. Is there anything in there under the name Dean Macall?"

His fingers fly over the keys again, and he shakes his head. "No." Typing something else, a new screen pops up. "There is a name here, though, that's all over these files. Samuel Watkins, an army general."

I lean over, reading the name on the screen. "I've seen that name before. He was in charge of rehabilitation."

Shadow starts typing again. "That may be what they listed, but he was definitely involved in Project Ignis. It says here 'regulation, recruitment, and arms training.'"

"Finally, a link." I rub my hands together. "This might be just what I need. I can take this to the Alliance, and we can depose Watkins and hopefully get to Winston. We can get whoever is behind these guys."

He scoffs. "Kid, if you want to get to the bottom of this, you're gonna need to do it yourself."

"What? Why?"

"Okay, first and foremost, how did you come by this information?"

My mouth drops and I glance at the laptop. The laptop I stole.

"Secondly, Winston is so clean, you'd look like a fool just accusing him. There's a reason Griffin entrusted him with all of his assets after he went to prison. And even if you did somehow manage to get someone to believe you, you'd be caught up in so much red tape trying to get the information, it'd take years."

"What about Watkins?"

"Same thing. If he's involved with Daedalus, and this project they were working on, he'll be protected. You're going to want to go directly to Watkins. Find out if Daedalus is even up and running still. Project Ignis could just be spillover. Loose ends that they never closed."

"How am I supposed to get to Watkins? And these fire guys still out there, they said they escaped."

Shadow shuts the laptop, removing the metal disc.

"They escaped? Then your only option *is* to go to Watkins. Tell him you're investigating them. Hell, he may even help you if he doesn't have a handle on it. And if Daedalus is up and running, you can use this to your advantage."

I nod. General Watkins is my only lead now. "You wouldn't be able to find out where I could locate him, would you?"

Shadow gives me a sly grin, pulls out a separate laptop, and begins typing. "He's working for another subdivision. The official line of their project is called AdvanceGro, *supposedly* working on developing new limbs for amputees."

"You don't think that's what they do?"

He shakes his head. "Everything under the Griffin empire is either for self-gain or retribution. Griffin may be locked up in Chromium, but even behind bars he wants nothing more than for his name to be attached to the fall of all superheroes."

"That guy has some serious issues."

Standing up from the desk, Shadow walks over to another table and picks up a small, rectangular-shaped box, which looks like it could hold business cards. It shines like onyx under the dim lights, and he twirls it in his fingers.

"I know Mimic is off-world," he says, looking over at me. "And I know you're suspended." I gulp. "What are you really doing here?"

Staring back at him, for the first time I'm not frightened like he's the boogey man. He's older and more experienced, but I feel like I'm actually talking to someone on even ground. Not like I'm being talked down to.

"I've screwed up these past few weeks. But I know what I'm doing, Shadow. I just want to help and get to the bottom of this."

He nods, keeping his eyes locked on me. "Fair enough." He throws the black box at me and I catch it. "We don't learn from making the right decisions, Worm. We learn from making the wrong ones."

"What's this?" I ask, holding it up to him.

"Keep it on you. It's an alert system. You hit that small button on it, and I'll be in contact."

"Oh. Thanks." I tuck the box away in the inside of my jacket. Turning my attention to the laptop, I pull out the flash drive. "Can you decrypt this for me in case it's tracked?"

He rolls his eyes, but plugs it into his laptop, and a couple of minutes later hands it back to me.

"Okay. Um, thanks again." He doesn't answer, instead continuing to type away at his computer. "Right."

Taking one last look around, I'm just about to teleport back to my Alliance bunker, when he stops me.

"You did good out there. Remember, sometimes you need to break the rules in order to get the job done."

I nod, taking in his words. I don't agree with his philosophy, of the ends justifying the means, but I did break the rules tonight. And I did get some results. Teleporting back to my bunker at headquarters, I fall back down to my bed. I've been out all night, but I finally got a lead. Undoing my jacket, I inspect the device Shadow gave me, before sliding it back into my pocket, throwing my jacket aside, and fall asleep.

23

I wake up the next day to a phone call from my mom. Whenever I stay the night at headquarters instead of going home, she always makes a bigger deal out of it than I think it needs to be. The ringing buzzes through the air, and I squint my eyes, grabbing my phone. Looking at the screen, there's no incoming call, but the ringing continues, and I realize I've grabbed the burner phone.

"Hey, Ma," I answer, groggily.

"Roberto Esteban Garcia! Where are you?" she yells, and I move the phone away from my ear.

"Mom, calm down. I'm at headquarters. I'm fine."

"You don't text. You don't call. I'm over here worried sick. At first, I thought it was an emergency, but oh no! I've seen the news."

"What are you talking about?"

"You and kissing girls on the streets."

"Oh my God!" Her accusation jolts me awake. "I wasn't out kissing girls."

She sighs. "I know this is uncomfortable—"

"Please don't say it."

"And I know you're a smart boy, but please. Be safe."

"That's it. I'm hanging up."

"I'm being serious—"

"So am I. I love you, Mom, but I'm hanging up and going back to sleep."

She lets out another deep breath. "Be home tomorrow. We're visiting your tia."

"Okay. Bye, Mom."

"And please—"

"Bye, Mom!"

I hit end and set the phone back down, throwing an arm over my face. Another buzzing slices through the air, and I grab the phone in frustration, sliding the talk button.

"Mom, please! I wasn't out with a girl last night. I'm at headquarters right now, which is exactly where I was last night. I didn't get any sleep until practically dawn, and I really don't want to have the birds and bees conversation with you right now."

"Aw, does that mean I don't get to meet *your* parents?" a soft voice asks.

My eyes shoot open, and I do a double take at the phone. It's the burner phone. Jasmin's number is displayed as the contact.

I let out an uncomfortable cough. "Crap ... um, hey."

She laughs on the other end. "I'm glad to know you weren't with any girls last night. I guess I didn't wake you?"

"No," I mutter, thankful for the voice modulator installed in the phone. "My mom just called, freaking out on me. Evidently, she saw the picture of us kissing, and now has this idea that I'm out there picking up girls."

"You're not, right?"

"No." I finally calm down, lying back on my bed. "Well, I

mean, there is this one girl. But I don't know how she feels about me."

"Oh, what's her name?" Jasmin plays along.

"I just call her cutie."

She giggles. "Well, that's very endearing. She probably likes you. I mean, you are a sidekick after all."

"True, but she doesn't really know me."

"Maybe you should tell her."

"Maybe I should ..." I trail off.

I'm not sure if it's the conversations, or the fact that I was out all night dodging attacks and I'm so worn out, but it's on the tip of my tongue to spit it out and tell her the truth. Common sense finally gets the better of me, and I change the subject.

"So, what are you doing?"

"I saw that you messaged me last night and thought I'd try calling you. I wasn't even sure if it was going to go through."

"I'm glad you did. It's nice to hear your voice."

"Yours too. Even if it does sound all weird."

I laugh. "I could change the setting and I'd sound like a chipmunk."

She giggles. "I love chipmunks!"

"I know."

"What?"

"Er—" *Crap!* "I know it's ... the weekend, um ... Any plans?"

"Oh ..." She trails off, and I hope I was able to cover my tracks enough. "Actually, my mom's going to Metro City today, so I'm home alone."

"Oh?"

"Well, I was wondering ..." She stops again. If I wasn't so tired, I might pick up on what she's trying to say. As it is, I remain quiet, the sleepiness setting back in. "Well, since we can't go out anywhere, how would you feel …"

My eyes pop open, finally understanding what she's trying to ask. "Are you inviting me over?"

"If you're not busy. I mean, I totally understand if you are." The nervous sound in her voice makes me think she's blushing. Which, in turn, makes me smile.

"I'd love to." I sit up and look over at my small couch.

Seeing my jacket, the little, black box that Shadow gave me has slid out and lies on top, reminding me about the investigation I'm trying to do. I need to look into that if I'm going to try to get to the bottom of the fire guys.

"Dang it. I actually can't right now. I have this thing I'm working on. I'm sorry."

"Oh, no, that's fine. It's not a big deal. It's totally fine." She's trying to sound as nonchalant as she can, but I can hear the disappointment in her voice.

"Jasmin, seriously, I would love to come over, but I forgot I'm working on something. It's kind of off the books for the Alliance." I pause, thinking for a moment. "Hey, how about this? Have you ever been to New York?"

"Uh, no …" she answers in almost a question.

I chuckle. "Well, after I'm done, I'll text you. We'll go there. Not in the city, but there's this place I know. There are a few places, actually, but I have this great spot in New York I've been to a couple of times."

"Worm, I can't just go to New York."

"Sure you can. You know how people say a place is just a hop, skip, and a jump away?"

"Yeah?" Her voice drips with skepticism.

"Well, for me it's not even a hop away. Come on, it'll be amazing."

"I don't know …"

"Please?"

There's a long pause, and I have no idea what she's going to say. I get it. Even if I am a sidekick, she doesn't know me. She has no idea who I really am or what kind of person I am.

"Okay," she finally agrees, but again, it sounds like a question.

I smile from ear to ear. "I promise, it'll be great. You trust me, right?"

"I'm still deciding," she replies, a hint of humor in her voice.

I scoff. "Wow, really? You've made out with me twice. No, three times actually."

"Just because you're a good kisser, doesn't mean I trust you. Actually, it probably means I should be cautious."

"Oooh, so you think I'm a good kisser?"

"Well, you're okay." She sounds a little tense. "My ex-boyfriend was pretty good, so the bar is set pretty high."

Hearing her say those words should give me goose bumps, or chills, or some weird sense of pride. Knowing she thought I, Robbie, was a good kisser should do something to me. But I'm in Worm mode and I decide to kick poor little Robbie in the gut.

"He must be your ex for a reason. What an idiot."

The irony of that statement is not lost on me. If I ever stand a chance of getting back together with her as Robbie, I'm not doing myself any favors as Worm.

"Don't say that," she chides me. "He's just ... strange."

An awkward silence rests between us. I can only imagine what she's thinking about, her memories, most likely of me breaking up with her last year. Disappearing on her at different times when we were together. Who am I kidding?

There's no way I'll be able to get back together with her as Robbie.

"Anyway," I break the silence, "enough about that. I'll text you later, but it might be late. Is that okay?"

"I'll be waiting."

The second-guessing begins as soon as I hang up the phone. My New York spot has no one around, but should I even be doing this? To what end and means am I taking this? There's no way I can have a relationship with her as Worm and not out myself as Robbie, is there? And I've already been down the road of trying to be with her as myself, hiding my identity as Worm.

Throwing an arm over my face, I let out a reluctant groan, knowing I'm digging myself deeper into a hole I have no way of getting out of.

"Stop thinking!" I slap my hand against my forehead a couple of time. I have to focus. Today, I need to get answers. The only way to do that is visiting my only lead, General Samuel Watkins.

Watkins is a high-ranking official in the army. He served as the nation's security adviser for both terms of our last president. When the president's term in the White House finally ended, he went to work for Griffin, and has since been involved with the company, even with Griffin out of the picture.

Working with the company AdvanceGro, a company that develops cutting-edge prosthetics, it's seemingly an organization that's doing the world a lot of good. Their tagline as a company is, "Making the world better, one hand at a time."

But I'm leery after all of the information Shadow helped me retrieve. If this corporation has any ties to Griffin's conglomerate, and Watkins is working with it, I don't know what to expect. Is he truly trying to help people, and oblivious to the business he's connected to?

Running a search through the database, I surprisingly find AdvanceGro is located in King City. Three blocks away from King City Tower sits the Fleischer building. They own the entire building, with the first twenty floors filled with different offices and testing facilities. The last ten stories are listed as authorized personnel only. Not only searching our databanks, but even on their legit website, it says the area is strictly off-limits, unless you have the proper credentials.

This is going to be tricky.

Any of the credentials that might work I could probably get through the Alliance. But that means Doc will eventually find out. And since I'm not supposed to be anywhere near this investigation, that leaves me to my own devices again.

Heading to a supply room, I grab a backpack and take a pair of enhancement goggles, and an astralcube as a precaution. Glancing around the doorway, I see no one is around, so I zip the bag closed, throw it over my shoulders, and teleport to the top of King City Tower.

Knowing the safest thing, even if I don't get caught, is to not leave any trace of myself as Worm, I teleport over in my sneakers, jeans, and a black, hooded sweater. Sliding the goggles on, which look similar to a sleek pair of back sunglasses, I scan the area. Tapping the side of the frame, the lenses activate, and I can see three blocks over, the lenses scanning through the building in an X-ray effect. The different buildings are outlined in red, with the AdvanceGro building outlined in green.

"Isolate Fleischer building," I say, and the software in the glasses activates. Everything in my field of vision is removed except the building. "Architectural scan, top ten floors. Isolate heat signatures."

The lenses do their job, and the X-ray vision now includes heat signatures from different people walking the floor. With the sun already set, I'm not surprised to find the floors mostly empty.

"Enhance." The lenses zoom in closer. "Audio. Isolate males."

I hear common chatter among the voices, and everything seems normal. Someone's talking about a TV show, another person is complaining about not getting a weekend off.

"Scan and confirm heat signature DNA along with facial recognition," I whisper.

"Scanning," the voice from the lenses replies into my ear comm. "Found: Jerry Givens, AdvanceGro senior chairman. Found: Landry Rosenthal, AdvanceGro Chairman of Global Recruitment. Found: Michael Wils—"

"Stop." This could take a while. "Scan for Samuel Watkins."

"Scanning ..." I stare at the building, unsure he's even going to be there, when the lenses come alive. "Heat signature DNA and facial recognition found: Samuel Watkins, General of United States Army, and AdvanceGro executive vice president."

"Gotcha." I pull out my phone, activating an Alliance app. "Save architectural structure and location of Watkins."

Teleporting to the next building over, I look through the lenses, trying to match the architecture design I've received. There's an office two rooms over from Watkins' office that doesn't have any heat signatures in it. If I get in there, I should be able to sneak into his office, and hopefully ask him some questions without raising any alarms. He'll have to understand, right? We've got flying, pyro-maniacs running loose in the city.

After teleporting into the room, I slowly creep to the door, and crack it open. I hear a few muffled voices, and a telephone ringing in the background. Staring down the hallway, I discover that Watkins' office is twenty feet away.

"Scan interior office of Watkins," I whisper to the glasses.

The scan on the lenses shows a normal office with a desk, filing cabinets, and a heat signature sitting at a desk. With a clear landing spot behind the door, I teleport into the room, and find it empty.

"That's weird," I whisper, lifting the frames over my brow. Setting the glasses back over my eyes, I tap the frame of the goggles. "Scan room. Search for heat signature again."

"Scanning," the software replies, then beeps immediately. "General Samuel Watkins, United States—"

"End scan." I lift the glasses onto my head. My eyes narrow at the office that's empty but supposed to have Watkins in it. "Weird."

Cautiously, I walk over to the desk, but everything in the office seems normal. There's a payroll sheet, a few books, and stacks of papers with different employees, departments, and other information listed on the desk. Walking around, I pull out the chair and take a seat, opening up the laptop on the desk. A password screen flashes across the monitor, and I pull out my flash drive, but second-guess myself. After last night's debacle, I don't want to sound any alarms again.

A picture sits on the desk of who I'm assuming Watkins is, with two small children, presumably his grandchildren. Another picture sits to the left of that one, one of the general in his full uniform, both sides of his jacket covered in medals and pins. He's smiling with the kids, but a stern and focused gaze in his army picture. Sporting a short, gray buzzcut, square jawline, and wrinkles at the corners of his piercing blue eyes.

I'm in the right office, but nothing seems nefarious or evil. Is this all a cover? Or is it all happenstance, and AdvanceGro really is a great company, that just so happens to be associated with Griffin's empire?

I pull the glasses back over my eyes, looking over at the door. "Scan the entire floor. Rescan all heat signatures."

"Scanning ... no heat signatures found."

"What?" I jump out of the chair. "That can't be right, the floor was just full of people. Scan again."

"Scanning ..."

I hurry over to the door and crack it open, peeking through. Silence. No hustle and bustle I heard moments earlier. No phones ringing. Something's wrong.

"Scan complete. No heat signatures found."

Something is seriously wrong. "Scan floor for any intrusions or anomalies."

"Scanning ... anomaly detected. Lightwave wiring found within architecture."

"Oh no."

The lightwave wiring comes alive, and the office walls begin to glow, white bars forming about six inches away from each other. The bars cover the walls, floor, and ceiling, seeming to morph the small office into a cell, and I can't do anything but stay where they've locked me into.

Lightwave wiring is a special form of wire that can alter the wormholes, quantum jump spots, or the dimensional travel of people who use them. People like me. The Alliance uses it in containment cells in case someone has an artificial teleporting device in their gear or implanted themselves with. Once the lightwave is active, it begins to glow a bright white, like the walls are doing now, making teleportation out of the area almost impossible.

The door of the office opens, and in walks a man with a slightly worn face, gray buzzcut, and identical eyes to the one in the pictures on the desk. Watkins. His stocky build and broad shoulders, along with his dark gray suit and tie, gives him an authoritative arrogance. All of which is accompanied by a hostile smirk.

"Well, hello there. Security mentioned I had a visitor."

24

Shutting the door, he calmly walks over and pulls out the chair in front of his desk, motioning me to it. "Sit. Please."

I stand there, totally clueless as to what's happening. He smirks, raising an eyebrow, and then chuckles as he takes a seat behind his desk.

Keeping the glasses on, and my hoodie pulled up, I pray he'll think I'm some random intruder, and I can get out of here without him learning who I really am. I just need an opening to use the astralcube I brought with me.

"You're the teleporter," he says, and it catches my attention. "The one that broke into the Winston building last night."

My mouth drops, unsure how he knows I'm the one from last night, but I can't think of any words.

"Worm, you can answer me. I know it's you."

"How?" I whisper under my breath.

He lets out another chuckle. "We monitor all of our locations. To say I'm surprised that you're breaking and entering is an understatement. You're a fine young man, and an upstanding member of the Justice Alliance from what I understand."

My eyes narrow behind the glasses.

"So, please, what brings you here, Mr. Garcia? You have to know this level of AdvanceGro is off-limits."

My faces drops again. He not only knows I'm Worm, but he knows my secret identity, too. *Who is this guy?*

Trying to gain my composure, I take a step closer to his desk. "Sir, I don't know what you know, but I think Winston is behind something ... bad."

"Oh?" He studies me curiously.

"The fire guys that have been flying around King City, they have ties to something called Daedalus and Project Ignis. I've been investigating it, and it all led back to Winston Industries. That's why I was there last night."

"Tell me more," he says, almost as if he was listening to a story from his grandchildren.

"I'm not sure what else there is. I went to Lost Hills to try and find answers. AdvanceGro is a company that does some great things, sir. I was hoping you might have some more information we could use. Do you know anything that might help track down these pyro individuals?"

"Perhaps." He presses a finger to his lips. "But first, is there anything else?"

We wait, exchanging a silent stare, and I'm not sure if he's genuinely asking or he's trying to get a read on me. Does he really not know anything?

"Nothing else. Well, except someone named Dean Macall. He was a university professor that went missing last year. The last fire person I met mentioned his name."

He nods in thought, staring at me, then gets up from his desk. Organizing a few papers, he grabs the phone from his desk, and talks into it without pressing a button. "It's time."

Walking around to stand in front of me, he offers me his hand to shake.

"Thank you for all of the valuable input. Unfortunately, I've never heard of this Dean Macall."

I stare down at his hand, then back up at him. Something's off. Eyeing him suspiciously, I take his hand. "Okay, then. Thank you for your time, sir. Since you know I'm not a threat, I guess I'll be leaving now."

He doesn't let go of my hand. "No. You won't be."

"Sir?"

"I'm sorry, son, but you've caused enough trouble. You're being detained."

"What?" I scoff, yanking my hand free. "You can't do that."

"I can and I will. You broke into a privately owned building last night, and today you broke into a federally owned building. You're putting the jeopardy of the world at risk by these breaches."

"Jeopardy of the world? I thought this placed was called AdvanceGro. You work on limb replacement."

Grabbing the front of my sweater, he pulls me closer. "You know exactly what we do here."

"What are you talking about?"

Ignoring me, he presses a finger to his ear, speaking to someone. "Have a shuttle waiting, and make sure a cell is open at the Daedalus detention center. We've got a whale coming in."

My face drops. "Daedalus?"

"I am sorry, Worm." His tone and expression, to my surprise, are sincere. "You've done a lot of good for this city. But your powers? They're just too powerful to pass up. With your DNA we can usher in a new era of technology for not only accessing wormholes, but even possibly controlling them. Teleporters are so hard to come by."

With his last sentence, the sincerity vanishes, and he leers at me.

I'm still trying to digest the entirety of this situation, and I continue to gaze at him. "What ... you? You're behind Daedalus?"

He scoffs. "Of course, I am. Winston Industries is an offshoot that, thanks to you, I now know needs to be erased. Imagine, leaving valuable information just lying around in an office? Winston's an idiot. That buffoon wanted to prove he was capable of taking on more responsibility. Once Macall and the other two escaped, I should've known better."

I still can't believe everything I'm hearing. "So ... you *do* know Macall? And the other two fire guys?"

He lets out a deep, rumbling laugh. "Oh, I keep forgetting. You're a sidekick. You still think the world's all sunshine and rainbows, and that your godlike heroes will come in and save the day. Heroes like Supron."

The chuckle halts. His smirk is gone, and he delivers a swift punch to my stomach, dropping me to a knee. Kneeling down, he whispers closer to my ear.

"King City only has superheroes because I allow it. It's good to keep the façade. To make everyone believe the puppets are in control, while the puppet master stays in the shadows. I suppose you'll learn that firsthand soon enough."

Regaining my breath, I pull out the astralcube from my sweater. The basic, metallic square has a single button, while the rest of it is nondescript, about double the size of a golf ball.

I got the idea from Daniel last year, when he told me he had precautions stashed around the city. In case he runs into any hotspots, he has a device that can instantly create moisture, to which he can use to save himself. The astralcube is my failsafe.

The cube is just a component, a vital piece used to make a quantum ring, which is a device to create artificial wormholes to teleport from one location to another. They're like large gates. The Justice Alliance has used them when helping alien civilizations relocating or defending their worlds. But astralcubes aren't designed to be opened. This is a plan I've created but have never actually had to enact it.

Another light chuckle floats from Watkins as he watches me hold the cube. "Ah, the Justice Alliance and its gadgets. Whatever that thing is, it won't help you. My men are already on their way."

I fidget with the cube some more, pressing my fingers into the metal, but there's no way to crack it open.

"I want you to know, I'll make sure the city honors you. A sidekick, fallen in battle. You can't beat those type of headlines. I'm sure the Alliance will erect a statue for you. At the very least, they'll put up a plaque in your honor. I'll even make sure the Griffin Foundation starts a scholarship in your name."

"You're sick," I spit out.

"The world is sick, Worm. And Daedalus is going to cure it."

My head darts toward the door when I hear the footsteps of the security team he called for. They're going to be here any second. The astralcube isn't budging. I spot a paperweight on a bookshelf I'm next to, holding a stack of folders in place. Grabbing it, I smash the weight over the cube, causing it to crack.

"What are you doing, boy?" Watkins glares, though he still keeps his arms folded.

With it cracked, I jam my thumb into it, already feeling the quantum rays tingling my skin. The vibrations travel along my hand, the same way I feel moving through the astral plane. Smirking, I glance up at Watkins, who suddenly realizes something's wrong.

Quantum rays nullify any and everything that inhibits contact with the astral plane. So even if I'm in a room surrounded by lightwave wiring, hardware that's specifically designed to stop teleportation, the quantum rays override that. I feel the metal dig deeper into my thumb, but don't stop and tear it open, unleashing a bright orange glow in front of me.

"No!" Watkins screams out, but it's too late.

The glow washes over the white bars, and I focus, creating my wormhole and teleport out of the office. Jumping immediately back to headquarters, I get to the control room to find Daniel manning the desk.

"Whoa!" He jumps out of his seat. "Robbie? What are you doing?"

"Doc? Where's Doc?" I demand.

"I'm not sure, in his lab I think."

Without another word, I teleport to his lab, but he's not there. Teleporting back, my breathing picks up. "He's not there! Where is he?"

"Whoa, calm down. What is going on?"

"Daedalus! I found out about Daedalus and it's real. They created the fire guys and it's being run by this army general. I need to find Doc!"

He cocks his head to the side. "What are you talking about?"

"There's no time! Where is he?"

He stares at me, not nearly as concerned as I think he

should be. Instead, he's looking at me like I'm crazy. "I don't know. Try the conference room."

I grunt in frustration, and teleport into the conference room. Sitting at the table is Doc and Melissa. Without waiting, I barge into the conversation.

"Doc, it's real! Daedalus is real! It's being ran by a psychotic general, and they're using Winston Industries, and something called AdvanceGro as a cover, but Daedalus is what he runs. It's where the fire guys were created and escaped from. We need to arrest him. He's in charge of it!"

Both Doc and Melissa gaze at me like I'm crazy.

"Doc! Did you hear what I said?"

"I heard, Robbie," Doc responds, but his face is anything but concerned. Instead, he looks disappointed. Staring at the table, he takes a deep breath, then shakes his head.

A beep sounds off of his watch. "Incoming call. General Samuel Watkins."

"What?" I gape at him. "Doc, no. You don't understand, he—"

Doc holds up a finger for me to be quiet, and I'm so caught off guard by his reaction, that I follow his direction.

"This is Doctor Grandside," he answers the calls, placing a finger to his ear. "Yes, sir. No, thank you for taking the time."

My eyes jump over to Melissa, who looks like she's trying to understand what's happening. I, on the other hand, can't believe what I'm seeing and hearing.

"Yes, I understand. Absolutely. Thank you, sir. We appreciate your discretion in this matter. Of course. It'll be handled promptly. Good evening."

Pressing a finger to his ear again, the call ends. His eyes find me. "You're indefinitely suspended from any and all Alliance contact, effective immediately."

"What?" My mouth still hangs open.

Standing up from the table, he walks over to me. He's only a couple inches taller than me, but his demeanor and facial expression make me feel like a puppy that's being scolded by a giant. "What you did was reckless, dangerous, and if anyone found out, the integrity of the entire Justice Alliance would be compromised."

"Doc, you don't understand," I try to respond. "Watkins is the problem here. He's in charge of Daedalus, and the fire guys escaped from him. That company is behind all of this."

"And you chose not to share that information with us?"

"Well, I—"

"Robbie, I found out about Daedalus. I was hoping you were telling me the truth when you said you didn't have any other information."

"But Watkins is dirty!"

Ignoring me, he walks over to the door, opening it for me to leave. "Grab anything you need from your bunker and head home. You won't be back until Mr. Mimic returns, and I've reviewed all of the information with him."

Confusion and pain cover my face. "Why are you doing this?"

"Robbie, we know about General Watkins. We've known about him for years."

I look back over at Melissa, unsure if she knows any of this, but she shrugs. "You have?"

"We've had tracers and undercover operatives in place for years, but you have to be smart. Watkins could've run for president after he was security adviser, but he didn't. He knows the system and he knows the players. We know he's dirty, but the public only knows him as the man who's helped protect this nation a hundred times over."

"Wait, wait." I stand in front of him, as he continues to

hold the door open. "So, you're telling me the Alliance never made a move on Watkins because of appearance? Because everyone thinks he's some national hero? He's the bad guy, Doc! They'll get over it!"

Letting out a long sigh, he narrows his eyes at me. "What would you have us do, Robbie? Just march down there and arrest him?"

"Yes!" I scream. "He confessed. He told me everything."

"Did he?"

I jerk my head back, dumbfounded. "Of course, he did. He called a security team up to the office. He was gonna lock me away in some kind of lab. He said he was going to use my DNA to experiment on wormholes."

"And you've got proof of this?" Doc asks.

"No."

"So how can you prove it?"

"Doc, are you serious? Why would I lie? You seriously don't believe me?"

"Robbie, I believe you, but if we go after him like this, we wouldn't be able to even charge him with jaywalking. It's all about the how. People with the kind of power Watkins has don't get it by happenstance. His influence is so much wider than you know. If he's brought up on charges, they need to be airtight, otherwise he'll just have another pawn on the political board at his disposal."

"This ... this is unbelievable. I'm getting suspended and you're not even going to look into this because of politics?" I glance back at Melissa, who seems to be following everything, but I can tell from her face she's siding with Doc. "So, he just gets to do whatever he wants? The fire guys are still out there, he's still controlling Daedalus, and God knows what else he's cooking up."

"We will stop him. One day. But today is not that day.

Today, we have to figure out how to stop the men who seem to want to burn everyone."

"But, Doc!" My shoulders drop, and I feel all of my energy draining, running around in this circular argument. "Watkins has to know how to stop them. If we just—"

"That's enough!" Doc barks. "You're done here. For now, you need to go home." Not waiting for a reply, he looks back over at Melissa. "Due to this recent turn of events, I'd like to ask you to stay on for a bit longer. Just until we have this situation with the pyrokinetic individuals resolved."

"Stay on?" I do a double take, looking at her.

"When this is over, I'm leaving," she answers, but doesn't meet my eyes.

"You're leaving?"

Her vision finds mine for only a second, before she stares down at the table, nodding. I turn back to Doc, shell-shocked. I figured out who was behind the fire guys, who'd have the answers to stop them, and an entire company that's dealing with underhanded activities, and it's all for nothing.

25

Looking around my bunker room, I realize I haven't kept a lot of stuff in here. Grabbing my uniform jacket, I roll it up, stuffing it in my backpack. I also take the burner phone, throw it in my bag, then scan everything else. As much time as I've been spending at headquarters, I didn't bring a lot of personal items from home. I put my ear comms in a side pocket, zip up my bag, and am turning to leave when a knock sounds at my door.

Melissa peeks in. "Robbie?"

I stand there, not sure what else there is to say, even though I know I still have an immense apology I need to go over. Now, after everything today, I don't have it in me. "Hey."

She takes a step inside and shuts the door. We stand there, gazing at one another. I don't know what she's thinking, but dozens of thoughts run through my head. Ninety-nine percent of them start with "I'm sorry." Instead, I tug the backpack over my shoulder. "Well, I guess I'll see you around."

I move to walk by her and she blocks my path. "So, you're going to leave? Just like that?"

I close my eyes, letting out an unbelieving chuckle. "Yeah. *I'm* gonna leave. Just like that."

Reaching out, she places a hand on my shoulder. "That's not fair, Robbie. It's just ... everything's been so crazy lately."

"Yeah," I respond, but feel the guilt build up. She sounds like she's apologizing to me, and she has no reason to. It's enough to finally break down that wall. "I really am sorry. For everything. There probably isn't a number of times I can say that to make up for what I did, but I am. I know I messed up, but I didn't think you'd leave. I never wanted that."

"I know." She turns her face away from me. "I didn't think I would either, but after I heard what you told Daniel ... I can't stay here. It hurts too much." A lump forms in my throat. "Robbie, why didn't you tell us about all of this other stuff though?"

My memories flash back to the initial meeting with everyone and Forge. Feeling replaced.

"I was going to, but when I saw you guys and Forge? I know I screwed up—" I scoff at myself. "I was just an idiot, that's what it boils down to. Besides, I figured Doc would eventually find out everything. I didn't think it was a big deal."

"And confronting Watkins?"

"I thought he might just be a cog in the machine or something. And now." I grit my teeth. "I can't believe he gets off scot-free."

Gazing at one another, the silence fills the air. There's nothing left to say. She's going to help Doc and Daniel get to the bottom of the burning men, while I'll be twiddling my thumbs at home, waiting for Mimic to get back. Who knows what'll happen after that. I want to give her some kind of heartfelt good-bye. Something that tells her how sorry I am about everything. But I can't.

Instead, I give her an apologetic smile, one she returns, and walk past her. "You take care."

Walking into the hall, I wait for just a split second, taking in my surroundings, and teleport away. Instead of going home, I decide to head up to the top of King City Tower. The shine of the moon and stars cascade over the neighboring buildings and their windows. No matter what happens, at least I still have my power. At least I can still take in this gaze over the city that I love. The thought reminds me of Watkins. His words about how no one really knows who the puppet master is. It leaves a bitter taste in my mouth.

The burner phone buzzes from my backpack. Pulling it out, I see Jasmin's number flashing across the screen. This afternoon, I couldn't wait to finish up investigating then teleport us to New York. Sure, I'd still be undercover as Worm, but it was going to be amazing. Now, with my world falling apart, I hit the ignore button.

I can't do this to her. Against all logical reasoning, I ventured down this road, somewhere in the back of my mind knowing it'd never turn out like I dreamed it could. I tried this already. Last year. We can't work. My life is too dangerous. Even if when Mimic comes back, even if I'm not a sidekick anymore, I still have these powers. Our worlds are too different.

Letting out an annoyed and disgusted grunt at myself, I shove the phone back in my bag.

I feel my throat tightening up, and the sting at my eyes. I want to cry, but what would I even be crying over? Everything that's happened these last few weeks is on me. I did this. I didn't call for backup. I went after the fire guys. I broke into a private business, and then challenged a high-ranking government official who I am now clearly on his radar. And he knows my secret identity. Every mistake is of my own doing.

The phone buzzes again, and I pull it out to turn it off. Instead of a missed call, it's a text message.

Jasmin: You there?

I let out a frustrated exhale, unsure what to do. Shaking my head, I send back a message against my better judgment.

Worm: Yeah

Why? Why can't I drop this?

Jasmin: Everything ok?

"No, not really," I whisper to myself.

Worm: …
Worm: It's fine

The phone starts vibrating again, and again I hit ignore. Exchanging messages is one thing, but I can't bring myself to talk to her. To hear her voice.

She sends another message.

Jasmin: What's wrong?
Worm: Today…
Worm: Things aren't good right now.
Jasmin: Then talk to me. Tell me.

Filling my cheeks with air, I lie over the side of the skyscraper, letting my arm hang off of the side, and stare above at the dark sky. Maybe I should teleport back to the headquarters, get rid of this phone and never talk to her again. But then I'd feel like a jerk for ignoring her. I do need to talk to someone. However, I can't dump everything on her. There's Pete, but now that he's dating Daniel, how awkward is that going to be with me being indefinitely suspended.

The phone buzzes.

Jasmin: I'm calling. Don't ignore the call this time.

The phone starts ringing for a third time. I stare at the number on the screen, my finger hovering over the ignore button. If I was smart, I'd do everything I just thought of. I wouldn't even have to go back to headquarters, I could just teleport somewhere and throw the phone in the trash. Out in the water along the docks. It's a burner phone, with no tracking. No one would miss it.

But I'm not smart. That should be evident by the massive blunders I've made. Even worse than being ignorant or stupid—which I seem to be both—I'm selfish. I want to talk to her. So, I answer it.

"Hey," I answer, somberly.

"Hey," she replies. I can hear the concern in her voice.

The phone's voice modulator is still intact, but I'm sure my voice sounds even more distorted with the sad demeanor echoed in it. "Sorry for not answering. Today's been ... not good."

She's quiet for a moment, before she finally speaks up. "You can talk to me, if you want. I may not know who you are, or what you're going through, but I do know when things are bad it helps to talk to someone."

My lips fight to smile. "Thanks."

Sitting back up, I stare out over the skyline. "I don't know ..." I struggle for the right words. "You're amazing, Jasmin. But my life? My life is insane, and I can't put you in danger."

"There it is again."

"What?"

"The way you talk. The way you say my name. It's like you know me." I shake my head, wishing I could tell her the truth. Then her next words catch me off guard. "Do you know me, Worm? When you're not under the mask?"

I swallow the panic and nervousness. *No, I can't do this.* Before I can try to come up with a lie, she continues.

"You passed on the question of what school you go to the other day. So ... do you know me? Do you go to King City High?"

Panic shoots through me. I cough, letting out an uncomfortable chuckle, struggling to cover. "Psh, no. Come on, that's crazy."

I hear her laugh, but it's not humorous. "I don't believe you."

"There's a bunch of different high schools I could go to. I could be homeschooled."

"What classes do you have? Do you have Mrs. Douglass for English?"

"Jasmin—"

"Are we in the same grade? Or are you a junior? A senior?"

A nervous chuckle escapes me. "Okay, this is getting out of hand."

She pauses for a moment. I think she's about to start a new round of questions, when she lets out a soft laugh of her own. "Well, at least you don't sound like death anymore."

"Was it that bad?"

"Yes." She laughs, and for the first time, it sparks a genuine one out of me. "So, are we still on for New York? I'm all bundled up over here."

I pause, unsure what to say. "I would love to, but ..."

"You did say it was just a hop away for you."

"No, I know I did. It's just ... I've been ignoring what I've been told lately, and I don't know if it's the best idea to still do that, especially with you. I can't let anything happen to you."

"Aw," she replies with a hint of sarcasm. "Well, I could just go back to asking who you are, if you want. Would that be any safer?"

"No, not really." I snicker.

"Well then?"

She waits on the other end in silence, as I ponder the move, still gazing out over the city. Unlike every other move I've made lately, I *know* this is not a good idea. I know I shouldn't. I'm not doing it to help the team or protect the city. I'd be doing this solely for myself. And like I said, I've been stupid and selfish lately.

"I'll be right there."

Teleporting to my house first, I change into my uniform, before jumping to Jasmin's fire escape. She's sitting on the edge of her bed, bundled up, and the smile that lights up her face as I appear outside of her window starts to make me forget what a crappy day this has been.

"So, how does this work?" she asks, standing next to me on the escape.

"As long as I'm holding you, you'll go where I go." She nervously looks around. "You'll be totally fine." Giving me a weak smile, she nods. "Will you close your eyes for me?"

"Why?"

"I want it to be a surprise."

Nibbling on her lip, I can see the nervousness across her face. Nodding again, she closes her eyes, and I wrap an arm around her.

"Oh," she lets out a timid whisper, and I remember what it felt like the first time I teleported. You almost don't realize you're in another spot, your feet seemingly never leaving the ground, but your insides know. Almost like a sudden jolt of temporarily feeling weightless.

She keeps her eyes closed through the jump, and I keep my arm around her as we land in New York. More specifically, a very cool spot I've visited a couple of times; the top of the torch of the Statue of Liberty.

The New York City skyline lights up with the moon and stars above, twinkling lights bouncing off of buildings.

"Okay," I whisper, leaning closer to her. "Open your eyes."

An audible gasp falls out of her. She raises her hands to her mouth, and I watch her as her eyes jump from building to building, across the entire skyline.

"What do you think?"

"It's ... this ... it's beautiful." Her eyes find my visor for a split second before they look around, and double in size. She takes in what we're standing on. "What in the? Are we ..."

"Yup." I smile.

"This is amazing."

Scanning back over the city, her eyes glisten as she takes in the view, and mine never break away from her. If nothing else, I'm glad I'm able to give this to her. I don't realize my arm is still around her until she moves it. At first, I think she might be giving herself distance. However, instead of moving away, she stays close, and takes my hand.

Glancing back over at me, her smile's superglued in place. "Thank you. This is so amazing. You're amazing."

I shake my head. "Don't say that. I'm not. I've been making mistake after mistake lately." I let out a sigh, then stare off in the distance of the city skyline. "This is also a mistake if I'm being honest. But I am glad I can share this with you."

"How is this a mistake?"

Looking back at her, she waits, and the feelings of guilt build up again. "Jasmin, this world? My life? I ... I'm being incredibly selfish right now. If anyone, anywhere, ever found out who you are, you'd be in so much danger. But ..."

I trail off, not wanting to finish my thought. Then she does it for me. "But you can't." I shake my head in agreement. "Why not?"

Don't do it, Robbie. I swallow the nerves and look away but keep my hand with hers.

"You *do* know me, don't you?"

"Jasmin—"

She doesn't let me give her another excuse. Wrapping her arms around me, she presses her lips to mine, and I slide my arms around her waist. It's in this split second that I decide. Maybe it's because of where we're at, or because she's kissing me again. Maybe it's from everything that I've been going through, that I just want to let it all out. Whatever the reason, I decide right here and now to do it.

Her lips break away from mine and a pink blush brightens her face. "I'm sorry. I don't know why I did that."

A low chuckle comes out. "You don't have to be sorry. I'm the one who should be sorry." I take a step back.

"For what?"

"I can't do this."

Her face crumples, a frown instantly replacing her nervous smile. "Oh, no! I'm sorry. I didn't mean to—"

"Not that. This." My hand slides over the emblem on my chest. "I can't keep this from you anymore."

Reaching over to the side of my helmet, I take in a long breath. Her eyes widen, and her fingers cover her mouth in shock. "What are you—"

"I have to. I need you to know."

I have no idea how she's going to react. She has every right to yell and slap me across the face. But I'm on the verge of losing everything, and I've already lost her once. If nothing else, she'll finally know the truth and hopefully realize how I really feel. How I've always felt, no matter what I told her.

Hitting the button, the helmet retracts, and I close my eyes. Swallowing the lump in my throat, I let her see my face, unsure what her words are going to be. Instead of hearing a response, I feel one. Her hand comes up to my cheek. The touch is enough for me to finally look back at her. She's not hurt. Or mad. It's more of incredulous revelation.

"How long?" are her first words, her gaze locked on mine.

"Since the summer before high school started," I answer, the words seeping out in a croak. She closes her eyes, letting out a scoff. "Jasmin, I promise, I wanted to tell you. There were so many times I wanted to tell—"

"I'd like to go home now."

She doesn't look at me. Instead, she keeps her eyes on the city, and I stare at her, realizing this is the last straw. Nodding, I take her hand, and teleport us back to her fire escape.

Knowing there's nothing left to say, I wait for her to crawl through her window. After staring inside for a few seconds, she turns around and faces me.

"I want the truth, Robbie."

I lift my shoulders, nodding. "This is the truth, Jas. I'm Worm. I'm sorry I never told you but—"

"No." Her command makes my eyes find hers. "Not that. As shocking and even as incredible as this is, I want the truth. Once and for all."

Her words jolt my mind, and I do a double take. "What truth?"

"Last year you said you lied. You said you were never into me, even though before that, you told me you'd liked me since fifth grade. We went to homecoming together, and I could've sworn I was falling in love with you ... and then you told me I never meant anything to you. So, I want the truth. Right here. Right now."

Of all of the outcomes, in all of the different ways I ever thought of revealing myself to her and her response to that secret being revealed, I've never in a million years would've thought this would be how she reacted.

"The truth." I stare down at the metal rail we stand on, before finally meeting her sight. "The truth is, when freshman year started last year, I was still crushing on you like I had been for years. Mimic told me I need to be careful, and you are the last person on Earth I'd ever want to hurt. Even with that, I still couldn't stop the way I felt. The way I still feel. And then, Craig stole your phone and it freaked me out. I thought he could've hurt you, or worse. So, I lied.

"I told you I never liked you because I wanted you to hate me. It was the easiest way to do it, at least, that's what I thought. But the truth is, I'm in love with you. I always have been. I hurt someone I care about because I couldn't get over you. I don't know if I'll ever get over you, and maybe the worst part is no matter what happens, I don't know if I'll ever *want* to get over you. And now I'm being incredibly selfish because you knowing who I am adds another level of danger to your life, but I can't help it. I love you."

I wait in the dark, watching her bite her lip in thought, her eyes locked on to mine. I see a flash of a smile cross her face, before she quickly wraps her arms around me, kissing me again. We made out plenty of times last year. I've kissed her this year while under the mask. But this kiss? This is the first true kiss between us. No secrets, no masks. Just us.

Pulling her lips away, she leans her forehead against mine. "I told you," she whispers.

A light chuckle escapes me. "You told me what?"

"That you knew me."

"You caught me."

26

Teleporting back to New York, I grab us a pizza, and for the rest of the night we hang out in her room, eating pizza and talking.

We stay up until the early morning and the words just fall out. I tell her how and when I got my power, the training I've gone through, being assigned Mr. Mimic as my mentor. I get into talking about Pete and how I accidentally teleported into his room one night when I almost died, and that's how he knows. I tell her everything.

Then I get into all of the drama this year, especially the fire guys I've been investigating. That leads to everything I've done, and how that's shaped the situation I'm in now.

Through it all, she listens to everything. Quiet, always attentive, almost hanging on my every word.

"And now," I finish explaining breaking into Watkins' office today, "I don't even know if I'll be a sidekick when Mr. Mimic comes back." I scan her room and can see the break of the sun outside of her window. "Wow, we've been up all night. I should get going."

Trial By Fire

Following me to her window, she grabs my hand. "I don't know what to say."

Turning, I grab her other hand, and hold her close. "You don't have to say anything. You have no idea how good it feels to tell you everything." Leaning closer, I'm about to kiss her, when we hear the buzzing of an alarm outside of her room.

"That's my mom!" Her eyes widen. "She has a morning shift at the hospital."

A mischievous smile crosses my lips. "Hey, does this mean we spent the night together?"

"Seriously, Robbie?" Her jaw drops.

"Just saying," I laugh. "Okay, I guess I should go home." Raising a hand, I run my thumb over her cheek. "Thank you, Jasmin. For everything."

Teleporting home, there's no wiping the smile from my face. I look around, almost giddy, not wanting the feeling to end. I teleport back to her room, and she jumps, startled.

"What are you doing?"

"I forgot something."

"What?"

Pulling her close, I finally get to relive the moment of our kiss again. A real kiss with no secrets between us. She wraps her arms around my neck, and I keep mine tightly around her, drawing in her scent.

She breaks way just enough to let out a small giggle. "Okay, you really have to leave now."

"I know."

But I don't. I kiss her again, and again she leans into me.

"Seriously," she says, her lips still against mine. "If my mom hears something and catches you, your secret identity is going to be the least of your problems."

"Okay, okay." Kissing her one last time, I finally teleport back to my room.

Falling down on my bed, I'm in a state of euphoria. Any and all problems and concerns that surround my life are gone, at least for the time being. All I can think about is Jasmin, and that she finally knows. And even better than that, we're together again.

Getting to school, I get a text message right before my first class that keeps any and all drowsiness that I should be feeling at bay.

Jasmin: Hey <3
Jasmin: I think we should wait to tell Pete and Maria about us.
Jasmin: It might be a little suspicious.

This girl is amazing.

Me: I agree.
Me: How u feeling? You gonna make it thru the day? LOL
Jasmin: I think so. I mean, I don't have a superpower, but maybe a kiss from you later will keep me awake ;)
Me: Don't tempt me. I'll teleport us out of school right now.

Our plan to keep Maria and Pete out of the loop doesn't go very well. First of all, we cross paths between classes, and after the second time, I hear Maria scold Jasmin. "What is going on with you?"

"Nothing," Jasmin answers, but starts giggling.

Pete bumps my shoulder a little while later, as we make our way toward the cafeteria. "Hey, I haven't heard you talk about anything that happened this weekend."

Trial By Fire

I should be annoyed, knowing he's found everything out from Daniel, but I'm not. "It is what it is."

"But aren't you concerned about what's going to happen?"

I laugh. I actually laugh and slap his shoulder. "Pete, I can't change anything. I just have to wait and try to explain my side."

He quirks an eyebrow at me, and we take our seat at our table.

"Jasmin, seriously," Maria chides her as they approach the table. "Stop messing around. You're hiding something, I know you are."

Jasmin smiles at me. "I'm not hiding anything."

"Then tell me if you talked to Worm this weekend?"

They take their seats, and Pete takes a drink of his water. Jasmin's eyes find mine, and she's holds back a grin. "Yeah, you could say that."

"Wait, what was that?" Maria asks, pointing at me.

"What?" Jasmin questions.

Pete's eyes dart back and forth between me and Jasmin, and Maria continues questioning. "You two ... what's going on here?" Her finger bounces back and forth.

"Nothing," I say, trying to fight off my own smirk.

"No, there's something," Pete jumps in. "And you've been weird all day."

"You're crazy," I brush him off.

"No, he's right," Maria adds. Jasmin bites her lips, looking down at the table. "Ohmygod!" Maria slaps Jasmin's shoulder. "No. Don't tell me. You two aren't back together, are you?"

Jasmin's face turns crimson. I bite my lip, and Pete's head snaps back to me.

Before either of us can answer, Maria grabs Jasmin's arm.

"Jas, no!" Looking at me, she puts a finger in my face. "How many times did you bail on us last year, Robbie? And that was before you broke her heart."

"Maria." Jasmin pulls Maria's hand back, reprimanding her.

A guilty lump forms in my throat, but I don't get a chance to respond. Pete jumps up from the table, gabbing my arm, and pulling me way. "We'll be right back."

A few eyes in the cafeteria follows us, as I try to shake him loose, but his fingers have a vise grip around my wrist. He drags me outside of the cafeteria, and off in a corner near a group of lockers. "Tell me you didn't."

"Didn't what?"

"You know exactly what!"

I stare at him, unable to keep the smile off of my face. "I don't know what you're talking about."

Stepping closer, he lets out a visceral whisper. "You and Jasmin! You told her, didn't you?" I lift my shoulder. "I can't believe you!"

His insult and disproval strike a chord inside of me. I put my hand in his face. "Hey, it's my secret and I can tell who I want."

His face cringes in insult. "How dare you! She's my friend, too, Robbie! I don't want something to happen to her. Especially with—" His mouth snaps shut.

"Especially with what?"

He doesn't hesitate, so I know he's really upset. "Especially with how you've been acting lately. Daniel told me everything."

"Whoa, now who's out of line?"

"But we've talked about this. I told you, Mighty was a better fit for you. Your world is dangerous, and you've been reckless doing your own thing. Look, I'm not going

Trial By Fire

to pretend to know the choices you've had to make, but—"

"But nothing! You're right, you *don't* know. And guess what? They're *my* choices! You've got no room to argue this with me. Not only do you know my secret, but you're also going out with Hydro. How different is your situation than hers? It's not, that's how. You're my best friend, but you've got no right to tell me how to live my life just because you have experience dating a sidekick."

"But he's been one longer than you."

"By one year!" My scream brings me back to reality and I double-check our surroundings. "Look, I'm sorry you don't agree with this, but do you know how hard it was to break up with her last year? Do you know what it feels like when you're being tortured, rendering your powers useless? Do you know what it's like to walk in on a team that you think is a second family, only to find them replacing you?"

His face crumples. "I'm sorry ... I didn't know all of that."

Other than our argument last year, before he learned my secret identity, this is the biggest fight we've had. I want to feel a little bad for yelling at him like I am, but I can't. I feel like everyone is looking at it from every angle except from mine.

He opens his mouth to continue, but is cut off by Jasmin, standing behind us. "Did I interrupt?"

Pete stands there, shocked. "How much of that did you hear?"

She lets out a half-hearted laugh. "Enough to know you're going out with a sidekick, too."

Pete shoots his head back at me, looking at me like I should say something. I shrug my shoulders. "You're the one who started talking about it."

He folds his arms. "Fine. You know what? Let's talk

about this then, all three of us."

Jasmin walks over, standing next to me.

"Jasmin, okay, you know now," Pete starts. "But do you have any idea how dangerous it is?"

"Pete, I get it. But *you* know, right? Nothing crazy has happened to you."

"That's not the point—"

I cut Pete off. "No, that's exactly the point. My sidekick life has not affected you in the least. Well, unless you call hooking you up with Hydro affecting you."

"You didn't hook us up."

"Oh, yeah? Who got you into Alliance headquarters, buddy?" Pete stands there, speechless. "Look, that's not even the point. The point is, nothing has happened to you. Is it dangerous? Yes, but I've been careful. I make sure my private life, stays private. Nothing is going to happen."

As if Murphy's Law is waiting for those very words, a huge explosion rocks the hallways. All three of us fall down to the floor, crashing against the lockers.

"Attention, students," an electronic voice chimes out through the hallway. "This is not a test. Please report to your homeroom. Faculty, lock the doors, and wait until authorities have arrived."

It's a code black. The school runs them once every quarter. It's like a fire drill, but for any type of emergency that involves supervillains being in or around the school. Because superheroes and villains are so prevalent, half of the student body never takes them seriously.

"You guys okay?" I ask, and they both nod. "Get to safety."

I turn to run outside and figure out what's going on, when Jasmin grabs my arm. "Where are you going?"

"I have to go see what that was."

"But—"

"Jasmin." I hold her closer. "I have to go." Glancing over at Pete. "Pete?"

He nods. "Come on, Jas." He holds his hand out to her.

She looks back at his hand for a moment, before wrapping her arms around my waist, kissing me. "Be careful."

"Always," I reply, smiling. "Go."

More students are filling the hallway, running to rooms, while others are running toward the exits to see what the commotion is. I take off, sprinting down the hallway, and get to the front of the school. My eyes bulge, as I stare into the sky, stunned.

Flying above the school is not one, but two fire guys. One of them hovers high above, while the second flies below, shooting out fireballs from his hands, hitting the roof of the school. He spins in the air and starts shooting into the student parking lot, making cars explode.

I take the opportunity to jump to the rooftop while everyone's attention is diverted. Everyone except the fire guy still hovering high above. His gaze meets mine and he floats down to the rooftop, landing across from me.

The air thickens with the heat. As he lands on the roof, the flames around his body begin to die out. His body emits a heat I haven't felt from the other two. The roof begins to melt under his feet, as smoke rises from his body. Every step he takes melts the tar lining the roof. The flames finally die out, but it doesn't reveal a body. Instead, he glows, as if his body is covered by lava.

His face is nondescript, though I can tell he has a mouth and a nose under the lava. His eyes are pitch-black, other than pinholes in the middle that glow an intense yellow. There's no way to tell who he is, but I know.

It's Dean Macall.

27

Daniel flies in from the side, gliding on a sheet of water, and lands next to me. Looking back at the parking lot, I watch as the fire guy blasting cars left and right is interrupted by Forge, and both take to the sky. Daniel steps in front of me, creating a huge wall of water, while Macall stands where he is.

"Robbie, what are you doing?" he shouts. Melissa drops out of the sky, unsheathing her sword. "You need to get to safety!"

"Are you serious?" I yell back, readying myself. "I may be suspended, but there's no way I'm not helping in this. That's Dean Macall. I know it."

Melissa calls back, keeping her eyes on Macall through the wall of water. "Robbie, you need to get out of here!"

"What?" I yell at them both. "You want me to just stand around and do nothing?"

"Watch out!" Daniel yells.

A huge blast of fire shoots through the water barrier, sending us all scrambling. Macall's body ignites, and he hovers above the rooftop. Raising his hands, he sends another attack, only this one is different. It's not fire. It's magma. The lava sludge splatters around me, sending steam, smoke, and a nose-cringing smell. Attacking again, I dive out of the way, but a few specks hit the sleeve of my hoodie, igniting it. I scamper out of the sweater, tossing it away.

"Robbie, get out of here!" Daniel orders and flies away on a bed of water.

Launching a huge stream of water down at Macall, his entire body glows a bright orange, and he forms his own barrier. The scorching heat forces me to back away, and as soon as the water hits the lava wall, steam clouds the air.

I teleport home and grab my uniform, changing as quick as I can, then I teleport back. Melissa's trying to go on the offense, swinging her sword at him, but he forms a rock-like shield on his arm, blocking her attack.

Launching a huge projection of magma into the sky, it forces Daniel to move out of the way. Macall turns his attention back to Melissa, and rapidly fires what looks like bullets made of lava at her. She raises her shield, but I know there's no way that it'll block everything. I teleport over to her, and take us both down to the ground level, near the parking lot.

"Thanks." She gives me a nod.

"Hey, hothead! Up here!" Forge yells.

We both turn around to see the other attacker on the other side of the parking lot. He shoots up into the air, and Forge circles around, making him chase him. The fire guy nears, and Forge unleashes an attack of his own, striking him in the face with a huge blast, sending the fire guy to the ground.

Forge keeps the attack up, continuing a steady stream of fire down upon him, and the man in flames waits on one knee, trying to withstand the attack. For a split second, it looks like Forge has him. Still on his knee, Macall's partner screams out, and then begins glowing a bright orange. I suddenly remember the first fire guy, Gunther's face, how he glowed a bright yellow and orange before releasing his final attack.

"No!" I scream, running over to them. "Forge, stop! Move!"

His stream of fire lets up just a bit as he tries to hear me, but it's no use. The fire guy explodes, and throws me back into a car, knocking the air out of me. Looking back up, I watch as Forge takes the brunt of the attack, and begins to fall out of the sky. I move to teleport over to Forge, to catch him before he crashes to the ground, but the attacker sends a new round of flames at me. Diving out of the way and behind a car, I can do nothing but watch Forge's body fall from fifty feet, slamming down onto the parking lot pavement.

Macall's partner takes off, back into the air, and Melissa gives way to chase. I teleport over to Forge, and have to hold my stomach back from spewing its contents. He's burnt. Bad. Pieces of his uniform still cling to him, melted to his skin. The exposed parts of his skin are scorched, steaming, and bubbling over. One of the goggles on his mask is busted open, and his eye's swollen shut. Chunks of his hair are gone, leaving a burnt scalp. For a split second I think he's dead. Then he lets out a cough, trying to move his arm.

"No. Don't move," I whisper, dropping to my knees.

I'm about to radio to Doc, when I hear a scream. Daniel is back on the roof, trying to block an attack from both men. Melissa's nowhere to be seen.

Jumping to my feet, I teleport up and land on the back of Macall's partner. Instantly, I feel my gloves and the front of my uniform burning. Losing his balance in the air, he begins to fall back to the ground, and I teleport off of him just in time to see him hit the cement with a hard thud. The flames over his body die out, but he starts to glow, and I know he's going to try another power attack. Rushing over to him, I don't give him the chance.

Slamming my knuckles across his face, I feel the crunch of his bones, but also the heat coming off of him. He falls down, and I stomp my boot as hard as I can into his chest. He grabs his sternum in pain, and I jump on top of him, swinging my fists wildly across his face, feeling the pain from his blistering skin, but not stopping.

Getting back to my feet, I grab his arm, and drag him closer to the parking lot, trying to think of how to contain him. Unsure what to do, I swing him around, teleporting him across the parking lot, using the force of the teleportation to smash him into a vehicle. His back crashes into the windshield of a bright red hatchback, and he screams in pain.

As he lies motionless over the car, I glance down at my hands, now red and starting to blister. Looking back over at the rooftop, I see that Melissa has joined Daniel, and they face off against Macall. She swings her sword, but he blocks it with a huge mound of lava over his fist. The blade gets stuck in the lava, which morphs into Macall's hand. As Melissa tries to pull it away, the blade begins to melt in his hand.

He backhands her across the face, sending a spray of sparks and cinder into the air. She falls back, but regains her balance and dives over to Daniel, who has set up a new defensive wall of water.

Teleporting up to them, I get to the roof just as Daniel tries to douse him again. He knocks Macall off-balance for a moment, but he regains his footing, and starts to hover in the air once more.

"Hydro," I call over to him, as he tries to catch his breath. "Waterball."

He quickly glances at me, nodding. If we can hit the same move we did when we took out the Turbo Trio, we have a chance of stopping this.

Staring back up at Macall, my eyes find his. Through his glowing lava skin, I can see a sinister smile. Feeling the light mist in the air, I wait with my hands up, as Daniel begins to form the huge ball of water in the sky.

I look over at Melissa. "I'm gonna need a boost, Mighty."

Her hesitant eyes linger on me. "Are you sure about this?"

I nod to her, then look back to the sky, amazed at the amount of water Daniel is forming. My vision jumps back over to Macall, who calmly stays in place, watching what we're doing.

"Now," I call out to Melissa, and teleport to the edge of the building.

Running back to her, I sprint as fast as I can, and she uses her strength and my momentum to launch me into the air. Diving through the orb Daniel's created, I keep my arms spread wide, and teleport the entire ball of water onto Macall, before teleporting back down to my friends.

Looking back up, I watch as Daniel controls the orb, compacting the water tighter and tighter. For a moment, Macall moves his arms, as if he's looking for a way out. Then he cocks his head to the side, an eerie calmness taking over him, and stares at me.

"We need to teleport him somewhere," I call out to them.

"Crisis room!" Melissa shouts back. "Doc's been working on a freeze chamber for them. He thinks it can hold him."

I nod and look back at Macall. He grins at me, and through the water, begins glowing bright orange and red.

"No, no, no!" I turn around, screaming at them. "Get down!"

A huge blast, which feels ten times more powerful than the other two attackers' blasts, explodes out of the water orb, instantly evaporating it. We all dive out of the way of what feels like a furnace blasting at us.

Melissa and Daniel get to their feet first, and as I get to a knee, Macall screams out, unleashing a new burst of heat. Only this time, magma shoots out, and I roll to the side. Melissa gets blasted from the roof, as Daniel forms a water barrier.

Pushing myself up to my feet, my hands stick to the roof and the now melting tar. The heat is almost unbearable, and I glare back at Macall, who's actually starting to laugh. His body is covered in a glowing magma, and each step he takes on the roof melts more of it, sending plumes of smoke into the air.

Pushing himself into the air, Daniel floats on his water, readying himself. Looking over at me, I can tell he has no idea what to do. I don't either.

Macall begins to form his own barrier, only it's not around himself. It's around Daniel.

"Hydro, get out of there!"

He's formed ice in the past, but I've never seen him cover himself in it. Now he does, along with freezing the water he's on top of. The walls of lava smash over Daniel, as his ice barrier begins crushing under the molten rock.

"No!" I scream, and rush over to him, but Macall waves

his hands, and knocks me down off of the rooftop, with a fiery spray.

Receding the scorching bedrock from Daniel, Macall lifts him up. He hangs there, motionless, and Macall throws him down to the ground, next to Melissa.

Rushing over to him, I see that he's not burnt up like Forge, but dehydrated. Almost to the point where it looks like there's no water in his body. His usually filled out shoulders are reduced to small mounds, and the black uniform hangs off of his body, as his muscles have seemingly been reduced to nothing. His scalp is burned and his face sunk in. He coughs, then groans in pain.

Macall breaks my attention. I hear him land in the parking lot and look over, as he inspects his partner.

"We have to get Forge and regroup," Melissa says, holding Daniel's head in her arms. "Worm, are you listening to me? We need to fall back."

My fists clench and I get to my feet. Macall looks across the parking lot and sees Forge.

Teleporting over to Forge, I grab his arm and he lets out a painful scream. I teleport him back to Melissa and Daniel, and turn my attention back to Macall, who stares at me, shaking his head.

"Fine," I hiss out, staring at him.

"Worm, no—"

Teleporting back to the cars, I touch a small, gray sedan, and drop it on top of Macall, who dives out of the way just in time. Turning to another car, I grab the side mirror, and try to teleport it as fast as I can. This time he doesn't move, but instead, blasts it out of the sky as it comes hurdling toward him. A mist of lava flies everywhere.

The cars spark a new idea, and I teleport to random cars on the lot, touching different ones, sending them all at

Macall. He blasts the first one, then the second, but by the third, he has to dodge out of the way. A fourth, fifth, and sixth all come crashing down over Macall, who rolls to the side.

Mighty rushes over to me, and I see Daniel and Forge, Daniel holding Melissa's shield.

"How is he?" I ask.

"I broke a sprinkler head. It's enough to get him mobile, but that's pretty much it. Forge needs help now though. What do we do?"

"I don't know," I scream out, running to another car and teleporting it over. "I'm gonna run out of cars pretty soon."

Macall stops running with the last car attack and begins to form a mound of dirt and lava, with some of the cars adding to the barrier. I take a deep breath, finally able to stop, and the burns start to set in more. The parking lot looks like a demolition derby that took place inside of a volcano.

"Give yourself up, Macall!" I yell.

A creaking of metal from cars being pushed begins. I ready myself and feel Melissa tense beside me. Macall's defensive mound cracks, and then he breaks out. It's not an explosion though. Instead, it's a gooey run of lava that drips from him, and forms puddles as he steps. The fire guy holds himself up, next to him, grabbing his side in pain.

"Macall?" he yells back. "That man died when Daedalus kidnapped me. You can call me Magma."

"Fine! Whatever!" Melissa yells. "There's nowhere to go. It's time to end this."

He lets out a sinister chuckle. "I underestimated you. But that doesn't mean I've lost."

Instead of continuing, his eyes shoot to the side of us. I follow his field of vision and see Forge writhing in pain, as

Daniel continues to try and hold a defensive position. I think he might try to attack them again, when his head snaps to the side, at his partner.

"You didn't kill the fire one?" he asks him, grabbing him by the throat.

The fire guy coughs, trying to fight off Magma. "That blast took almost everything out of me. If I would've hit him with everything I got, I'd be dead. Like Gunther."

"You failed the cause," Magma spits out. "This cause requires you to give your everything. Even your life."

The partner struggles to break free but can't. "Screw you! I haven't seen you kill the teleporter yet."

"Imbecile!" Magma swings his lava-covered fist into the man.

"This isn't my cause," he chokes out, trying to catch his breath. "It's yours. I've only stayed with you because you're in my mind. I hate these heroes as much as you, but I ain't dying for them. Or for you."

Magma slaps him across the face, unleashing another round of lava splatter, sending him to the ground. Mighty and I exchange curious glances.

"You're right," Magma says, stepping on him. The partner bursts into flames, but it does nothing to stop Magma, whose skin begins dripping of lava. "This is my cause. And your use for it has come to an end."

"This is not good," I whisper over to Melissa. Grabbing her hand, I teleport us back to Daniel. "Hydro," I whisper over to him, "can you form any water?"

He lets out a deep, painful breath, holding his chest. "For what?"

"This might be our last chance to take him out."

"What? No, Robbie." Melissa pulls at my arm. "Look at us." She waves her hand between the four of us and I take us in. Forge is out of commission, Daniel can barely stand, and both Melissa and I are burned, scarred, and our uniforms are barely holding themselves together.

I nod. "You're right." I look back at Daniel. "If you can form enough water as a barricade, we can make a break and regroup back at headquarters."

Daniel stares past me. "I ... I can try."

Before we can act on any type of escape plan, Macall's attack on his partner explodes. Scanning the area, Macall turns to us and begins floating in the air, hovering over a pool of lava.

"Go, go, go!" I scream at them. Daniel gets to his feet, and Melissa picks up Forge, draping his arm over her shoulder.

I move to run over to the parking lot, but Melissa grabs my arm. "Where are you going?"

"We're not gonna have enough time. You need a diversion."

"Robbie—"

"Go! Now!"

Without another word, I teleport to the other side of the parking lot. Melissa flies up to the rooftop of the building, holding Forge. Daniel floats through the air slowly, mustering up as much water as he can. Macall's vision locks on them, and he looks like he's about to attack, when I grab another car and teleport it at him, knocking him out of the sky.

Twisting around, a furious scream echoes around us, and he sets his sights on me. "Fine!" he screams. "You'll be the first to die!"

He unleashes a new round of magma at me and I teleport to another section of the parking lot. It splashes against the car, sending bits of lava everywhere. The steam rises from his steps as he stalks me, and he raises his hands again.

I wait until he's just about to throw another attack, and then teleport to the side, watching as the lava comes out in full force. Then, as if it's a garden hose when the water pressure's being turn off, the lava starts to fade.

Macall pulls his arms up, staring at his hands. Dropping to a knee, he raises his fist, and I watch as the magma on his skin begins to recede. From lava, to fire, then suddenly to regular hand.

"No!" he screams out. "No, I need more time!"

The rest of his body begins to shift from the molten lava that he's been parading around in, into now glowing red rocks. Dropping to both knees, he begins coughing, and I'm reminded of Gunther, who started to cough up ash and smoke. The same thing is happening to Macall.

I glance back up at the roof, and see Melissa and Daniel, watching the scene unfold.

The glowing rocks over Macall's skin begin to crumble and break away, revealing normal skin. Dirt and ash are smeared across him, but he's a regular man. Wearing the same kind of sheer, black uniform as the others, his hair looks like it could be blond, but it's covered in grime.

Pulling out a small device from behind him, he continues to gag, spitting out more lava. He hits a button on the device and a soft blue glow begins to form around him.

"No!" I yell out and try to teleport over to him, but by the time I get to his spot, he's already used the beamer to transport himself somewhere else. "Damn it."

I spin around. With the artificial teleporter, he could go anywhere he has the homing beacon set up, but I'm hoping it's somewhere close I can see. It's not. I frantically search the area and the rooftops of neighboring buildings, but don't see anything.

"Worm!" Mighty calls out. "We need to get Forge and Hydro back to headquarters."

I teleport up to the roof and take Forge from Melissa, who's also helping keep Daniel standing. Taking one last look around, I still see nothing. Melissa nods over to me, and I teleport myself and Forge back to headquarters, before coming back for them.

28

Daniels lies in a medical bed, his burns bandaged up, along with three IVs being administered. Doc tends to Melissa, applying ointment to her burns, from where she sits next to Daniel. She looks back at him, and they both exchange knowing nods.

"The ointment should help heal the burns within a couple of hours," Doc says. "You two are lucky."

Unfortunately, Forge isn't.

Casting a sideways glance at me, Doc walks over to Forge, lying in the bed next to Daniel. Doc attended to him first when we got back, so his entire body is covered in bandages. His right shoulder and the right side of his face is left open, but everything else is wrapped. Piercing the bandages are tubes connecting to both arms and one inserted into his neck.

I watched as Doc initially bandaged him up, his skin blistering, pockets of blood formed under his skin. But the worst part is what's happening to his insides. Due to the blast that hit him, and his already altered physiology with his superpower, his internal organs are overheating. Doc has a continuous drip of a cooling serum that is being pushed through his system, so his internal organs don't overheat.

Doc walks over to the EKG that's attached to Forge and shakes his head. "This shouldn't be possible." He looks back at me. "Forge's body is able to withstand temperatures up to four hundred degrees Celsius. For this type of damage to happen to him he'd have to come into contact with something as hot as magma."

Melissa and I both look at one another.

"That's what Macall called himself," I reply. "He said Dean Macall died the day Daedalus kidnapped him and now his name is Magma. He was so much more powerful than the other two. Sometimes, he didn't even have flames. He was just shooting molten lava at us."

Daniel nods, then gazes up at the ceiling. "Then he killed his partner."

"That isn't good," Doc says, stroking his beard.

"What are we going to do?" I ask.

He stares at me like I'm crazy. "*We* aren't going to do anything. You're still suspended, you shouldn't have even been out there."

"You can't be serious. If I wasn't there, this would have been a whole lot worse. Forge could be dead right now."

"He's right," Melissa says, making me shoot her a look of surprise. Between her and Daniel, I definitely did not think she would be coming to my defense. "Magma is way too powerful. We need Robbie's help with this."

Doc locks his gaze on mine. "Fine, but only until this is over."

Without hesitation, I immediately start throwing out an idea. "He changed. Somehow, he depowered and became a regular-looking guy. I think his power might've been drained from everything. Maybe all of the fighting and then taking out his partner was too much on him. If we make a plan and attack him head-on, we could take him."

"Absolutely not," Doc rejects the idea.

Daniel sits up in his bed. "He blasted through my water, but I could tell it was taking a toll on him, if only a little bit. Perhaps if we cause a distraction—"

Doc shakes his head. "You all barely got out of there. We have to do this the smart way. If we run in trying to attack him head-on, who knows what his power level will be. We set up defensive plays, get King City PD alerted, and make sure this is contained."

"But if we—"

"No, Robbie. This is the plan. We have to be smart about this."

"I know. But, Doc, why were they at my school? It has to be Watkins. Isn't it suspicious that Magma attacks my school after I confronted Watkins?"

"We're not discussing this right now. Macall is the priority."

I glance around at all three of them, Melissa and Daniel stare back, unsure. Don't they see the connection? Watkins is the key here. "I can't be the only one who sees this."

"Did you not hear anything I told you?" Doc takes a step forward, asserting his leadership. "Watkins cannot be strong-armed into cooperating. We've had him on the bubble before. We know of things that he's connected to, but we have no proof. He's the one with the power. If we confront him, even if we find a link to the experiments, he's covered his tracks. We need to focus on Macall."

Taking deep breath, Melissa gives me a knowing expression. It's a look I've seen before. An expression that tells me I need to listen to him because it's the smart and safe move.

It's not that I don't see his point, but there has to be some way to connect Watkins to this and force his hand.

Walking closer to me, Doc puts a hand on my shoulder. "Please, Robbie. Listen to me on this. Griffin was the same, and you might not have been here then, but you know the toll that took."

Before Justin Griffin was sent to prison, he was Supron's main concern. But how do you take down a genius billionaire with countless devices and companies at his disposal? You don't. And even though Supron knew Griffin was dirty, there was no way to connect him to the multitude of underhanded dealings he was involved in. The first time Supron did make a move, Griffin launched a world-wide smear campaign against the Justice Alliance.

Reports on how superheroes can't be trusted or were a rogue band of misfits—even if we are registered under the Super Human Registration Act—and how we take the law into our own hands. The allegations were just that, but once they were made public, it cast a shadow of doubt over the Alliance.

Griffin was eventually caught, and even though the majority of the population now know the truth of who Griffin really is, and that the Justice Alliance is here to protect the public, there are still pockets of doubters. Going after Watkins would no doubt do the same.

I finally nod, agreeing to Doc's terms. "Then what do we do?"

"We send King City on high alert and wait for the first sign of him. We call in backup. Lazerbeam from Parkfield, and Tremor from Queensbridge. We make sure everywhere is monitored. We can also get backup from Granite. That will give us the necessary reinforcements. With three superheroes, three sidekicks, and the police force, when he makes a move, we'll be ready."

My defeated feeling spreads, and I slump my shoulders. "Great. We just wait for him to attack again."

"Not exactly."

His rebuttal perks up my mood. "What do you mean?"

"You're right about your identity, he must know who you are. Even with his power, I'm sure he won't attack us here. But if he attacked King City High in an attempt to draw you out, I say we give him another shot." I quirk an eyebrow. "He'll be on the lookout for you. Stay in uniform and teleport around the city. We'll draw him out."

Finally, something that feels proactive. "Let's do it."

After Lazerbeam and Tremor meet up at headquarters, Doc has Granite covering the north side, assisting police.

Tremor has been serving as the superhero in Queensbridge for nearly five years. He's called Tremor because he can send out vibrations through the air, or if he wants to, vibrations through the ground or other objects.

Lazerbeam patrols over the harbor district of King City, while Tremor keeps watch over the financial district. After a few more hours, and IVs, Daniel is in better condition, so he and Mighty stay close to the east side. Everyone waits on me as I teleport from spot to spot, hoping to catch any sign of Magma.

After a few hours, the sun begins setting, with clouds still hanging up above. When school started this morning, the weather said we might get the first snowfall for King City. Nothing substantial, but a light dusting, nonetheless.

It's cold, but there's no sign of snow yet. After another teleportation run, I teleport to the top of King City Tower.

Across the street is a huge media-conglomerate building with screens and advertisements playing. It always reminds me of Times Square in New York City, though in King City no one pays real attention to it.

"*Police are cautioning citizens to be on high alert,*" a screen shows the transcription of a news report playing. "*The suspect, now known as Dean Macall,*" the screen displays a picture of Macall, one which looks like the picture he would've used when he was still a professor, "*has caused substantial damage throughout the city. The Justice Alliance is reporting him a priority level red threat, and anyone that has any information is implored to contact the authorities.*"

Despite the message of caution being played, the street down below looks as full as always. With King City home to three of the most famous and powerful members of the Justice Alliance, along with their sidekicks, the city's become lax and takes for granted the threat that supervillains actually pose.

Yes, flying men on fire are on the loose, who've also just blown up parts of a school, but that's just another day in King City. The good in the city far outweighs the bad, but it makes it difficult when someone as serious as Magma could be ready to strike at any time. Citizens expect superheroes to save the day, no matter what. With Mimic and the others gone, I'm hoping we can still do it.

Teleporting again, I jump to another rooftop.

"Anything yet?" I radio in to Doc.

"All's quiet," he responds. "Police scanners are silent. With all of you out there even the low-level thugs seem to be keeping a low profile. We'll continue for a few more hours."

I nod, letting out a sigh. "All right."

Standing on top of a building, I scan over the city blocks. A light breeze runs over me, and I gaze up to find snow falling. The white dust floats, making the city lights look serene, with the fading light almost gone from the sunset. The view is a stark contrast to what our actual mission is tonight; trying to lure out a madman.

I press a finger to my comm. "It's snowing. That could help, right? Hydro, can you use that to our advantage?"

"It's perfect," he replies back confidently. "I'm already feeling better."

I let out a chuckle, teleporting again. Jumping over to a nearby rooftop, I gaze down upon King City Hospital, and suddenly remember Jasmin and Pete. I haven't seen or talked to either of them since the incident at the school. Pete's probably kept in contact with Daniel, but Jasmin looked terrified when I left her.

Knowing Magma could still be watching me, I teleport over to the west side, trying to keep my guard up. I jump into an abandoned building, then over to a storefront that's closed, trying to avoid rooftops. Teleporting into the lobby of the neighboring apartment building, I look up and see Jasmin's fire escape. Moving up to it, I knock on the window lightly. She jumps as she turns around, and I smile. It instantly vanishes when I see her worried expression.

I teleport in, and her arms wrap around me before I can take a step.

"Robbie!"

I chuckle. "Okay, we're gonna need to work on the whole secret identity thing."

She doesn't reply and my laughter evaporates. With her arms still around me, I can feel her shaking.

"Hey." I pull back, holding her face. "It's okay. I'm okay."

Her eyes are red, and she lets out a sniffle. "I was so

worried. At first, everyone at school was acting how they normally do, pulling out their phones and everything. But when the first explosion hit the cars ... I thought ..."

I retract my helmet, pressing my forehead against hers. "Jas, I'm okay."

She nods, and more tears fall. "I just didn't ... I didn't know it would be like this."

I swallow the guilt I've been keeping at bay from revealing everything to her. This is what I wanted to avoid. Then I remember the horrible feeling of breaking up with her last year. Telling her I never liked her. Keeping her at arm's length. As much as it hurt me, it's far better than causing her this kind of sadness and worry.

"I'm sorry," I whisper, still holding her. "This is exactly why I never wanted you to know. I never wanted to get you hurt, or have you feeling like you are now." Hitting my earpiece, I pull my helmet back up. "When this is over, when we stop Magma ..." I turn away.

Say it, Robbie. What did Daniel say? It's called growing up.

"I can't be the reason you're hurt or scared. Knowing you're safe is far more important than what I want." Walking away from her, I stare out of her window.

"What are you saying?"

"Jasmin, I won't be the reason—"

Cutting me off, she steps in front of me. "No, you can't do that. That's not what I want."

"It doesn't matter what you want, Jasmin. It matters what the right thing is."

"No." She presses a finger into my chest. "It absolutely matters. Was I terrified today? Yes. But this is King City. There's always going to be danger, whether I'm with you or not. And the good far outweighs the bad."

"Please, it's better if we—"

"Do you remember last year when I told you about my uncle?"

I nod my head, remembering the story.

We were going out and it was one week before homecoming. Her uncle is a doctor, like her mom, and his wife was an officer for King City PD. They were married for twenty years. One night while he was on duty at the hospital, an officer that had been shot was taken to the emergency room. He saw his wife being rolled into the hospital, bleeding out. He tried everything, but she died.

"This isn't the same thing."

"You're right, it's not. But I remember what he said at her funeral. He knew every day that she was out there, doing her job, protecting the city. When they were in college and he found out she wanted to enroll in the police academy, he said he was scared. He said he asked himself if he could live a life where the woman he loved was doing something that might take her away from him. And the answer was yes. Because as painful as that might be, being with her was worth it to him."

I shake my head. "Jasmin, they were married for years. This isn't the same. We're in high school. As much as I want this, I refuse to be the reason you suffer that kind of pain. What I want is not nearly as important as making sure we both live past high school and into happy lives."

Her eyes still puffy, her face turns hard. Her vision pierces my visor. "Take your helmet off."

"What?"

"You heard me," she demands. "Take it off."

Doing as she says, it retracts. She remains determined.

"Was I scared today? Hell yes. But you're being selfish right now, Robbie."

"Excuse me?" I ask, looking at her like she's gone crazy. "*I'm* the one being selfish? How so?"

"Because you keep saying what *you*. *You* can't let me. *You* won't do this. But what about me? What about what I want?" I wag my head side to aside, about to counter her, but she cuts me off. "What I want is to be with you. You can try and argue with all of the supposed logical and practical reasons why we shouldn't be together, but I know who you are. Not this guy"—she jabs a finger into the star on my chest, then raises the hand to my cheek—"but this guy. Who once told me he had a crush on me for years. Who runs out to help people while the rest of us try to find safety."

Tears well up in her eyes and feel the same happening in me. Leaning closer, her lips graze mine, and I press my forehead against hers. "I can't be the reason something happens to you," I whisper.

"Then don't be," she whispers back, before firmly planting her mouth over mine.

If the first kiss with no secrets between us felt like my first real kiss with her, this one is one with a promise. I can't give her up and she won't let me, so I'll do everything in my power to keep her safe. No matter what. Safe from harm, from hurt, and from feeling like she'll lose me.

Finally breaking away, we keep our foreheads together, and for the first time, she smiles. "You're looking at this like it's the hero who gets the girl," she says, smiling. "It's not. It's the girl that gets the hero."

I can't keep the grin from my lips, and I'm just about to kiss her again, when my ear comm starts.

"We got something," I hear Tremor say.

Nodding to Jasmin, I pull my helmet back up. "What is it?"

"Not sure," he replies. "People are running around like

crazy over here. It sounded like a bomb just went off, but no sign of fire."

"Should I head over there?"

"No," Doc interjects. "All readings on the control panel say it was some kind of sonic bomb. King City Fire is on the way. Hydro, I'm picking up readings of higher temps from underground where you're at."

"I'm seeing it," Daniel responds. "It looks like steam coming up from the manholes."

"The water by the docks is picking up action," Lazerbeam says next. "It's starting to bubble."

"Three cars just blew up here on the north side," Granite radios.

"It has to be a diversion," Melissa tells us. "I've got action on my side, too. Multiple fires started. At least five different buildings."

"Worm, get to the south side," Doc calls out. "Help with the fires. I'll keep scanning in case he shows up."

"Got it." I look over at Jasmin, my smile fading a bit. "It's time to get back to work."

"I know," she says, before kissing me again. "Just make sure you come back to me."

"Always."

Teleporting out of her room, I land on the rooftop across the street. Off in the distance I can see the light from the fires Mighty called in. Just before I teleport, a huge explosion rocks me from behind, sending me to my knees. Rolling over, I look across the street to see the top of Jasmin's building blown apart.

"No."

The blast takes out the top three floors, with her room right beneath it, fire and smoke seeping out of her window. Jumping over to the fire escape, I land on the metal bars and they come loose, falling apart, so I have to teleport back across the street.

"No!"

The blood from my face drains, and I try to peer into the flames and smoke, hoping for some sign of her. About to teleport into the fiery room, a terrified scream comes from the next building over. I look up and my body goes rigid.

Horrified, Jasmin stands at the edge of the rooftop. Macall, in his regular form, clutches the back of her neck.

29

Down below, debris from the explosion litters the street. The area isn't heavy with traffic, but neighboring residents have started coming outside to see what's happening. My mouth goes dry.

My training instinctively kicks in, and I take everything in; scanning my environment, hearing people scream below, but nothing can keep my eyes off of Jasmin. Macall holds her, still depowered, and leers at me.

"Worm," I hear a voice in my ear, but I'm completely numb. "Worm!"

Slowly, I creep to the edge of the roof I'm on, my eyes jumping back and forth between Macall and Jasmin. Her lip quivers and tears run down her cheeks. A sick and sinister grin hits Macall's face. Then he leans closer to her, whispering something to her.

"No!" she screams at him.

"Do it!" he shouts, and when he looks back at me, his eyes are glowing.

"Robbie," Jasmin whimpers out. "Help me."

"Worm, what's happening?" I hear Doc shout in my ear.

"It's ..." I swallow the fear. "It's Macall. He has Jasmin."

"What?" someone shouts back, but I'm not sure who.

"Again!" Macall screams at her, and she cringes in pain and fear.

"Robbie ... help me," she cries.

I'm in a trancelike state, inching closer to the edge of my roof. "Doc ... he has her."

"We are sending support right now. Don't advance on him."

"He has her!" My breathing picks up, and I clench my fists. "He must've ... he had to have been following me this whole time. Oh my God. He has her, Doc."

"Don't advance!" Doc calls out, and Macall still stands there, holding Jasmin, the evil grin plastered to his face. "Tremor and Hydro are en route. Do you hear me, Worm?"

I hear the words, but my entire mind is focused across the street. Macall nods to the side of the building. If I don't go, he could kill her. If I do go, it's most likely a trap. But I have no choice.

Jumping to his rooftop, I put my hands up. "Let her go, Macall. She has nothing to do with this."

He curls a lip. "Yes and no. But we'll get to that."

He's cleaned up from the battle in the parking lot. Wearing the same kind of bodysuit as the others, his blond hair waves in the night breeze, the light dusting of snow instantly evaporating as it touches his skin. He looks worn. I've seen the picture from when he was a professor, and I can tell it's the same man, but he looks like he's been through hell. His eyes are sunk in, a stubbly beard over his face. He seems to be a man at the end of his rope, holding on to the final string before falling into an abyss.

Staying where I am, I keep my hands high. "How'd you know who I am? Watkins? He's behind all of this, isn't he?"

He rolls his eyes, releasing a disgusted groan. "I hate that bastard." Raising his free hand, he stares at it, and it begins to glow. "He did this to me. But, in the end, I guess I do owe him an ounce of gratitude. Information, upgrades, and a clean slate." He lets out an evil chuckle. "Kid, he wants you bad."

If I keep him talking, maybe that'll buy us time until Daniel and Tremor show up. "What's that supposed to mean? And how's this all connected to Daedalus? Is that where you escaped from?"

"I did. And I had nothing but revenge on my mind. First it was going to be you. All of you. Then I'd go back for him. Imagine my surprise when he found me, and not only offered to stabilize me, but wipe me off the grid. All for the low price of tracking you down."

"You actually made a deal with him?"

"In a way." He grins. "He gave me your info. Your name, your parents' names, even people like her." He nods to Jasmin. She continues to stand there, tears silently falling. "Oh, and let's not forget Peter Malory or Maria Ruiz. Friends of yours?" I swallow the panic and try to stay calm. He lets out another sinister chuckle. "Watkins is so full of his own crap he gave me everything. He thinks I'm gonna trap you and hand you over. Nope. You're the first on my list to burn. And when I'm done with you, I will be going back for him."

I take a step closer. "Let her go then. She has nothing to do with this."

"On the contrary, she has everything to do with this." I narrow my eyes, confused. "All of you heroes deserve to die. You just left me. Left us. When we disappeared, no one came for us. Gunther had a son. Frank took care of his mother. And I—" His hateful gaze finally breaks. He looks down at the ground, almost remorseful. Shaking his head, he looks back at me. "No, you'll suffer. Like I suffered. That's what she has to do with this."

His free hand begins to glow again, only this time it doesn't stop. The skin starts bubbling, then the lava begins to cover his arm and hand. He raises it to Jasmin's face, who cringes and whimpers in pain.

"No!" I rush over, but he raises the hand back at me, stopping me in my tracks.

"That's far enough."

His entire body begins powering up, magma covering his legs, crawling up around his waist and chest. The lava slithers up his neck, then over this face, leaving the only part of his body untouched by the lava the hand holding Jasmin's neck. I can feel the heat from the few feet away of where I stand.

"Please," my voice cracks. "Please, let her go. I'm here. Take me and do whatever you want. Just let her go."

A thin smile spreads across his now glowing lips. "Don't worry, I plan on doing whatever I want."

Forming his hand as if he's making a gun with his thumb and index finger, he raises the finger to Jasmin's temple.

"No!" I scream and run at him again. This time he throws his hand out, splashing lava down in front, only an arm's length away. "Please! I'm begging you. Please, don't do this. This can't be what you really want? You want to hurt me, right? Us? She doesn't have anything to do with this."

He sneers, and the glowing magma over his skin begins to recede, until he's normal. Everything except his glowering orange eyes.

"Haven't you been listening? Her death makes you suffer. And that's exactly what I want."

"But why?" I scream.

"I lived in this city my whole life. I was just like everyone else. Don't worry about it," he says, waving his hand around in disgusted arrogance. "Supron and the others will clean it up. And then I learned firsthand that they only care—you only care—about the big stuff. No one cared about a biology professor who went missing. And when you failed to save me, you killed my family."

"I'm sorry, okay? But you're just hurting innocent people now!"

"Exactly!" he shouts back. His skin begins glowing again. "They're dead! The night we escaped Daedalus, I went to find them. But I couldn't control it. I killed them! I killed my own family. I had a wife. A daughter. I had the perfect home and you all took that from me."

Looking over at Jasmin, I see her eyes drip with fear.

"I lost everything," he repeats, almost in a whisper. "Now, you will lose everything."

Throwing Jasmin down in front of him, his entire body shifts solely into Magma. Raising his hands, lava bubbles over, with flames floating over his fists. I drop to my knees, about to wrap my arms around her, when he throws a glob of lava between us.

"Wait!" I scream. "Please, please ..." My voice quivers. "I'll do anything. Anything. Just ... don't kill her. Kill me instead. I'm begging you."

For a moment, he stands there staring at me. An ounce of hope floats inside, praying that a sliver of the family man he described is still inside of him, and he'll take mercy and grant my request. As quickly as that moment of hope flashes, it's gone.

He curls his lip with a devilish smile.

"Robbie," Jasmin's terrified whisper of my name floats in the air.

Trial By Fire

Molten lava explodes everywhere. I scream out in anguish, sorrow, and fear. I reach out to her, hoping that somehow, I'll be able to reach her and teleport us away, but I feel the singe of the magma on my fingers. The scorching flames burn through my uniform and I feel the sear of the heat burn my throat as I scream out.

30

In an instant the burning subsides. The heat around me is gone. Then there's nothing.

No snow, no smoke, no lava. No noise from the city, no hateful Magma, and no terrified Jasmin. Still on my knees, I look around. I'm surrounded by what I can only describe as a floating orb. Everything around me is pitch black, except for the orb, which gives off a blueish glow. I'm in a bubble that seems to be floating through an infinite void.

Getting to my feet, I peer around, but there's nothing. Just me inside of the blue orb. I motion to take a step, and suddenly the orb zooms forward, into the blackness. I feel the motion but see no outward signs of moving past anything. Then a small, gray cloud appears in the distance.

Without having to wait, the cloud immediately surrounds the orb, and gold lightning scrambles around the outside of the sphere. The orb stops moving and the lightning crackles, then shoots into the cloud. An eight-pointed star, the same shape as the insignia on my chest, somehow burns into the gray cloud.

Getting closer to the sphere wall, the insignia stays, and

Trial By Fire

then the orb speeds through it, and I'm flying through fog. Lightning dances over the mist and I see images. Scenes from ... something. I peer as close as I can, almost pressing my face against the sphere, trying to discern the scene in the cloud. Then my eyes pop open. It's me.

I'm drinking orange juice out of the carton and my mom scolds me. My dad's reading his tablet. It's the morning my mom thought I was out with a girl the night before.

"What?" I mumble to myself.

The orb speeds forward and comes to a sudden stop in the hazy cloud. Another scene appears. Melissa and I are lying down on my couch, in my Alliance bunker. Three zombie movies lie on the ground and we're kissing.

"What is this?"

Lightning strikes through the cloud and I'm on the move again. The crackle of the electricity rings around me, and then strikes the cloud. I see Pete and myself, and we're standing outside of our homecoming dance last year. He's yelling at me. It's the night he came out to me. Observing the scene play out, another lightning bolt strikes the cloud, and the scene shifts.

This one is of me in my uniform. I'm standing on the sidewalk, with Jasmin next to me. Then we kiss. I see myself teleport up to the roof, and then watch her go down the subway station tunnel.

"What is this?" I yell again.

Thunder sounds, and a huge lightning bolt strikes the orb, dropping me to a knee. The orb moves and the cloud surrounds me. Jasmin's face pops up, and she's crying. I see the whole scene of what just happened. Magma throws her to the ground, and I reach for her, but he puts the lava between us. I don't hear anything but can see Magma's lips move. Then he shoots out the lava.

The out-of-body experience, as I watch the lava cover over both of us, snaps something inside.

"No!" I slam my fists against the sphere. More lightning crackles around, and it shoots through the scene.

It continues on, though I don't remember any of what's playing now. Jasmin and I lie motionless on the roof, covered in lava. Magma explodes, sending the scorching material everywhere. Daniel flies into the picture, only to be knocked out of the sky by a huge fireball. Tremor dodges fiery projectiles, and then another explosion. A huge blast covers him in magma. The scene pulls out wider and the entire block explodes.

"No, no, no!" I slam my fist against whatever I'm trapped in. Each time, the lightning sizzles, and a new round of thunder sounds. "This isn't real! This can't be real!"

Screaming, I kick the orb as hard as I can, and the lightning that's been circling outside, suddenly penetrates inside. As if it's a floating snake, the lightning has a mind of his own. It twists and turns, edging closer to my face. Then it shoots through my chest.

My body convulses. Every muscle tightens, and I drop to my knees, writhing in pain. Letting me go, I stay seated and the lightning forms a circle. Starting to spin like a pinwheel, it explodes, and I feel it splash across my face. I gasp for air, but I can't breathe. I can't see. I hear nothing but silence. Forcing my eyes open, I see an intense light, and reach for the electric-white nothing in front of me.

Suddenly, I'm floating. The electricity is gone. The white, the pain, the orb, and the cloud. It's all gone. In a single instant, I'm floating in nothing, and then my senses explode.

Gasping for air, I feel a cool breeze. I feel light and sun. My chest heaves, and the brightness around is hazy, but I'm hearing voices. I'm sitting in something and I tumble to the ground, still heaving. I try to gasp for the air I should be breathing normally, but it's as if I've been suffocating and I can't breathe properly.

Stumbling to my feet, I trip and hold myself up, on what looks like the edge of a table.

"Worm? Worm, what's wrong?"

I gasp again, hearing the voice, but unsure what's going on.

"What's happening?"

"I don't know, he was fine and then he just started doing this."

"Worm? Can you hear me? Robbie?"

My vision comes in a little clearer and I see Doc. He's holding me up, and I look around the area. Forge is lying in a medical bed. He's bandaged up. Snapping my head to the side, I see Melissa standing next to Daniel, who's sitting upright in his bed.

"What ... what is this?" My eyes jump everywhere.

"Robbie, what's wrong?" Doc asks again.

"I'm ... I'm at headquarters?" Trying to get my breathing under control, Melissa shoots me a concerned glare. "I'm ... wait." I scan the room, trying to understand. "Wait ... Did we catch him?"

"What?" Melissa asks.

"Worm, you guys almost died out there."

"Who?" I ask, grabbing Doc by the shoulders.

He peaks an eyebrow. "You three. At your school."

"School?"

"Yes. Now that you're reinstated for this mission, we need to get to work. We need—"

"Wait, wait. Reinstated?" Melissa and Daniel stare at me with worried gazes. "Reinstated ..." I glance over Forge and his bandaged body. "Oh my God! This is today. This is today!"

"Melissa, grab my medical kit," Doc instructs her. "Robbie, take a seat. We need to—"

"No!" I yank my arm away from him. "Magma. Holy crap, it happened. It actually happened."

"Robbie—"

"Doc, I did it! I don't know how, but I did it!"

"What did you do?"

"I time traveled!"

His face drops. So does Daniel's and Melissa's. "As in, right now? Right this instant?"

"Yeah. Or, no. I don't know. I've lived this day already." I take another look at Forge. "Doc, it doesn't work."

"What doesn't work?" Melissa asks.

My solemn expression finds her. "Everything. Our plan doesn't work. We try to patrol, cover everything and hopefully catch him, but he's ready for it. He follows me. He knows who I am."

"How is that possible?" Daniel asks.

"Because I screwed up," I answer, looking at Melissa. "I screwed up everything."

Doc places a hand on my shoulder. "Robbie, we need to tread very softly here. I know very little about the time continuum, but what I do know is that it's fragile. Extremely. We have to make this work."

"No, aren't you listening? It doesn't work." My voice rises, shoving his hand off of me.

"We can't alter something because the plan doesn't work. All theories on time travel are extremely uncharted. How are you even here, in your present form, with future knowledge? Nothing makes sense. We must press forward,

Robbie. Changing how time plays out can send shockwaves through the continuum ... theoretically."

"Doc!" I scream, catching everyone off guard, including myself. "I die! Jasmin dies. He knows who I am, and he follows me. I go to make sure Jasmin is okay, and he blows up half her building, before blowing us up. Then the whole city block."

Gazing down at the ground, I feel all of the emotions all over again. The pain and the fear. I clench my eyes shut, wishing I could forget those feelings on the roof.

"He takes her to the roof and tells me everything. Watkins told him who I was so he could find and kill me. He wants to kill all of us, but not just ..." I trail off. "Wait, he told me ..."

"What?" Doc asks.

"Before he killed us. He said we were to blame for this."

"Who?" Melissa questions.

"All of us. He was taken. Kidnapped. Daedalus experimented on him and made him into Magma. But he escaped. We knew that part, but he went home. He told me he went home and killed his family. It was an accident. He didn't know how to control his power. That's why he hates us."

"By the gods," Melissa whispers, horror spreading across her face.

"I begged. I begged him to let her go, but he wouldn't. He wanted to make me suffer, and then he blew us up."

The silence in the room is palpable. Daniel stares at Doc, unsure of what to do. Melissa gazes at me, fear and sympathy across her face.

A flash hits me. Wherever I was, I remember seeing something. My face drops and I look to Daniel. "You die." Glancing back at Doc, his stunned expression is locked in place. "Tremor dies. It doesn't work, Doc. We need to try something else."

He shakes his head, stroking his beard in deep thought. His eyes jump from all of us, then down to the floor. "We've tried tracing heat signatures. Either his DNA isn't traceable, or he's depowered, and we can't get a read on his location. Planting a flag and calling him out is out of the question. He's too powerful, especially if what you say is true. Robbie, are you sure—"

"Yes!" I scream. "I know it sounds crazy, but I'm telling you the truth. I don't know how, I don't know where I was, but this has happened." Taking a deep breath, I rack my brain, thinking of some other way to face him. "Right before it happened, the city was going crazy. Buildings on fire, an explosion— Wait. Boiling. The water in the harbor district, by the docks. It was boiling."

"How?" Doc asks.

"I don't know, but we thought it might be a diversion. Now I know it was. He was doing it to keep everyone occupied so he could tail me."

"I hate to be the one to say it," Daniel speaks up, "but I'm not hearing anything about how we can change the future here, guys."

Doc nods. "Hydro's right. There's only one thing we can change that might affect this and that's you, Worm. You need to stay on the line. If you don't go to Jasmin's, he won't be able to follow you there."

I shake my head. "No, he knows who she is already. Watkins gave him everything. My parents' names, Pete's name—"

"What?" Fear spreads across Daniel's face.

"He knows everything about me."

Doc lets out a long sigh, scratching his beard once again.

Trial By Fire

He looks shaken. Completely flabbergasted. "This is beyond me. I've never dealt with time travel before."

"There has to be something we can do," I plead with him.

He gazes at me, completely defeated. "I'm sorry. If he knows who she is, and your family, he'll be keeping eyes on their locations. There's no way to make a move without him being aware. Whether it's trackers or he's hired some thugs to keep watch, there's no way of knowing. He'll be sticking to the shadows, and when he sees you that's when he moves. Our only chance is to reinforce that area. I can call in more help and—"

"Keeping watch …" I whisper aloud, breaking through Doc's words. "Keeping watch … he's sticking to the shadows …"

"What are you talking about?"

My mind races. There's a plan there. "He's sticking to the shadows …" A million-watt light bulb goes off. "Of course! We can do this. We can beat him."

"Robbie?" Daniel questions, getting out of his bed, holding his ribs tenderly.

"What do you mean?" Doc asks.

"He's keeping an eye on them. He's waiting to see where I go first and that's where he makes his move."

Melissa gives me an unsure look. "Yeah?"

"I know how we can stop him."

"How?" Doc asked.

"By doing exactly what you said. Stick to the plan."

All three of them drop their jaws, giving me a crazed-eye look.

31

Doc calls in Lazerbeam, Tremor, and Granite like before. And, just like before, Melissa and Daniel patrol their sections of the city. I teleport around the north side of King City, stopping at all the rooftops I previously did. Finally, the snow begins to fall.

"Snowfall," I say into my comm. "Hydro, you ready?"

"Are you sure this is gonna work?" he asks.

I can hear the hesitancy in his voice. I'd like to sound confident. I want to act like I know exactly what I'm doing, and I don't have a doubt in the world. Instead, I feel ten pounds of nerves in my stomach.

"It has to."

I finally jump over to Jasmin's building. Unlike the first time, I don't bother trying to sneak around through empty rooms and buildings. I know he's waiting. Getting to her fire escape, I tap the glass and she jumps.

"Robbie!"

Teleporting inside, I chuckle as I did before. "Okay, we're gonna need to work on the whole secret identity thing."

Wrapping her arms around me, I'm hit with déjà vu.

This has to work.

"Hey, I'm okay," I whisper to her.

Looking up at me, the same red and puffy eyes gaze into mine. "I was so worried. At first, everyone at school was acting how they normally do, pulling out their phones and everything. But when the first explosion hit—"

I kiss her, cutting off her words. This is my second chance, and I'm going to make sure I do everything possible to save her.

"Jasmin, I'm so sorry. This is why I never wanted you to know. This world is dangerous, and I wish I could explain more to you right now, but I can't."

"What?"

"Remember when I told you I love you?" She nods. "I meant it. And I know this isn't going to make any sense right now, but I need you to do something. Slowly, walk over to your door, and hit the light switch."

"Robbie, what are you—"

"Please." Even with the red eyes, a new concern covers her face. "Jasmin, please just do this. I'll explain everything later."

She nods. "Okay."

Walking over, I can tell she's nervous. Turning to face me, she raises her hand to the light switch.

"One more thing. As soon as you hit that switch, you won't be here anymore. Don't freak out, okay?"

"Robbie, you're really scaring me now."

"I know, I'm sorry. But you'll be safe, I promise. I love—"

"Don't say that." She shakes her head. "You tell me that when whatever this is is over."

"Deal." I nod, giving her a small smile. "Hit the switch."

I don't wait. As soon as it goes dark, I teleport to the top of the neighboring building, knowing she's safe for the time being, and now I'm praying that this is the right decision.

Just like before, the explosion knocks me down. Turning around, I see that the top three floors are gone again.

"She's safe," Shadow's gruff voice echoes in my ear. "Top three floors were cleared, too."

I let out a sigh of relief. "Thank you, Shadow. Granite will rendezvous with you near the north side. Hydro, we'll be coming down fast."

"You sure about this, kid?"

I pause, taking a look around. I don't see Macall anywhere yet. "It'll work. It has to."

Finally, Macall steps out from behind a stairway exit. He stares at me, already fully powered. I teleport to him, readying myself. "It's over, Macall."

"I told you already, my name's Magma. You hid the girl?"

"You're not gonna hurt her. You aren't going to hurt anyone!"

A low, evil laugh seeps out of him. His eyes glow brighter.

"You think you're so smart?" He shoots lava out from his hands, forming a pool of it around his feet. "You all deserve to die! You let this happen to me!"

Throwing his hands up, he launches the scalding magma at me, and I teleport out of the way.

"I know, and I'm sorry!" I yell out from the edge of the roof. "I'm sorry we weren't there to save you. I'm sorry that your family died."

Spinning around to find me, his magma bubbles over him, dripping all around, and he screams again. "They didn't die! They were murdered! And it's your fault. Every last one of you."

He sends another round of lava at me, but this time I

take off running. Sliding to a stop near the edge of the building, the snow around us is falling harder now, melting to mist as it nears us and the heat. Turning to face him, he calmly stalks over to me.

"There's nowhere to run. Wherever you go, I'll find you. Or someone you love. And I'll make you suffer. Like I suffered."

"I know," I answer, dropping to my knees.

He releases an undaunted smile. "Finally, you're coming to your senses. I'd like to say I'll make it painless, but I won't."

From on my knees, I look up at him, torn with sympathy. "I'm sorry we didn't save you."

Reaching down, I press my hands into the cement edge of the building as hard as I can. A rumbling starts, and the rooftop starts shaking. Pausing, he looks around. "What are you doing?"

I don't answer. Instead, I keep my hands pressed against the roof, and grit my teeth. The rumbling gets louder, and the shaking worsens. He loses his balance and takes a step back to stay upright. I let out a scream, trying to focus as hard as I can on my task.

I've never teleported anything like what I'm trying to do. And even if the size wasn't a problem, I've never teleported only *part* of something. Anything I touch and teleport, I always take the complete object. Teleporting the entire roof of the building, but not the building itself, along with me and Magma wouldn't be anything I would've ever thought of in the past. But this has to work.

"What are you doing?" he screams again.

Every muscle in my body strains, and I clench my eyes shut. Trying to block everything out, I only focus on the roof. I've done this long enough that, when I teleport, it comes as natural as breathing. I can peer through my wormhole in the milliseconds I have and know where I'm going to end up. But this is something I never even thought to experiment with.

I feel the power of the astral plane rippling across my skin. But I can also feel the energy from the rooftop. It's hard to explain; it's like the molecules of the matter that the roof is composed of run up my arms and around me. I grunt, almost trying to dig my fingers into the cement, and then feel heat.

Squinting through my visor, I see Magma starting to spread lava over the entire rooftop. He tries to move but can't. Struggling with his legs, which are stuck to the roof, the lava flowing over his feet. "What is this?" he yells at me.

For the first time, there's no anger or hate in his words. There's fear. I block it all out, screaming, and focus harder on the roof. Exerting everything I have, I watch as the magma rolls over toward my hands, but see it's being held at bay by an invisible field. The astral plane.

Releasing one last primal scream, a large crack shudders around us, and he falls down. I feel the roof moving. I'm doing it. I converge every last thought on where I want us to go, and we're instantly weightless. It only lasts for a moment, and then we're falling back down to Earth. I didn't focus on a specific spot, or how high I wanted to take us, I only wanted to get as high as possible.

Pieces of the roof fall to the side, but the bulk of it stays intact. Tackling me, I feel the heat from his hand around my throat. He's depowered but it still burns my skin.

"You think this will stop me?" he screams.

The roof begins to drift away from our bodies and now we're free-falling, with the roof beneath us. Falling through the clouds and snow, I see the city below, but it's a blur.

Twirling through the air, our positions shift, and I finally get in a strike, hitting him across the face.

A piece of the rooftop floats up, and I grab it, slamming him in the head, but it doesn't do any damage. Spinning more, we start to float farther apart, and neither of us can control our direction. While the clouds and snow continue to stay amid us, a sudden flurry of snow comes out of nowhere.

Continuing to fall, the snow begins sticking to my body. More steam mixes with the clouds as it hits Magma's body. Gazing down below, the buildings come in clearer, and it's only now I'm realizing the speed of our descent is slowing. The flurry continues, and I see the storm get denser around Magma. Nothing is sticking to him, but the whiteness surrounding him makes it so I can barely see his body.

"It's working, Hydro!" I finally call out into my comm.

We're closer to Jasmin's building, and I finally see Daniel off to the side, controlling the snow.

"Now! As much as you can!"

The moment I say it, the snow turns to water. What feels and looks like thousands of gallons of water splash over us in a huge ball. I can feel the water heating up, and as the buildings get closer, I teleport myself out of the sphere of water and down to a rooftop, rolling to a stop.

"Hit him with everything you got!" I scream out to Daniel, who's on the next rooftop over.

With a savage yell, he holds his hands to the sky, and it looks like every snowflake within viewing distance all converge onto Magma, turning into water, the orb of liquid growing larger. My eyes widen as I watch the water begin to freeze. The ice cracks from Magma trying to fight it. Then it erupts, ice and lava spraying everywhere.

Hissing sounds echo around us with the magma

burning into buildings, cars, and street signs. "That won't stop me!"

"Now, Tremor!" I scream, and Tremor jumps out of the shadows, right on cue.

Unleashing his powers, he points his fists at Magma, and sends shockwave after shockwave through the air. The lava covering Macall's body begins to get pushed back, as if it's being forced away by a powerful spray. He raises his hands to block the shockwave, and Daniel hits him again, catapulting as much water as he can, encapsulating him.

Teleporting over, I run past a car, reaching out and teleporting it over him, letting it fall. He crumples underneath the vehicle but blasts it off of him. Tremor and Daniel continue the onslaught, and Macall starts to lose power. Not waiting, I teleport in front of him, slamming both fists into his chest, feeling my gloves burn.

"More!" I scream out to Daniel.

"You're in the way!"

"Do it!"

Without another word, the snowstorm surrounds us. He's now completely depowered, and he raises his glowing orange arms to his face, trying to block the snow and shockwaves. Rushing at him, I tackle him to the ground. We exchange a flurry of punches and kicks, and even though he's not covered in lava, every time I come into contact with him, I feel the burning through my uniform.

I kick him off of me, and teleport to the side, but still within the makeshift blizzard. He tries to shoot magma from his hands, but the snow and water stop it from traveling more than ten feet. He tries again, and this time, he can only shoot a couple feet in front of him.

I press a finger to my helmet. "Doc, we're coming in."

Running at him full speed, I dive and tackle him

through the flurry of water, snow, and the shockwaves. Instead of falling to the ground, I teleport us both into the crisis room at headquarters.

It's completely dark, with the exception of a small spotlight that we're lying in the middle of. I quickly roll off of him, feeling the heat of his body.

He lets out an exhausted grunt. "What is this?"

I know we all have to accept the consequences of our actions, but I still feel sorry for him. Sorry that we weren't able to save him from what Daedalus did. And sorry for what's about to come. I want to give him a chance, but I've already seen the hate-filled torment in his eyes. He won't take it. And he won't stop until I'm dead.

Getting to his feet, he raises his fist, and his skin begins to glow red. "It'll only take a minute to recharge enough to kill you." He flashes a sinister leer. "After you're dead, she's dead. Your family's dead. Everyone you've ever loved will die. But not before I kill you."

I shake my head, discouraged. "I wanted to give you one last chance, Macall. But I see now there's no room left in you for anything except pain and suffering."

"Don't you dare lecture me on pain and suffering. You know nothing—"

"No! I've felt pain. I've felt suffering. But I was given a second chance. I wanted to give you the same thing."

"All you've done was delay the inevitable."

I let out a long sigh. Taking a step to him, I can feel the heat emanating from his body. "I'm sorry, Macall." His hateful gaze stays on me as I lift my hand and press it again his chest, feeling my glove start to burn.

Unsure of what I'm doing, he goes with my movement and takes a step back, into the darkness surrounding us. He's only halfway within the shadows and I hear clawing.

The gnashing and the growling. His face instantly drops—all hate and enmity gone, replaced with terror.

"Wh-what is this?" he screams, and I hear the creatures chomping. He bellows out in pain. "No! What is this?"

I take a step back, feeling like I'm listening to and watching a nightmare. He struggles to get out of the shadow, but he can't. "No! No!" he yells out in pain once more, and begins to slide in against his will.

He reaches out to me. "Help—" His plea is halted by another primal scream, and he sinks deeper into the darkness. I swallow the lump of fear that's forming in my throat. Then, in a snap, he's pulled completely into the Dark, and the screaming and growling silences. Shadow steps out of the Dark, and into the middle of the spotlight, next to me.

He stares at me, silently. The ghoulish creatures he calls Feeders that live in the Dark do nothing to ease my mind about Macall escaping.

"End Darkness Protocol," Shadow says in a gruff voice. The crisis room comes alive, and the entire area lights up, leaving Macall nowhere to be seen.

"Is he ..." I glance at Shadow, not wanting to finish the thought.

"He's not dead, but he's not alive either," Shadow explains.

"Do I want to know what that means?"

"No, you don't," he deadpans.

"Will he be able to escape?"

He turns and faces a light gray wall in the room, but he stares at it like he's peering into the Dark. "Nothing escapes the third layer."

Without another word, he turns and begins toward the exit. I rush over to him, grabbing his arm. "Wait." Eyeing my hand, I cautiously pull it back. "Sorry. I just wanted to say thank you."

"No need to thank me."

"There really is." I shake my head, thinking back to the entire events of the day, half of which I relived. "We wouldn't have been able to do this without you. Even if we caught him, the chamber Doc was working on is nowhere near ready."

Shadow smirks under his black cowl. It's a little creepy. "I like you, kid."

I stare at him, genuinely shocked. "Really?"

He nods. "Like I said before, sometimes you need to make some bad decisions. That's because then you'll know what the right decisions are later."

"Thanks ... I guess." He takes a step, but I move in front of him. "Sorry. Jasmin? She's safe, right?"

Another odd smirk from him. "She's safe. First, I took her to my place. After you and Macall left the street, I transferred her to your bunker here."

I quirk an eyebrow. "My room? How did you know which one mine is?"

"Even Alliance headquarters has shadows." He flashes a sneaky grin.

I wrinkle my nose, unsure what I'm more nervous about; the fact that he can slip into headquarters anytime he wants, or the fact that he made a creepy joke about it.

With a disturbed expression, I nod. "Okay ... thanks again."

The doors open and he walks out. I scan the crisis room and the lights shining down all around, with not a trace of Macall or the Dark in sight. It's over. It's finally over.

32

I'm not sure what to expect to find when I enter my room, but seeing Jasmin sitting at my desk immediately fills me with relief. She's scouring multiple tabs on a laptop, all of them on news websites. Hearing the door close, she turns and sees me, then jumps out of the chair, wrapping her arms around me.

"Ow." I cringe, but still keep my arms around her waist.

My helmet already retracted; she puts her hands to my face. "Oh my God. You need to be in a hospital."

I finally take myself in. My uniform is bloodied, burned, and torn to pieces. I can't imagine what my face looks like, but I know it can't be much better. "I'll be okay."

"How?"

Her question makes me chuckle, and with more of the adrenaline wearing off, the breathing sends a stabbing pain to my ribs. "Ow."

"Sit down," she orders, and I take a step over to my bed.

"Hold on." I raise a finger and teleport to one of Doc's labs, grabbing a medical kit, and then jump back to my room, emptying the contents on my bed as I take a seat.

Grabbing some gauze and ointment, I tear open the packages, but she takes them from me. "Give that to me."

I chuckle at her reaction, and again grab my ribs in pain. "My mom may be the doctor, but I can disinfect and bandage blindfolded thanks to her."

Releasing a great sigh, I reach over and stop her hands from moving, resting mine over hers. "I'm so sorry." Memories roll around of what happened the first time around, and I hold back thankful tears I was able to change it.

"For what? You saved me. You guys saved everyone."

"Yeah." I nod, staring at the ground. "It could've been ..." I can't get the words out. How do I tell her she died and somehow, someway, we've avoided that? "Jasmin, we can't ... This world is too dangerous for you."

For a split second she has the same face that she wore when she told me about her uncle. The same expression of countering my argument. Then it vanishes, and her eyes dart around the room. "Weird."

"What?"

"I just had the strangest feeling of déjà vu."

I swallow my nerves, and Doc's word echo through my brain of how fragile the time continuum is. I don't know how I did what I did, and now I don't know if things have changed for the future.

What is this power?

"Anyway," she starts up, continuing to bandage my arm, "you're not getting rid of me now, Robbie Garcia. Do you remember when I told you about my uncle last year?"

I can't help it. Another chuckle floats out.

"What?"

"Nothing. It's just ... yes, I remember. And you don't need to explain it to me, I think I could live a hundred different lives and you'll probably say the same thing every time."

Pausing, she lifts a brow. "What does that mean?"

Smiling, I lean over and kiss her. "Nothing. It doesn't matter. No matter what I say, anything you counter with I'll accept. I've always been yours, Jas."

A wide smile spreads across her lips, her cheeks turning pink. Returning her attention to my arm, I try to mull over what to tell her. *If* I should tell her. Maybe later, in the next few days or weeks. Right now, we survived, and that's enough for me.

"I have to go soon," she speaks up, finishing the bandage.

"Why?"

"My mom. She saw the news and I got about a hundred text messages from her. I told her I was fine, and the police escorted me to a safe site, but I didn't know what else to say, and acted like my phone was losing service."

"Right. Of course." I move gingerly, getting to my feet, and hold out my hand to her. "Come on, I'll take you."

"Are you sure?" she asks, taking my hand. "I really think you should have Doctor Grandside check you out."

"I'll be fine," I whisper, pulling her closer. "I'll get some more treatment later, but nothing works as well as having you close."

She snorts, rolling her eyes. "Okay, I think you may be overestimating your feelings for me just a tad."

"Let's see."

Rushing my lips to hers, I don't know if its adrenaline picking back up, or the thought that we're both alive, but I do feel better. She wraps her arms around me, and I swear I can stand in this spot kissing her for hours. Days even. Then, there's a knock at my door, and it slides open. She breaks away, a new shade of red covering her face.

"Oh, pardon me," Doc says. I turn and give him a nod. "Robbie. Ms. Fuentes."

"Sorry, Doc. I was just about to contact you."

"Good. Fire and rescue are on the scene, and all of the diversions have been taken care of."

"Should I join up with Hydro and Mighty?"

"No need. After I check you out, you'll be relieved until further notice."

That's right. I'm technically suspended until Mimic comes back. "Okay," I answer, gazing at the ground.

"Ms. Fuentes"—he looks past me—"you've been registered into a safe site a few blocks from the incident. I believe your mother has already contacted the site, so we should get you over there."

"I was just going to—"

Doc cuts me off. "I've asked Hydro to accompany her."

"Oh ..." She looks over at me, then back at him, unsure. "Okay."

Giving her hand a squeeze, I offer her a soft smile. "It'll be okay. I'll call you later."

She nods and then Daniel steps through the doorway. He squeezes my shoulder and smiles, while I cringe at his touch. "Oh, sorry." He chuckles. "I seriously didn't know how that was going to go down. But awesome job out there, man."

"I wasn't sure myself, but thanks. And you, too."

Letting out a sigh of relief, he nods with a smile. Then he looks over at Jasmin. "I can take you now, if you're ready."

Offering me one last wave, she follows Daniel down the hallway, and out of sight. Doc takes a step closer to me. "Let's get you checked out, Robbie."

After the inspection, I head back to my bunker and finally get into clothes that aren't covered in ash, blood, and dirt. Taking another look around, I want to believe I'll be back here, but I have no idea. Yes, I helped stop Magma, but I've still done a lot of stuff while Mimic's been gone that could spell the end for my sidekick career. One last look over my room, I turn the lights off, and decide to walk out through the front of headquarters.

Coming in from the other side of the hallway, Melissa approaches, covered in dirt and ash herself.

Stopping in front of her, I give her a heartfelt smile. "Hey."

"You look horrible, Robbie."

I chuckle. "So I've been told." I run my fingers over the multiple bandages Doc applied to my chin, cheeks, and nose. The pain around my back and ribs has died down a bit from the healing serums he used. "Everything okay out there?"

She nods. "King City Construction is surveying the main damage to the buildings. The diversion spots were pretty minor."

"That's good ..." I take a deep breath, keeping my gaze on her. "Mel, I know I already said it, but I truly am sorry. For everything."

"I know you are." Her vision breaks from mine for a moment, and she bites her lip. "Daniel explained to me a little about your history with her. It was a really crappy thing to do, Robbie, but ... I get it. And that's also why I can't stay here. Majestic's worked with a few other superheroes in the past. I'm gonna work with a couple of them and see where I fit best. I like Earth too much to leave, but I can't stay here. I'm sorry."

I shake my head. "You have nothing to be sorry about. When are you leaving?"

"Tomorrow."

"Oh," I respond, a little surprised. "Okay."

I feel like I should say or do something, but what else is there I can say? Nothing can make up for how I acted. Clearing my throat, a memory surfaces that I hope will ease the tension.

"We'll always have *Die, Zombie, Die*."

For a moment she narrows her eyes. Perhaps I shouldn't have made a light-hearted attempt to keep things neutral. Maybe it's too soon to make a joke. Then her face softens, and she punches my shoulder.

"True," she says with a chuckle. "I better get going. I just came to grab a few supplies, and then I'm headed back out there."

"Okay."

I watch her walk past me and down the hallway. Before she turns the corner, she looks back and offers me a simple wave. I wave back, and then she's gone.

33

It's been three weeks since Magma attacked. Three weeks since Jasmin and I died. Since I somehow traveled back in time and reset what would've been the end of so many things. And I still have no idea how I did it.

The following two days after the attack, the school was shut down for repairs, but it's since opened back up. And, just like any other time a major battle happens in the city, every student has gotten back in the flow of things, with Magma barely being a topic of discussion. Such is the life in King City.

The first day we met up at lunch it was awkward. Maria was the first one to point it out, telling me I was being weird, Jasmin was being too quiet, and Pete was out of it. I do feel bad keeping Maria out of the loop. I've known her as long as I've known Jasmin, but the safest thing to do is to try and keep her safe. If she ever finds out, I hope she doesn't kill me or Jasmin for keeping it a secret from her.

I've kept in contact with Daniel, mostly through Pete. He told me that Mimic and the others finally got the advantage in the battle and are due back this week. With no training or practice to enact on, I'm lying across my bed, aimlessly flipping through my geography textbook, wondering when I'll be called to headquarters for my comeuppance.

An alert sounds on my phone, and I see Doc calling.

"Hey, Doc."

"Robbie, how are you?"

Puffing my cheeks full of air, I let out a drab sigh, and flip another page. "Oh, you know. Studying for high school geography exams. It's a regular party over her."

He lets out a low chuckle. "Sounds like your sense of humor's still intact. I'll be sitting in on your overview, so if you'd like to come down, we can get this all taken care of."

"Yeah, sure," I respond about as dull and reluctant as possible. "I'll be right there."

I don't bother changing into my uniform. In my jeans and a gray hoodie, I teleport into my bunker which looks the same as it did the last day I was here. Exiting, I see Daniel across the hallway, walking into the control room, giving me a nod. I wave back at him, and head to the conference room.

Walking inside, Mimic and Doc sit on one end of a long oak desk. Only one other chair is present, sitting at the other end. It catches me slightly off guard, since the last time I had a hearing, Majestic and Supron were also present.

"Robbie, good to see you," Mimic calls over, smiling.

"Glad you're back home safe," I reply. "I guess you—"

"Take a seat, Robbie," Doc cuts me off. I lift my shoulders and follow his command.

"So," Mimic begins, "it sounds like you three had quite the altercation while we were gone."

I look over at Doc, and then back at Mimic, confused. "Uh, yeah. It was ... insane."

"That's what Doc said." Mimic grins.

"Robbie," Doc starts, "I took it upon myself to cover all of the necessary details with Mimic."

I nod, feeling the lump form in my throat.

"I have to say," Mimic interjects, "teleporting half of a rooftop? The concentration alone must've been excruciating. I'm extremely proud of the plan you devised. And calling in Shadow? Very smart."

"Um ... thanks." My eyes narrow and dart over to Doc.

"As I was saying," Mimic continues. "The insubordination when you faced Frank Gomez, the second fire guy in the high-rise office, is being noted. Though, because of the circumstances, there will be no penalties assessed to your training. But everything else is being recorded in your file. The infiltration and reconnaissance mission of looking into Daedalus, and your confrontation with General Watkins. The Alliance silver ops code will be attached."

"Silver ops?"

"Again," Mimic speaks up. "I'm extremely proud of you, Robbie. Silver ops missions are highly dangerous, and from what Doc says, you handled everything as best you could. Using an astralcube to escape the lightwave trapping was quick thinking. We might not have anything that can stick to Watkins, but we will. Eventually."

I know exactly what Alliance silver operation missions are. A kind of black ops mission, but instead of plausible deniability for those, silver ops are held under sealed files and can be broken open if needed in a court of law. I also know what I did was never even hinted at being one of those.

Both of them stand up from the table.

"If you don't have any questions, you're dismissed," Mimic says. "And I'll see you this weekend for training and patrol."

I'm trying to digest everything that's happening. Doc's covering for me, but why? A part of me wants to ask, but another part tells me to stay quiet. I know what I did went against orders, but I truly was doing what I thought was best. Is that why Doc did this?

"Yeah. I mean, yes, sir." I get up and follow them out of the room. "Thank you."

Mimic leaves the room first, followed by Doc. I trail behind them and want to jump up and down in joy. I want to call Jasmin, and Pete, and teleport to the top of King City Tower, and scream out in excitement. Before any of that, though, Doc heads to his office and I run to catch up to him as he opens the door.

"Doc?"

Turning, he offers a smile. "What is it, Robbie?"

I look around, unsure if I really want to ask this. "Um ... can I ask why?"

Nodding to me, he walks into his office. Shutting the door behind me, he leans against his desk. "Did you not want me to?"

"Oh, no. Of course not. I'm ecstatic about it. But ... you just seemed ... I mean, I know I messed up. I really was doing what I thought was best, but I know I broke protocol."

"You did." Giving me the familiar Doc expression, he strokes his beard. "But after everything that happened, and I've had these last few weeks to analyze everything, Robbie, I'm not sure any of us would be where we are if it wasn't for you. I'm not going to discipline you for that." I smile. "You know Mimic as well as anyone. He's not a simpleton. I didn't explain everything, but he knows the main issues. And he knows you. Do you know what he asked me when I finished my report?" I shake my head, almost unsure if I want him to say it. "He asked me one question; Do I trust you? I do, Robbie."

"Thank you."

"Plus, we have something on Watkins again. He's made the first move. He went after a member of the Alliance and used Macall to attack you. We have to be very careful going forward. Daedalus is a true threat now."

I nod, the weight of everything coming down around me. Macall was intense. Deadly. And he almost won. I shudder to think what Watkins will try next, especially after Macall's words that he wants me.

"Thanks again," I tell him and turn to open the door.

Swinging it open, I'm instantly in a blue orb. The memories come flooding back, and I hear the crackle of lightning riding over the outside surface. Just like before, I'm floating through a dark void, when instantly a gray cloud surrounds me.

"Doc? Hello? What is this?"

Slamming my fist against the orb, I notice my hands. I have my gloves on. Looking down at my body, I discover I'm in my uniform. A loud rumble vibrates the orb, and a huge lightning bolt strikes the cloud, revealing a moving image.

It's a girl, standing in the middle of the ocean. She's wearing some type of teal dress that looks like it's covered in shimmering ocean shells. Her hair glows orange and red. The scene zooms to her face and she's crying. A tall man in some kind of Atlantean or Merkian armor places a crown over her head.

"What is this?" I scream out, and another lightning bolt hits the cloud.

A new scene appears.

"Diego!" a lady calls out, laughing on the side of a boat. A young guy, maybe my age, sits next to an older man, who's holding a fishing pole. The younger one, Diego, lies back over the front of a ship, taking in the rays of the sun, while what appear to be his parents laugh and talk.

"Why is this happening?" I scream. "What is this? Let me out of here!" I pound my fist against the orb and the lightning strikes it, knocking me down.

Outside of the orb, a man floats. Short black hair, he's wearing black pants, and a long, black trench coat. His eyes narrow as he looks at me. Waving his hand, the lightning pierces the sphere, and though it seems impossible, his body appears to morph for an instant, into crackling lightning. Then he's in the orb, standing in front of me.

"I told them," he says quietly, shaking his head. He looks around and I peer up at him, seeing a tattoo on his neck. It's the same symbol I use as my insignia. The same eight-pointed star that you'd see if you're looking through am astral-scope to see me teleport.

"What is this?" I get to my feet. "Who are you?"

Ignoring my questions, he walks around me. "But they didn't listen. I said to not take you for granted. When they first sent me, I could feel it. The power you have. Sometimes they let their egos get in the way of making the right decisions."

Clenching my fists, I step closer. "Who are you?"

"I'm sure they could feel it, too, but they didn't want to believe it. There has never been two chronowalkers born under a century apart from one another."

"Stop!" I yell at him. "I have no idea what you're talking about."

Still ignoring me, he turns and peers out into the void. "Still, I know why they weren't concerned. You're young. Chronowalkers never come into their full power until they master jumping planets. I learned to control that in ten years, and they tell me that's above average."

"What are you talking about?" I scream at him.

Spinning on his heels, he steps closer, pointing his finger at me. "Robbie Garcia, your world as you know it has changed. And you're the one who changed it."

"Okay, that's enough." I take a step to grab his arm and take him down with a flip. I'm getting answers now. Before I can grab his arm, he teleports behind me, catching me completely off guard.

"I won't let you flip me," he says, his back still facing me. "And when I turn around right now, don't try to take my legs out from under me."

"How ..."

"No, you can't out-teleport me. And no, you can't teleport us both out of the orb. I'm controlling the astral-sphere. No, this isn't a mistake. And yes, you are the right person."

"Stop! How do you know what I'm thinking?"

"I don't," he answers, finally facing me. "I know what you're going to do. I've replayed this moment a dozen times to get your reactions."

"I ... I don't understand."

"Look." He turns and waves to the surrounding cloud on the outside. Gazing out, I see the scene I was watching before. Then another appears. Me with my parents. That switches to me eating lunch with Pete, Jasmin, and Maria. Another lightning strike, and now I'm talking with Mimic at headquarters. Following that, I see Jasmin and Maria watching a movie. Then Pete kissing Daniel.

"These are all moments in time. Moments that were. Moments that should have been. And moments that have yet to happen. And because of your actions, you've created a chrononexus."

"Chrono-what?"

Waving his hand, the scenes vanish. One replaces them all. It's frozen, like a scene paused on television. Magma is about to unleash his lava over Jasmin and me.

"A chrononexus. A fixed point in time that has been altered. And because of that, the future is now changed. Forever."

My mouth drops, still staring at the scene on the cloud. "But ... I had no choice. You don't understand, we were going to die."

Chuckling, he turns to me. "Really? Didn't Doctor Grandside tell you your body has the ability to regenerate. And even if it didn't, isn't that part of your job? To take those risks?"

"Not hers!" I finally find my courage, putting a finger in his face. "How do you know any of that? Who the—" My words freeze. His face. I remember it now. It's the same face I saw of the man Doc said was a time traveler. "You're him."

He nods. "My name is Cade Fremont, and I'm a chronowalker."

"And what does any of this have to do with me?"

"Everything. You altered your timeline. And the Eon Watchers are not to be trifled with. That's why I've brought you here. This is the easiest way to travel to a fixed spot in time, and somehow, you accessed it accidentally. But accident or not, Robbie, you've changed time. So, I've been sent to give you a warning."

My body tenses with suspicion. "A warning?"

"Two actually." He waves his hand, and the rooftop scene disappears, revealing the swirling cloud again with lightning traveling on the outside of the sphere. "I've been assigned as your time sentinel. If you try to change anything again, I'll be there. And I'll stop you."

His warning sounds nothing short of a threat.

"But I don't even know how I did what I did. All of a sudden, I was here and then I was back at headquarters. I didn't know what I was doing."

"It doesn't matter. You did it. Accessing the time continuum is similar to accessing your powers to teleport, only on a much grander scale. Your emotions, your subconscious, you have to focus on all of that just to make the jump. You're being watched now. You may not be a chronowalker, but you have the power. And if you interfere with time again, I'll have to deal with you."

Our vision locks on one another. I'm trying to understand everything he's telling me, while he seems calm and collected.

"Since your timeline has changed, there are still great things that could happen in your future. But you did alter it. Now the course has to be adjusted. You need to be careful, Robbie. You're about to enter a very dangerous time in your life."

"More dangerous than Magma? What does that mean?"

Ignoring my question, he turns around and peers through the orb. "Time is incredibly delicate. Every choice a human makes alters time and what it will become. Ripples in a pond, as it were. And sometimes, those ripples can produce a riptide."

"This doesn't make any sense. You're talking in riddles." I look around and see nothing but the vast darkness. Turning to face him, I discover he's gone. "Hello?" I call out, but only hear the crackling of electricity. Then a sudden burst of lightning runs through the sphere, striking me in the chest.

"Robbie?"

I take a deep breath, shaking my head, and try to focus.

My hands don't have my gloves on them anymore. I'm back in my jeans and hoodie.

"Robbie, did you have anything else to add?"

"What?" I spin around and find Doc still leaning against his desk.

"Are you okay?" he asks, and I realize I'm back in his office. My hand is still on his door handle. "Is everything all right?"

"Yeah." I nod, trying to remain calm and remember what Cade was talking about. "Yeah, everything's fine."

EPILOGUE

Atrimi looks over the ocean horizon, two of his guards standing by his side. His armor hangs off of his wide shoulders, lined with hardened starfish, conch shells, and shark teeth. Their ship can submerge to depths no humans can reach, which serves as a protection, but today he's getting much-needed aid. For his insurgence to overthrow the king, he'll need it.

"The serums we've been using have had ..." General Watkins pauses, almost grinning. "Unusual side effects."

"Land dwellers and your human concoctions." Atrimi rolls his eyes. "You know our blood is unlike anything on Earth. You should—"

"You should"—Watkins puts a finger in his face, establishing a dominant stance—"know who you're talking to. I know who you are, Atrimi, and I know what you want. Your people know of the Justice Alliance, right?" Atrimi nods. "Then you realize I'm your only hope in getting what you want and helping to do it without having to deal with superheroes getting in the way. Know your place, Atrimi. You're no king yet."

Watkins glances over this shoulder and motions to his guards to load on five huge, wooden cases.

"Project Ignis was a success, but I doubt you'll find any need for fire. There are many other things you can use these serums for though. We've only been able to test them on normal blood."

Atrimi nods. "Very well then."

A silent standoff takes place between the two alphas. Atrimi moves first, turning around, and motioning for his men to follow him. Watkins returns to the small boat that's drifting next to their ship, and one of his guards loosens the rope that's keeping them tied together.

"Sir, was this a wise move?" a man whispers over to him, as Atrimi's ship begins to descend into the ocean water. After a moment, it's fully submerged and gone. "With the teleporter having more information on you than anything the Alliance has had before, shouldn't we be concentrating on him and not this Merkian civil war?"

"Two birds, one stone," Watkins retorts. "The Alliance won't make any moves. Robbie Garcia may know more than others, but he has no proof. What we truly need is access and blood, and the Merkian insurgents will be able to provide both. Let them fight over the water. Project Rebirth is exactly on schedule."

ABOUT THE AUTHOR

Raised on a healthy dose of Saturday morning cartoons, video games, and Captain Crunch cereal (with crunch berries, of course), I write books that capture my imagination.

When I'm not writing, you can probably find me plotting my next story, playing video games, or at the movies with a large Diet Coke and a large popcorn.

www.rontuckerwrites.com

Made in the USA
Columbia, SC
30 April 2020